W9-BQJ-868

Praise for Frances McNamara's previous novels

"McNamara has a keen eye for zeroing in on how a metropolis
can fuel and deplete the human spirit."
*Chicago Sun-Times*

"This is a fun, satisfying read for a summer afternoon à la
hammock or back porch."
*The Barnstable Patriot*

In this novel a "little romance [and] a lot of labor history are
artfully combined… Creating a believable mix of historical and
fictional characters…is another of the author's prime strengths
as a writer…[she] clearly knows, and loves, her setting."
Julie Eakin, *ForeWord Reviews*

"The combination of labor unrest, rivalries among local families,
and past romantic intrigues is a combustible mix, an edgy
scenario that is laid out convincingly… A suspenseful recreation
of a critical moment in American social history, as seen from the
viewpoint of a strong-willed, engaging fictional heroine."
*Reading the Past*

# Also by Frances McNamara

❧

## The Emily Cabot Mysteries

*Death at the Fair*

*Death at Hull House*

*Death at Pullman*

*Death at Woods Hole*

# DEATH AT CHINATOWN

Frances McNamara

ALLIUM PRESS OF CHICAGO

Allium Press of Chicago
Forest Park, IL
www.alliumpress.com

This is a work of fiction. Descriptions and portrayals of real people, events, organizations, or establishments are intended to provide background for the story and are used fictitiously. Other characters and situations are drawn from the author's imagination and are not intended to be real.

Book and cover design by E. C. Victorson
Front cover images:
Ida Kahn and Mary Stone in Western dress
Courtesy of General Commission on Archives and History,
the United States Methodist Church
and
"Traditional Chinese Pattern" by John Lock/Shutterstock

Library of Congress Cataloging-in-Publication Data

McNamara, Frances.
   Death at Chinatown / Frances McNamara.
      pages cm. -- (An Emily Cabot mystery)
   Summary: "In the summer of 1896, amateur sleuth Emily Cabot becomes involved
in a murder investigation when a herbalist is poisoned in Chicago's original China-
town"-- Provided by publisher.
   ISBN 978-0-9890535-5-6 (pbk.)
   1. Chinese Americans--Fiction. 2. Murder--Investigation--Fiction. 3. Chinese
Americans--Illinois--Chicago--Fiction. 4. Chinatown (Chicago, Ill.)--Fiction. 5.
Mystery fiction. I. Title.
   PS3613.C58583D36 2014
   813'.6--dc23
                                    2014015348

*To Charles LaGrutta, my fellow student of all things Chinese*

# ONE

**M**r. Cormick here suffered injuries from a shotgun blast a month ago." The surgeon gestured and looked down, but I kept my eyes on the balding patch just visible on the top of his head. "We were unable to locate all of the pellets at the time of original treatment and he has been in continual pain ever since. Today, gentlemen…and ladies," Dr. Erickson said, with a bow in our direction, "we will, for the first time, use a new technique which the German physician Dr. Roentgen discovered while experimenting with a Crookes tube." He paused to point at a round glass bulb mounted on a wooden stand.

My husband, Stephen, stepped forward, holding up a photographic negative against a white sheet, which Dr. Erickson pointed towards. "With the help of Mr. Emil Grubbé and Dr. Stephen Chapman, we are able to use the Roentgen rays to find the problematic pieces of lead still in the man's thigh. Mr. Grubbé will explain the methodology."

A slightly disheveled young man with stringy black hair shambled over to the negative and mumbled about the plate used, the method of placing the limb between the tube and the plate, the exposure of forty-five minutes, and the procedure for fixing the image. He pointed out a copper wire around the leg, which had been used as a marker, and the pellets visible six centimeters below it. So this was the work that Stephen had been spending so much time on. He had tried to tell me about it, but I was distracted and, I had to admit, uninterested. In the current circumstances, however, I couldn't help being impressed. In fact, I was fascinated as I realized the machine could show the inside of the body. I had to admit to myself that it really was an amazing discovery.

"And now we will be able to address this man's pain through removal of the missing pieces," Dr. Erickson explained. It was obvious he was impatient with the mumblings of the technician, and it was clear that he saw Stephen as nothing more than an attendant, as he directed him to hold the negative so that it could be examined. "Now we are ready to remove the material." He nodded to the nurse administering the chloroform. "The patient will be unaware of the procedure. Gentlemen…" he said, addressing several younger men standing nearby, "…you will secure the limbs to prevent any unconscious movement."

Dr. Erickson wore a conventional herringbone suit, although he removed his jacket and vest, handing them to a nurse. After he rolled up his shirtsleeves she brought a basin for him to wash his hands in. Once he'd dried them he donned a white apron. All the while, he talked about how the unfortunate Mr. Cormick had been treated for his wounds and the surgical procedure he planned to perform.

I ventured a quick glance at the patient, but he was laid out on a stretcher sheathed in white sheets. His face was indistinguishable, as a nurse held an overturned wire netting over his nose and mouth. It was stuffed with gauze and she carefully drip, drip, dripped a liquid from an amber-colored glass jar onto the gauze. I could smell a cloying, sweet scent that made me want to pinch my nose, but I restrained myself.

It was clear to me that Dr. Erickson wanted to make sure we had an unobstructed view. I would have liked to demur, to leave even, but I sensed that would have reflected poorly on Stephen, so I said nothing and attempted to concentrate my attention on the least shocking sights in the room—thus my interest in Dr. Erickson's head. Staring at it kept me from glancing down at the injured man and the knives and the bandages, the thought of which I found somewhat alarming.

The surgeon was a tall man with prominent cheekbones, and had a full white beard and mustache, very neatly trimmed. His cold gray eyes were on a level with mine. As he spoke, I paid attention to each movement of each wrinkle on his well-lined face, intent on *not* looking down at the man on the stretcher below us.

I noticed that Stephen now stood in a corner of the stage, but I knew that he could still see me. Conscious that I was there at his request, I was determined to endure the experience, despite my quite natural revulsion. I could face anything if I had to. I had seen seriously wounded and ill people before, and even encountered dead bodies in my past, but I had never observed a surgery where they purposely cut into human flesh.

Dr. Erickson appeared to be ready, and I let my gaze drift up to the ceiling, hoping to avoid the sight of blood as he wielded the scalpel, but he hesitated.

"Unless we can prevail upon one of our visiting physicians to demonstrate the skills they have learned in Michigan? Dr. Stone, you told me you are trained as a surgeon, is that not the case?"

꩜

When I had first met Dr. Mary Stone and Dr. Ida Kahn in the lobby just a short time before, I was disappointed. They seemed so very ordinary. It was only much later that I realized it must have required a great effort to transform themselves chameleon-like for American society. For, despite their very American-sounding names, they were very thoroughly Chinese.

I knew they had come from China four years previously with Miss Grace Howe, a missionary, to study at the University of Michigan. And I knew they had completed medical degrees that spring of 1896. They were visiting Chicago all summer before returning to their homeland to open a clinic. For months, I had been hearing about them from my husband. I suppose I expected something more exotic than the two slim figures in ordinary walking suits with flat straw hats. They could have been any of the women scholars at the University of Chicago in those days. They had the almond-shaped eyes of an Oriental, but nothing beyond that to mark them out as extraordinary. Held up as paragons by my husband and others, they were said to excel in both social and professional spheres. Yet, when I introduced myself to them in the comparatively cool corridor of the Rush Hospital on that blazing hot August day, I was not overly impressed.

"We have heard so much about you from your husband," Dr. Mary Stone told me, as she accepted my extended hand in a firm shake. The gloves we both wore did nothing to relieve the oppressive heat. My skirts felt like a heavy drag, my hat a burden, and my jacket too constricting. I struggled to ignore my physical discomfort and to pay attention as she turned to the other women in her group. "This is Dr. Ida Kahn and her adoptive mother, Miss Grace Howe, who has accompanied us during our stay here."

Ida Kahn seemed a copy of Mary Stone except for the round spectacles she wore. Miss Howe was a large-boned woman whose face was flushed with the heat of the day. I nodded to each, not feeling it necessary to extend my hand, since Mary was gesturing to two other women as well. "And this is Mrs. Laura Appleby—she is the widow of an eminent physician and has been most kind to us during our stay—and Miss Charlotte Erickson. Her father is the distinguished surgeon who will be leading the demonstration today."

"Pleased to meet you, Mrs. Chapman," Miss Howe told me. "You are also here for the demonstration? Mary and Ida are anxious to see it. Not my cup of tea, but our time here is for them to learn as much as they can before we return to China. Your husband made special arrangements for them to attend and we are very grateful for that. I must say, he has been extremely helpful with introductions to many people in the medical community here. I know the girls are in his debt for that."

I clenched my teeth in an effort to refrain from commenting on my husband's activities. That summer Stephen had been spending more and more time away from home. His activities had taken him into the city, leaving me in our Hyde Park home with our children. It was not uncommon for him to even spend overnights in the city without notice. When I protested, he parried with enthusiastic descriptions of various new procedures or research he had seen, and then invited me to attend demonstrations. He was deaf to my insistence that I was needed at home and he had become slippery as an eel in slithering out of arguments. It had come to a head the evening before in a big argument, and ended in his insistence that I attend this demonstration and meet the Chinese doctors. That morning he had departed early, leaving me to find my own way to the hospital and to introduce myself to these women. I would not let them see my annoyance, but I was hard pressed to conceal it.

Before I could reply we were interrupted. A tall man in his fifties strode across the corridor towards us. He planted his imposing figure in front of Miss Erickson and accosted her with no consideration for the rest of us. "Charlotte, what are you doing here?"

The young woman was of medium height. She wore the black of deep mourning and she cringed away from the man's towering figure. Mrs. Appleby, who also wore black, stepped between them, as if to protect the young woman. "Isaac, please, I asked Charlotte to join us. After the demonstration there is a luncheon to honor our Chinese guests. I thought it would be a fine thing to have another young woman in the party."

"Madam, I will not allow it. I will not have you influencing my daughter. Is it not enough that you assisted her in poisoning her own mother? How dare you continue to force your attentions on her when I have forbidden it?" He frowned at his daughter, who appeared to wilt under his furious gaze. Brushing past the older woman, he took his daughter by the arm and led her away.

"I apologize," Mrs. Appleby told us. "Please do not mind what he says. He has not recovered from the death of his wife. She was one of my dearest friends. When she suffered pain in her final struggles she asked me for help in finding herbs that could provide some relief. Like many physicians, Dr. Erickson has an unreasonable prejudice against homeopathic treatments. He knows perfectly well that nothing we gave her harmed her. He just needs someone to blame for his loss."

It was an awkward moment. "I am so sorry Miss Erickson will not be able to join us for the luncheon," Mary Stone commented.

"I have heard that Dr. Erickson does not believe women are suited for medical research or surgery," Ida Kahn said.

"He hasn't always been that way," Mrs. Appleby hastened to comment. "He has changed since the death of his wife. Before that, he helped to train women physicians at the women's hospital she supported. And I'm afraid that is not the only change he has undergone." She shook her head. "He has resigned from most of his appointments at local medical establishments, and much of his practice. It's unusual for him to even do the kind of surgical demonstration he's doing today. Please forgive any rudeness. I believe he still suffers from a painful grief."

I thought this did not bode well for the coming demonstration. If the surgeon disapproved of women physicians, the presence of the Chinese doctors would be awkward, to say the least. Restless with a certain apprehension, I looked around in vain for Stephen. He was the one who'd insisted I attend this session, but where was he?

At that moment, a young man came and asked us to follow him to the demonstration. When I realized that Miss Howe and Mrs. Appleby had no intention of attending, I thought of remaining with them. But I remembered Stephen's insistence, and reluctantly allowed myself to be herded to a nearby doorway.

We mounted a few steps and found ourselves in an operating theater. I was shocked. When Stephen had suggested I attend a demonstration, he had not mentioned that it was surgical. The room was a small amphitheater with boxy wooden desks lining the rows. They were mostly occupied by young men in suits, who I assumed were medical students. I hoped we could remain as far as possible from the floor of the room where the operation would happen. But as I moved toward one of the last rows, we were hailed from below.

It was Dr. Erickson. "Come, come, gentlemen. I see our lady visitors have arrived. Make room, make room. You must allow them seats in the front row." He waved at the young men in the first row and they promptly gave up their seats, much to my dismay. I had no choice but to follow Mary and Ida down the steps and to slip in behind a desk. It would be the only thing between us and the operation about to take place below.

❧

And now, here was Dr. Erickson asking Dr. Stone, one of the Chinese women doctors, to cut into the man lying on the stretcher. The very thought made me cringe with anticipation. I thought it was cruel of the doctor to challenge her in that way. My husband had been a surgeon before he came to Chicago to do research, but that skill was forever lost to him when he was injured by a shotgun blast, several years before our marriage. I had never seen him perform surgery and had no desire to. How alarming it must be for Mary Stone to be dared to perform surgery in this rather antagonistic atmosphere, where the only other women were nurses or observers. I was almost prompted to protest when he badgered her.

"Come, come, madam. Did they not teach you that this is the essence of modern medicine? Or do you plan to merely prescribe herbs when you return to your country? Surely that is not what you came to here to learn? If you graduated from the great institution of the University of Michigan, surely they taught you to do simple surgery, didn't they?" He had an unpleasant grin on his face, as if he were happy to cause the young woman discomfort. It made me angry with him. I heard Ida speak softly to Mary in Chinese. I was sure it was a warning.

But Mary answered Dr. Erickson in a soft voice. "I would be most honored to participate, if you would allow it."

That surprised him into silence, for a moment at least, while she carefully picked her way through the row of spectators and down the steps to the operating area. My gallant husband stepped forward to help her descend. "You can see how we have used Roentgen's rays to make the image," he told her, leading her to the hanging sheet and placing the negative at her eye level. "There are all sorts of uses for this equipment. You must take one of these devices back to your country with you. People will be amazed by what we can see. I'm sure you will find use for it."

She followed him politely and put her face close to the image, glancing back at the patient from time to time.

"We will have to see if we can put together a setup and ship it to you in Jiujiang," Stephen said enthusiastically.

Satisfied with her inspection of the image, she gave him a charming smile. "That is so generous of you, Dr. Chapman. But I am afraid there will be no electrical power in the cities and towns where we will be working. You must save the equipment for places here where it can be used." She removed her hat and jacket and carefully rolled up her sleeves to the elbow. A nurse appeared at her side with a basin of water and she thoroughly soaped and rinsed her hands and arms, donning an overlarge apron that the nurse tied behind her back. Before turning to the patient, she walked to a small table with a curious-looking container, set atop a spirit lamp, that appeared to be giving off a misty spray. Smiling at it, she gestured to Ida, who nodded. Then she turned back to Stephen. Everyone else was silently paying attention to her every move. I thought they were watching for her to make a mistake but I saw that she was unmoved by that attention. "Perhaps the most important things we can bring back with us are the antiseptic procedures of Dr. Lister and the careful sterilizing of materials near open wounds."

"Ah, yes. Germ theory has been a great advance for all of us," Stephen agreed. His mentor at the university, Dr. Jamieson, had been researching germs, and that was what had originally drawn Stephen to his laboratory. I guessed, from what I knew of Stephen's work at the university, that the curious-looking container was spraying carbolic acid in order to destroy germs during the surgery. This was something the women doctors could take back to China without needing electrification to use it.

Dr. Erickson was getting impatient. Mary was clearly very knowledgeable and thorough in her preparations, but he stood with his hands on his hips, as if he was not at all impressed. He loomed over her as she approached the man on the stretcher, but she appeared to be unaffected. She was a petite, slight figure, tiny beside the tall men around her. Her Western-style dress and flat Oriental face contrasted with the suits and beards of the masculine figures. With utter calm, she took up a scalpel and I turned my stare to the ceiling.

By the rapt attention of the audience, I judged that she performed well. Certainly they would have reacted immediately to any error on her part. I was holding my breath without even realizing it. Then I heard a tink, tink, tink, then a general exhalation of breath, followed by, amazingly, applause. Looking down, I saw blood, but also a metal tray holding three shotgun pellets. Mary was still carefully working on the wound, as unaffected by the now positive atmosphere as she had been by the negative atmosphere that preceded it. I looked up again, avoiding the sight of the bloody sheets. After some time had passed, I glanced down and could see that she had sutured the wound. Finally, the still sleeping patient was wheeled away. I could breathe easily again.

# TWO

There was a general movement in the room. Everyone stood and shook off the effects of our intense concentration. Soon I was swept along the row and down the stairs, as all the spectators climbed down and spread out into the operating area. I was following Ida, being careful to navigate the steep stairs, when I felt a hand at my elbow helping me descend. It was Stephen. I tingled at his touch as he put his arm around my waist and led me forward through the crowd. The medical students had gathered around the Crookes tube, and the white sheet that held the film negatives pinned up for them to see, but they parted as Stephen guided Ida and me through.

"Mr. Grubbé, I have some ladies I would like you to meet."

The young man turned from the sheet, where he had been pinning more films, and gave a slight bow. Stephen introduced us. "Dr. Kahn, Emily, this is Mr. Emil Grubbé. Mr. Grubbé is a student at Hahnemann. Mr. Grubbé, Dr. Ida Kahn and my wife." I recognized the name of the school of medicine that specialized in homeopathy. I knew there was disagreement between those who provided that type of training and professors at the more traditional schools of medicine in the city. "But he already has a laboratory for X-ray treatment. He was one of the first to apply the work of Roentgen to actual treatment here in Chicago."

"Dr. Chapman has been very helpful in getting a hearing for me from Dr. Erickson and others." Mr. Grubbé smiled and I realized how very young he was, even younger than me. I thought he could not be more than twenty. "Come, let me show you how it is done."

As he began to demonstrate how to place a hand over a plate and then the tube over the hand, I looked across the bent heads and saw Dr. Erickson glaring at the crowd of men gathered around Mr. Grubbé. It crossed my mind that he might be jealous of the attention the younger man was getting. He certainly was not pleased. Perhaps Mary Stone also noticed his reaction. She turned her back on the X-ray machinery and attempted to engage the tall physician in conversation as he shrugged into his jacket. But he continued to frown and brushed off her attentions to march over to the edge of our group. Some of the young men moved out of his way with uncomfortable looks when they felt his presence behind them. Mr. Grubbé was pointing to some of the films pinned to the white sheet when Dr. Erickson interrupted. "Yes, yes, the pictures can be of some help. However, have you explained the dangers?" He reached out and took the younger man's left hand and raised it for all to see. It was scarred and mottled with what looked like a painful burn.

Mr. Grubbé pulled his hand back. "It is true. We are finding that the rays may result in burns. This very characteristic has led us to believe the rays may also be used for treatment of some cancers."

Dr. Erickson guffawed at that. "Nonsense, surgery is the recognized treatment for cancers."

"We're seeing some very interesting results from our treatments," the younger man insisted.

"Now that is not something that has been recognized. Not at all, young man. Perhaps your homeopathic studies lead you to misconstrue what you see, but these treatments are not recognized, not recognized at all." He turned to the crowd of young men who were, after all, his students. "The value of these machines is to show what is beneath the skin before the surgeon makes the first incision. That is all. Take this one." He pointed to a film that showed the bones of an arm marred by what appeared to be very poorly healed fractures. "It is far too damaged to warrant further treatment. You see the ulna here, and here? Beyond repair. Save the patient the trouble. But treating cancers, not at all. Now, it is time to proceed to lunch. We resume at two o'clock." He strode from the room.

During this speech I felt Stephen stiffen beside me. When I looked up, I saw his neck had reddened and I knew he was very angry about something. I assumed it was the way Dr. Erickson had dismissed the work of Mr. Grubbé. I put a hand on his arm to soothe him and he looked down at me as if he had forgotten my presence but, before I could talk to him, Mary Stone patted my other arm. "Mrs. Chapman, we are so very glad you could come to this demonstration."

"I was most impressed to see you perform the surgery. My husband told me about you and your plans to open a clinic when you return to China. However, we really must return home now. We have two young children, you know, and I have left them long enough for today. Stephen will escort me home on the afternoon train." I placed a hand on his arm.

"No, my dear, I must help Mr. Grubbé dismantle his equipment," Stephen told me. "But I understand there is a luncheon in honor of Dr. Stone and Dr. Kahn. I have secured you an invitation, so you should go along with them for that." He appeared quite pleased with his arrangements, but I was not happy. I had conceded to him by coming into the city for the demonstration, but this was the first I'd heard of luncheon plans.

It was too public a place to converse about private matters. The young medical students had wandered away, but Mary and Ida waited. I gritted my teeth. "That is most kind, but I am afraid I will have to give them my apology. I really must return home." I was at the end of my tether. I felt I had cooperated quite enough for one day. But Stephen was not looking at me and he moved to assist Grubbé in dismantling the Roentgen device without replying. It was obvious that he had no intention of accompanying me. "Fine, I'll expect to see you at home for supper," I told him, speaking to his back. I was preparing to leave when he suddenly straightened up.

"Emily, if you cannot stay for the luncheon, why don't you invite Dr. Stone and Dr. Kahn to tea tomorrow? I'm sure they'd like to visit the university while they're here."

I was ambushed. "I wouldn't want to take up their valuable time," I responded. "I'm sure they have too many appointments for such a trivial engagement."

Even I could hear a hint of discord in our exchange, but it was immediately smoothed over by Mary Stone. "Oh, no, we would be honored by the invitation. We have appreciated the visits we've made to several of the wives of physicians and missionaries during our stay."

In the end, I could not help but agree to the visit. Stephen seemed to lose interest then, and he turned back to helping with the equipment. It was clear that I would have to make my way to the train station alone. Mary patted my arm and led me out of the room to the foyer where we found Miss Howe and Mrs. Appleby waiting to lead the way to the luncheon. I stubbornly refused to go with them, but Mary insisted that we confirm the details of their visit the next day before she would leave.

I was preparing myself to exit into the heat of the day and find a cab when I heard my name hailed from across the room. Looking up, I recognized Detective Whitbread, my friend from the Chicago police department.

"Detective Whitbread! What on earth are you doing here?"

"My dear Mrs. Chapman. Just here to interview a suspect in a robbery case. He was stabbed before he could escape and they brought him here for surgery. I was able to get a word with him before they put him under. What luck to run into you. We've been missing you at the station these past few months."

The lanky detective had been my mentor when I first came

to the city. Working with him helped me to complete a study of criminal statistics in my first year, and that had been followed by a cooperation that led to my involvement in several investigations. But in the past year my family obligations had restricted my activities, so that I seldom saw him now. It was a compliment that he claimed to miss my presence, yet I'd felt obliged to turn down his invitations to return to our work together. My time was simply too taken up with my children.

He was rubbing his hands in anticipation as he stepped towards me. "This is quite fortuitous. I wanted to discuss with you how you want to structure our work this fall. I heard you'll be returning to your research. I have some ideas on how to take advantage of some new information we've been gathering." Ever since he'd first been approached, Whitbread was unexpectedly enthusiastic about the opportunity to work with academics from the university in the analysis of various aspects of police work in the city.

"And I have another problem that I think might interest you. I've just been informed of a death. In Chinatown. A herbalist has died and they've asked for the police. Very unusual for them, they usually fend off police investigation. Interesting that it should happen just when your Chinese lady doctors are visiting." It did not surprise me that Whitbread would be aware of Mary and Ida. There was little of importance in the city that escaped him. It was surprising to have him invite me to participate in an investigation. In the past, I had to argue for my inclusion. This time he was eager. "There's no telling how things can relate, is there? But, in any case, wouldn't you like to join me? I do believe this investigation may have some unusual aspects that may be of interest to you." He grinned at me. He had an infectious enthusiasm for even the grimmest aspects of his job and he always expected me to share it.

I explained that I needed to return home to my children. "Oh, but isn't Delia taking care of them?" he asked. Delia was a cousin of Whitbread's wife. Men! Like Stephen, Whitbread had no understanding of the deep responsibility and constant attention required to care for children. Both of them failed to understand that I could not just return to the activities I had participated in before the birth of my children. It exasperated me that they could not understand why I was needed at home.

When he realized he could not persuade me otherwise, Whitbread offered to deliver me to the train station and *that* offer I took gratefully. On the way, he tried to get me to agree to come into the city the next day to meet about work he wanted my students to do in the fall. Like Stephen, he assumed I would return to my lectureship when the next university quarter started. I knew in my heart that was unlikely, but I couldn't tell them yet. Instead, I told him firmly that I had already invited Mary Stone and Ida Kahn to tea. He snorted at the thought, but left off trying to convince me. I was glad, at least, to be in plenty of time for my train when he stopped at the station. I watched his carriage disappear into the crowded streets of the city with a tiny pang of regret. Before my children were born I would have happily gone with him.

# THREE

No, Jack, come back here." I hoisted my infant daughter on my hip while I grabbed my son by the scruff of his neck, dragging him back over to the pile of wooden blocks that I had laid out on the rug in front of the window seat.

They would be here any minute. I looked around anxiously. The scene was set, but my offspring refused to cooperate. Little Elizabeth squirmed in my arms and my fifteen-month-old son had recently discovered how to crawl with rapid crablike movements, escaping my grasp.

"No, Jack, stay. Play with the blocks, see?" They were given to us by Dean Marion Talbot, who'd been told by the top educators at the university that these were the most up-to-date learning toys available. I piled them up, hoping he would take the hint and imitate his beloved mama, but he was having none of it. He saw Kitty slip under the shawl I had draped over the desk and he wanted to follow. I clung to his little jacket as I heard the doorbell.

"Delia!" There was no need for me to yell. Our young maid was conscientious in the extreme. Stephen said she was afraid of me, but lately it seemed I could do nothing right in his eyes. "Straighten your cap," I hissed when Delia stopped in the doorway, confused. She was a slight, pale girl of fifteen with large blue eyes and hunched shoulders. "Go, answer the door." I let go of Jack to wave her away.

Sitting up straight, so as to be carefully framed in the bay window, I tried to smooth my skirts and arranged my little daughter

in my arms. I had chosen the sprigged muslin of my dress to complement the green velvet drapes hanging in the window. Making clothes for myself and the children had become an obsession of mine over the last year. But my skill with a needle was questionable. I looked down and noticed the dropped stitches in the seam of my daughter's matching gown. I plucked at the fabric and moved her to my other arm to hide the fault. Suddenly, I felt how very makeshift and cheap the whole place must appear.

The second-story apartment on Blackstone was the best we could afford. There were a few good pieces of furniture I had inherited when my mother passed away, but I had to scrimp and save and do my own sewing to try to achieve the level of gentility I remembered from my parents' home in Boston. Seeing the room through a stranger's eyes, I felt a complete fool. My efforts were so amateur. The two exotic women entering my home had been entertained in some of the finest drawing rooms of Prairie Avenue and Michigan Avenue. Whatever had possessed Stephen to invite them to tea in our pitiful little parlor?

Jack found his balance on all fours and moved towards the desk where I had so carefully set out tea and sandwiches. "No, Jack," I hissed. I could hear Delia directing our guests to the parlor door. I half rose, but suddenly Elizabeth screamed. I realized I had accidentally squeezed her little arm. She was red in the face with anger as I sat back down.

My children seemed determined to disrupt this important occasion. Sometimes I wondered how Stephen and I could have created our children. Jack was named for my father, Elizabeth for my husband's mother, but when faced with their contrariness, my children seemed far more foreign than any of the children of immigrants I had met at Hull House.

Lizzie screamed again and beat her little fists in my face. "Lizzie, no, here." I rocked her in my arms, but she only screamed louder. As I tried to quiet her, I saw a sudden look of alarm appear on Delia's face. Behind her, two round faces appeared, looking startled.

I turned to see what they were responding to, but I was too late.

I yelled, "No, Jack!" as my son yanked the shawl down from the desk, pulling the tea and sandwiches onto the floor. The hot tea splashed his shirt, he screamed, and the cat jumped out from under the desk, grabbed a sandwich, then escaped into the hallway with a scratch of her claws on the wooden floor. Lizzie hiccupped sharply and I looked down in time to see her throw up all over the front of my dress. And then, to cap it all off, I felt my whole face tremble and, to my immense embarrassment, I broke down in sobs. I wanted to sink into the floor and die. I just couldn't stop it. Trying to stop only made it worse. It was horrible.

Through my sobs I saw Delia frozen in the doorway. The poor girl had no idea what to do. Then, the two small women behind her glided in and brought order to chaos. Ida Kahn, the shorter one with round rimless spectacles, gathered up Jack, wiped the tea off his shirt and hands with a towel from the desk, and whisked him back to his blocks. With him ensconced on her lap, she was soon entertaining him by building towers.

At the same time Mary Stone whispered to Delia, who disappeared and returned with cloths the Chinese woman used to clean up the tea from the floor, righting the pot and placing it on the desk. Then she lifted my still wailing daughter out of my hands and gently hushed her. I gathered together the scattered sandwiches and retreated to the kitchen.

Delia quickly prepared a fresh tray of tea things. By the time it was ready I'd managed to bring my sobs to a sputtering stop and to sponge off the front of my dress, so I carried it out to the parlor. Mary passed Lizzie off to Delia, who took the baby eagerly, looking at me with apprehension. Despite the fact that she had been hired to help care for the children, I'd made it perfectly clear that I would not have my motherly duties usurped, so she was fearful of my disapproval now. I gulped and nodded, allowing her to relax as Mary led her to the rocking chair, where she was soon happily rocking with the baby.

I stiffened as Mary turned back to me with a cup of tea. I patted the damp spot on the front of my gown, completely humiliated by the chaos. With all the authority of a medical doctor she insisted I drink a cup of heavily sweetened tea, hovering over me until I obeyed. It calmed me, but I felt a knot in my throat that prevented me from speaking, I was so embarrassed. Even coughing would not clear it.

Refilling my cup and setting it by me, she took a cup for herself and sat primly in one of the chairs I had set out for my guests, hoping to impress them with a picture of domestic happiness. What a perfect mess my children and I had made of that! But now there was quiet, as Jack gurgled with joy in the games Ida played with him and Delia rocked Lizzie in mutual comfort.

Mary sipped her cup of tea as if none of the chaos of the past several minutes had ever happened. "We were so very happy to receive your invitation," she told me. "You are so kind to invite us into your home." She was a petite woman with a heart-shaped face, smooth as porcelain. Both women wore Western dresses in the most up-to-date fashion, with high-necked collars, huge leg-of-mutton sleeves, and waists cinched tight. Delicate tiny pearl earrings dropped from their ears on almost invisible wires.

I sniffled inelegantly and attempted to swallow. I still could not quite bring myself to speak.

"As you know, Ida and I have been here for several years studying. In Ann Arbor we lived with Miss Howe, Ida's adopted mother, who brought us from China. Of course, people were very kind to us and we had friends, especially among our Methodist congregation. But it was not so often that we have been welcomed into the home of a woman scholar such as yourself. We are very grateful to you for taking the time to see us."

Finally, I took a deep breath and, stretching my neck, spoke around the knot in my throat. "I must apologize for the confusion. I am so sorry."

"Oh, no, you must not say so. It is a great honor to visit you.

Ida and I have been able to spend our time studying these past years but that is nothing to your accomplishments. To be not only a scholar at the University of Chicago but also a wife and mother to two children, this is extremely impressive. I cannot tell you how much we admire you. Dr. Chapman has told us how proud he is of his most accomplished wife. We would learn from you," she said earnestly.

I ducked my head in embarrassment. It was praise I little deserved. I had been a scholar, it was true. Before the birth of my son I even held a lectureship. For that fall quarter I had managed to retain the position, despite the prejudice against giving any appointment to a married woman, and I had proven myself in my post. But, by spring, it was impossible to disguise my condition. There was certainly no precedent for a woman carrying a child to hold a lectureship, so I was given a leave of absence. It was against the policy of the university to employ married women, but the dean of women, Marion Talbot, argued my case. There was a tacit understanding that I would return to my duties the following fall.

I had my son in April, only to find that caring for a baby, and then moving into the apartment, was far more time-consuming than I ever imagined. When the summer ended I found myself again with child. With that discovery, I lost all hope of continuing. I was supposed to return to my appointment within a few months but, if I failed to take up the post this time, I knew I would have to give it up forever.

I realized Stephen must have told these Chinese women of my plan. It was a point of contention, one of many that summer. I knew it could only be a dream. I looked around the room, aware of the respite from the demands of my children, but I knew it was only temporary. That was something Stephen seemed unable to understand.

"No doubt you will one day have children of your own," I told Mary. Was I wishing her a blessing, or invoking a curse? At that time in my life, I was unsure.

She shook her head sadly. "It is not to be. I see you think I am modest, but that is not it. You see, in my country a marriage must be arranged between two families." She put down her cup. "You will find it strange, but in China a man will not marry a woman whose feet have not been bound. It is not something you have heard of here, I know. But it is the custom for a girl child to have her feet bound so they cannot grow beyond this." She made a gesture with her hands, indicating the size of a small box.

"How can that be?" I thought of the perfect little feet of my daughter and I was appalled.

"It is painful. They are strapped in, you see...not allowed to grow."

"How awful."

She smiled. "It is a custom. My father decided against it. My mother had her feet bound according to custom but, when it came time for it to happen to me, my father heard my cries and he decided it would not be. My parents are Christians, you see. They already had gone against the old practices of our country so they decided to take the Western way in this as well. But it means no man would have me as a bride." She seemed quite at peace with this. Her expression remained content.

"My father also met Dr. Kate Bushnell. She is a Western woman who had a clinic in our town. When he saw that, he was greatly impressed. He decided that his daughter, whose big feet would make her never marry, should become a doctor, too. So he took me to Miss Howe and asked her to help me become a doctor."

Ida looked at me over Jack's head, nodding in agreement.

"Miss Howe adopted Ida. She was the sixth daughter born to a good family. But daughters are not wanted so much, you see. Miss Howe also adopted some sons. She is the one who helped Ida and me to study medicine."

"My husband is most impressed by your skills, both of you," I admitted.

"But it is nothing to you, who are not only a scholar but also a wife and mother. This is most impressive. We will return to China to open a clinic in our native Jiujiang, but we will not marry."

"I once thought I would never marry," I confessed, surprised at myself for the sudden wish to confide in her. "You never know what the future will bring."

She smiled and looked across at Ida, who shook her head. It was as if they shared secrets I could never understand. But I felt myself older and wiser than them. I had not expected to find myself anchored down with children as I was. I felt sure the future could not be so easily predicted for any young woman. That conviction was based on my own experience, something they could not understand.

"I am curious about your names. I'm guessing that you changed them when you came to study in America."

"That is right. If you like, I could show you our Chinese names. I brought my calligraphy brushes along," Mary said.

"I would love to see that. I've heard that you did demonstrations at some of the other houses you visited. My friends were very impressed with the beauty of your writing." I made my way over to my desk. "I have ink right here."

"You are not to worry. I have special ink I use. See?" She pulled a bar of solid black ink out of her bag and held it up. Then she set her things up on the desk, insisting I should sit. She asked Delia to bring her a little pitcher of water, then moistened the ink and rubbed it back and forth on a stone. Once she had the correct consistency, she placed a sheet of paper on the desk, then uncovered a bamboo brush and placed it carefully next to the ink.

When she began to unbutton the sleeves of her dress, preparing to roll them up, I stopped her.

"Oh, wait," I said, "I have something for you to use." I went to the desk and pulled out some paper sleeve protectors. Mary was thrilled by the discovery as I showed her how to wear them. She insisted on demonstrating to Ida how they worked. Her excitement went far towards making me feel more confident than I had since the fiasco at the start of their visit.

Once she had her preparations completed she seemed to do

a little meditation, swirling the brush on the ink stone and trying it on a scrap for some moments before she began.

"Here is my Chinese name—Shih Meiyu." She drew several intersecting lines on the paper. "In Chinese, when you say a person's name, the family name comes first, followed by the individual's name. My family name, Shih, means 'stone,' so I picked that word for my English name." She swiftly drew several more characters. "And here is Ida's Chinese name—Kang Aide. She picked an English family name that sounded a little like her own. And now I shall write you a poem."

She set the first paper aside, then took a rectangle of paper and carefully folded it, over and over, until, when she opened it back up, the folds defined four squares across and five squares down. Holding the brush perpendicular to the paper she swiftly drew a little picture of a few strokes in each box. Starting from the upper right hand corner, she carefully filled in the five blocks down, then the next column top to bottom, and so forth, until the entire paper was filled. There was only one chance for each stroke, with no opportunity to correct a mistake. It made me hold my breath as she drew each square, the point of the brush held for a moment over the blank paper before it dropped down and was moved to form the image. Her concentration was so intense I hardly noticed the deep serenity of the room—Delia rocking with the baby, while Jack giggled quietly in Ida's arms and a tranquil breeze drifted through the open window.

When Mary put down the brush she smiled and translated. She explained that she had written out a Taoist poem and pointed to each character as she named it.

*A thousand mountains birds flying stopped*
*Ten thousand footpaths, man's footsteps dissolved*
*Alone in a boat an old man wearing a straw hat sits*
*Alone fishing cold river snow*

Somehow coolness pervaded the heat of midsummer in the room and all was at peace. If only it could last.

Suddenly the doorbell rang and there were heavy knocks on the door. My heart skipped a beat. The bell rang insistently, followed by more knocks. Mary began to move, but I put a hand on her arm, at the same time waving Delia back into the rocking chair. I would answer it. When I opened the front door, I was startled to see Detective Whitbread, his lanky frame looming over me, and two uniformed patrolmen lurking behind him.

"Mrs. Chapman, is Dr. Mary Stone here?"

"Detective Whitbread." I felt the blood move up my neck to my cheeks. What was going on?

"Dr. Stone?" He looked beyond me to where Mary stood in the doorway to the parlor. Ida, still holding my son, stood behind her. "Are you Dr. Stone?"

Mary nodded. "Yes."

"Dr. Mary Stone, I have a warrant for your arrest for the murder of Lo Sung Chi. I'll have to ask you to come with me now."

I was flabbergasted. I watched helplessly as the policemen hurried Mary out of our apartment and down the stairs. At a questioning glance from Whitbread, I protested that I could not leave. I gestured towards my children. What did he think? When they were gone, suddenly all of the uneasiness and conflict that had been simmering in my home that summer came to a head and I knew then that Stephen would never forgive me.

# FOUR

Stephen arrived home, unaware of the earlier drama. He came into the parlor full of energy, swept Jack up with his good arm, and planted a kiss on Lizzie's forehead as she lay in my arms.

"And how was your visit? I see you're still all dressed up, my little man." Jack giggled with joy as Stephen tickled him.

Delia stood in the doorway, a strained look on her face. "Take the children into the kitchen, Delia, while I talk to Dr. Chapman."

"Yes!" Stephen approved of this idea. "They can take their supper there." His eyes crinkled with a smile of triumph he was trying hard to suppress. He disliked sitting down to formal meals in the dining room and had been agitating to feed the children at the broad kitchen table. I put this down to the lack of formality in his own unconventional childhood but I was firm about the need to bring up our offspring to be able to move in polite society. It exasperated me that he assumed I would suddenly abandon my principles in the matter, but there were weightier issues to discuss. Earlier that year, Stephen had turned thirty-eight. He was twelve years my senior. His hair was always a little too long, as he would not take the time to have it cut, but his warm brown eyes were as deep and inviting as ever, even when I was exasperated with him.

As I transferred my daughter into Delia's arms and carried Jack after her, Stephen seemed completely insensitive to the air of anxiety still present in our apartment. When I returned, he was standing over the desk with a broad grin on his face as he looked at the sheet of calligraphy.

"I see she was here." He rubbed his hands together with glee. "Tell me all about it."

I felt sick to my stomach. "Stephen, there is something I need to tell you. They were here, Dr. Stone and Dr. Kahn." My head was filled with the memory of the scene with Whitbread. "But she was taken away." I gulped. "Mary Stone was arrested for the murder of that man in Chinatown."

His face went blank, like a chalkboard swiped by a wet rag. Disbelief grew in his expression, as I explained as succinctly as I could what had happened. He just stared at me for a moment, and then his brow contracted in an awful frown.

"Emily, what is going on?" He shook his head back and forth. "How could this happen?"

"I don't know. He just said it was for the death of a herbalist, in Chinatown. That was where he went when he left the hospital yesterday."

"But I thought you went with him?"

"No, I came home. For the children, Stephen. You do remember the children? He wanted me to go with him but I had to come home. I told him Mary and Ida were coming here for tea today. That must be how he knew to come here looking for them."

Stephen stared at me. "But then what happened? Why didn't you go with them?"

"Go with them? How could I go with them? I had to be here with my children."

"But surely you plan to help her? After all the times you've worked with Whitbread before? He'll tell you what's going on. How can you not? She needs you."

"Stephen, that was before I had the children. There's nothing I can do for her. Whitbread is the police. He'll handle it."

"Emily, how can you do this? How can you just stand there and do nothing?" He shook his head again. "Oh, and here I had thought you were finally coming out of the swamp of misery in which you have mired yourself for the past year. My God! When will you ever return to your interests and your work?" He gave a mirthless laugh. "I told myself—when you finally met Dr. Stone and Dr. Kahn yesterday—that you'd remembered your own passions and ambitions. What a fool I was to think that."

He raised a hand, not letting me speak, but I felt a searing flame of anger in my breast—that he would assume that meeting the impressive women doctors would in some way revitalize me. Why could he not understand the sense of responsibility I felt to our children? He was staring at me.

"You have no intention of resuming your work with Whitbread...none at all. You let him arrest Dr. Stone and you aren't going to help her. You don't care if she hangs."

"That is not fair," I finally retorted. "Apparently Dr. Stone was seen pouring something in a man's ear and then he died several hours later. There are witnesses and a warrant. Of course, when Whitbread told me that, I had to let him take her. What do you expect me to do?" I closed my eyes, trying to block out the memory of the calm and friendly young Chinese woman who had painted the lovely poem. "I'm sorry this has happened to her, but there is nothing that I can do about it."

"Since when have you become so helpless? You've never been like this before. What is the matter with you? You refuse to return to your studies, you refuse to work with Whitbread, now you won't help this woman who was arrested in our own home."

"I have not refused to return to my studies," I insisted. I was furious with that accusation. "I have two children to care for. I have a home and family to maintain. Why do you never give me credit for this? You can go out to your laboratory. You can attend meetings, surgeries, experiments. You barely see your children at dinner before you rush out the door to some lecture or discussion. Because you grew up in the slums of Baltimore, you have no idea what it is to have a normal childhood. We can't let our children run wild. They must be trained, or how will they ever be accepted?" I thought of Jack pulling down the teapot. Stephen was never here to help me keep them from behaving like that.

"Emily, I have told you, there is no need for you to confine yourself to the house like this. That's why we hired Delia."

"Delia is an uneducated maid. We cannot afford anything more. They are our children, our responsibility. But you barely have time for them. You are off doing your experiments and then you come home and sing the praises of the wonderful Dr. Stone and Dr. Kahn." I gulped back a sob, unable to believe I was saying this to him. It was a mistake to do so, and I knew it.

"If I have praised Dr. Stone and Dr. Kahn it is for the same qualities that you have always had. I have tried everything I can think of to get you to see that you don't have to give up your life like this, but you won't listen. Dean Talbot has held a position for you. I have urged you to join me in attending lectures. I hoped the help of Delia would allow you to spend time on your studies, but you insist on wallowing in self-pity."

"Self-pity! I do not."

"You do, you are. I have tried to be patient. I have tried to help you. But to allow this to happen to another woman and do nothing? That is not like you, Emily. It is more than I can sustain. I cannot and will not support you in this madness any longer." He stepped close to me and put his hand up to my cheek, refusing to listen to my attempts at rebuttal. "Emily, what has happened to you?"

With a violent shake of his head he turned away and I heard the front door slam as he left the house. I collapsed in sobs, my heart like a cold stone in my breast. The accusation was so unfair, but my inability to pierce his arguments was frustrating. He wouldn't listen to me. It was all very wrong.

# FIVE

S tephen kept urging me to go out into the world, so I did. I had no choice after he stormed out of our home. He did not return that night and, by morning, I had progressed from sorrow to guilt to anger. When I woke from a fitful sleep I was decided. I left the children with Delia and took the train into Chicago to go to the Harrison Street police station.

The sergeant at the desk downstairs did not recognize me at first. There was a time, when I was first at the university, that I visited the station several days a week. I'd worked on a project to collate information from boxes of identity cards collected during arrests all over the city. They had been gathered together by Detective Whitbread and he was tremendously excited that a scholar from the university would finally analyze the information for a sociological study. Soon, I was a familiar figure to the men who worked at the station. The fact that I was no longer recognized was a blow to my self-esteem, but I knew it was my own fault. I had stayed away too long.

I introduced myself, explaining my connection to Detective Whitbread. The tall, white-haired policeman on the desk finally remembered me but, before he could sign me in, he became embroiled in an argument with a woman who had barged up to the counter and stubbornly refused to be turned away.

"I insist on speaking to the officer in charge of this investigation!" I was startled to recognize Miss Gertrude Howe,

Ida Kahn's adoptive mother. Sure enough, Ida stood beside her quietly, her hands clasped at her waist, her eyes peering through rimless spectacles. The older woman had a tall, big-boned figure and plain features. She wore a rather severe black serge dress and jacket, and a broad-brimmed black straw hat with a jaunty set of standup feathers set off her determined-looking face. She was the epitome of a Methodist missionary, very earnest and straightforward. I'd learned earlier that she'd spent more than twenty years doing missionary work in China. Beside her, Ida seemed quite small. She wore a brown taffeta dress with large puffed sleeves, with a small cameo pinned at her throat and a wide sash at her waist. A small straw hat with silk flowers was perched on her head.

Miss Howe turned from the tall policeman to solicit my help. "Mrs. Chapman, it is a good thing you are here. Can you get this man to listen to reason? You have worked with the local police, or so your husband told us."

From the look of misery on the sergeant's face, I conjectured that this was not the first time Miss Howe had been to the station on Mary's behalf. I'd hoped to speak with Detective Whitbread privately, but reluctantly suggested that I could accompany the women to his office. The sergeant grimaced at the thought so we compromised by agreeing to have Ida wait below. The poor man truly did not know what to make of a Chinese woman in Western dress. I led Miss Howe up the worn stone stairs to the second floor, all the while feeling a pang of guilt. Stephen was right. I should have gone with them when they had taken Mary in the night before.

We found Whitbread in his office. While he showed no enthusiasm at our arrival, I was once again overcome by feelings of familiarity. I had spent so many hours in that high-ceilinged room with its window facing a brick wall. Within the room, a desk, hard wooden chairs, file cabinets, and academic tomes on criminology still filled the space. It was reassuring that the hand-lettered poster listing "The Best Rules for Health, Happiness, and Success" still hung between two cabinets. My eyes sought out number twenty. "If responsibility confronts you, seize it. Do not throw it aside—responsibility represents opportunity." It seemed particularly apt.

"I am in the middle of an interrogation," Whitbread said, halting our approach with an outstretched hand as he rose from his desk. In front of him were two Chinese men who presented contrasting images. One was a short, stooped man wearing broad cotton trousers, a loose-fitting cotton jacket, and a black cap. His hair was pulled back in a braid that fell down his back. The other was very jaunty looking, in a checked wool suit and bowler hat similar to one that any American man might wear. There was no braid down his back but under the rim of the bowler you could just see the taut end of a braid that must have been curled up round his head and hidden under the hat. I learned later that this was commonly done by Chinese men who wanted to appear more Western by hiding their queue of hair without cutting it. This man had a sizable diamond ring on one hand. He grinned at us, seeming at ease, while the other man stood with his hands clasped in front of him, looking at the floor. Whitbread looked even more tall and lanky than usual beside the two men.

"I am sorry to interrupt, but I came to ask you about Dr. Stone, and I found Miss Howe here trying to find out what is happening. She is Dr. Stone's guardian and accompanied her to the United States to study medicine. Surely you will want to talk to her. Miss Gertrude Howe, this is Detective Henry Whitbread. He is the one who arrested Mary."

Whitbread frowned.

"I really must know what has happened to Dr. Stone," Miss Howe insisted. "I brought her here from China to study and she has been awarded honors for her work. That you should arrest her is an outrage. I protest this action and I demand to see her and to know what is going on."

Whitbread rolled his eyes. He was no stranger to strong-willed women, his own wife being one. "I must finish questioning this man before I can discuss it. I suppose you may enter and wait for the interrogation to complete. Please come in and sit down." He waved at a couple of chairs in the corner and I took Miss Howe's arm and led her there while he continued. "This is Mr. Tan Tsao who saw Dr. Stone with the dead man, Lo Sung Chi." He gestured towards the man in Chinese garb. "Tan Tsao does not speak English, so this is Mr. Charlie Kee who has been sent by the Hip Lung Yee Kee Company to interpret for us." The bowler-hatted Mr. Kee smiled at us, nodding, while the other man continued to look at the floor. Whitbread turned back to them. "Ask him what he saw after he delivered his package to Mr. Lo."

Kee turned to the other man and talked to him in what sounded like a series of grunts to me, as I was unfamiliar with the Chinese language. In fact, the only time I had encountered any Chinese people, before Dr. Stone and Dr. Kahn, was when I visited that country's exhibit at the World's Columbian Exposition a few years before. Certainly the words they spoke to each other meant nothing to me.

"He says Lo Sung Chi greeted Chinese lady doctor as he leaves shop. Chinese lady doctor comes all the time. They argue about medicines. Lo Sung Chi makes Chinese herb medicine. Many people come to him when sick. Lady doctor tells him he is wrong, Western medicine good, Chinese medicine bad. He says they argue about it."

I felt Miss Howe move in the chair beside me. I turned and put a hand on her arm, silently imploring her to remain quiet.

"Then what happened? Did he see her leave? When did Mr. Lo become ill?" Whitbread asked.

Again there was back and forth between the two Chinese men. The man called Tan Tsao shuffled his feet and glanced up at Whitbread, quickly turning his eyes back to the floor again. Mr. Kee seemed to be telling him something at length. He replied. Finally, Kee turned to us with the translation. "He says lady doctor put something in ear of Lo Sung Chi. She leaves. Lo gets sick. Very sick. Sick for some hours, finally he dies."

Miss Howe jumped to her feet. "That man is lying!"

Whitbread rose to his feet as well. "Madam, please!"

"No, he is lying. That's not what the other man said at all." She frowned and shook her head. "What he said was that he did not want to get in trouble with the authorities and would Hip Lung protect him. He asked if Hip Lung would really forgive him his debt if he agreed to sign whatever the big nose white man wanted him to do. Kee told him yes, if he signed the paper, his debt would be forgiven. They didn't talk about Lo's death at all!"

She turned to the two men and barked at them in what must have been Chinese. This obviously startled them and they both stared at her as if she had grown an extra head. This was followed by a sharp exchange between Charlie Kee and Miss Howe. When Whitbread intervened, Kee just continued to repeat the story exactly as he had told it before, word for word, while poor Mr. Tan Tsao looked like he wanted to sink into the floor. Finally the detective sent the two Chinese men away.

Miss Howe was furious. "Where did you get that interpreter? He's awful. The tongue they were speaking is a dialect of Cantonese, of which I know only a little from when Ida and I lived in that area some years ago, but even I could tell that what he was saying to you had nothing to do with what he said to the man Tan Tsao!"

Whitbread sat down behind his desk and frowned at her. "The Hip Lung Yee Kee Company commonly provides an interpreter when any Chinamen have dealings with the police or courts. There is always a language problem. These people will happily communicate with white people when they want to sell them something or take their money in gambling but, as soon as there's a crime to be investigated, suddenly none of them understand or speak English. Hip Lung, who is also called

Moy Dong Chew, runs the company on South Clark Street and it is the center of Chinese society in the city."

"Ah, the senior Mr. Moy, of course I know of him," Miss Howe told him. "Well, he's forgiving the man's debt in order to have him tell that story."

Whitbread rubbed his forehead as if it ached. "Which doesn't necessarily mean it is *not* the truth. The local Chinese are a closed society. For the most part they police themselves. It is unusual for us to have to intervene. It's likely that they pay for the protection of the First Ward aldermen—Coughlin and Kenna. Coughlin tried to scapegoat them in his first race a couple of years ago, accusing them of smoking opium. But, since then, they must have started contributing to Kenna's protection fund. That's used to buy off police and politicians, to send prostitutes with TB to a sanitarium, and to keep lawyers on retainer if any of them get into trouble. But, frankly, from the point of view of the police, the Chinese establishments in that ward are among the least objectionable. So when Hip Lung sent Kee with this man as a witness we had to hear him out." He considered the red-faced Miss Howe, who was glaring at him. "You heard the story. This man who died was a herbalist. They're saying Dr. Stone visited him and argued about treatment. They're saying she visited him the day of his death, she treated him, and some hours later he died of poisoning. Are you disputing that account?"

"Of course Mary knew the man. She purchased herbs from him. Certainly they discussed the relative merits of traditional Chinese herbal treatments and modern Western medicine. She may even have treated him for some ailment. They were by no means enemies, even if they did disagree in some matters. But why ever would anyone think she would want to poison the man? It's absurd."

Whitbread looked uncomfortable. "It was alleged that she wanted to get rid of him to start a practice taking over his patients."

"Nonsense, where did you hear such a thing? We will be

returning to Jiujiang, China in the fall to continue our missionary service."

"It was representatives of the local Chinese community who approached the mayor and insisted on the arrest. They indicated the young woman might be suffering from a form of madness."

"Ridiculous! Mary Stone has been attending the University of Michigan for the past four years and she graduated with honors. I'm sure her professors will vouch for her sanity and professional skills. In addition, she has met with many in the local medical community during our visit here and I am certain that all of them will vouch for her as well."

"I've been made aware of her connections in the academic and medical community here," Whitbread admitted. "In fact, Dr. Chapman came to me last night, along with several other medical men, in an attempt to intervene on her behalf. I have no doubt these people, who are prominent members of society themselves, will exert their influence on behalf of Dr. Stone. But, meanwhile, we cannot just ignore the accusations coming from the Chinese community. Surely you can see that?"

"But why would they make such unfounded accusations? That's what I don't understand," Miss Howe said. "Where is Dr. Stone? Is she all right?"

"I assure you, madam, she is being treated with respect. She is housed separately from the common criminals in a special area. She is in no danger."

"Can Miss Howe see her?" I asked.

"I'm sure that can be arranged," Whitbread answered.

But Miss Howe was on her feet. "We will want to visit her later. But first Ida and I must go to Clark Street to discover who is behind this ludicrous accusation."

Whitbread was also on his feet. "Madam, I strongly advise you to refrain from any excursions into that area. As you are a stranger to our city you may be unaware of the types of establishments that are located on South Clark Street."

"Nonsense, Detective. You are wrong to think I am unacquainted with that area of your city. On the contrary, I have visited there many times during these past several years to obtain foods and spices not available elsewhere. And of course I am aware of the saloons, brothels, and gambling establishments. I have visited similar areas of cities all over the world, as part of my missionary activities. And, as it happens, we also have some powerful connections in that community and it is there that I will go to find the truth."

Whitbread shook his head as she stalked out the door. With such serious accusations lodged against her, I knew Whitbread could do nothing to get Mary released, so I decided it would be best for me to accompany Miss Howe and Ida. While I was familiar with those unsavory areas, I had never entered any of the Chinese establishments sprinkled throughout that section of the city. It was with some trepidation that I followed the two women out of the police station and towards Clark Street. If it was members of the Chinese community who had insisted on the arrest of Mary Stone, how did Miss Howe expect to overcome their accusations?

# SIX

I had to scurry to keep up with Miss Howe's long strides. Poor Dr. Kahn, with even shorter legs than mine, was practically running. It appeared Miss Howe knew exactly where she was going and soon we were on Clark Street, facing a storefront bracketed by two Chinese laundries. A large sign announced that it was the Hip Lung Yee Kee Company, with Chinese symbols in vivid red paint under each word. Miss Howe did not enter the open doorway, where men with pigtails down their backs or wound around their heads slouched. Instead, she proceeded around the corner of the building to a barely visible alleyway, marched up and pulled the bell beside a door in the wall.

The door opened, words were exchanged in what I assumed was Chinese, and then we hastily followed Miss Howe as she gathered her skirts to climb a narrow stairway inside the building. We seemed to be ascending to apartments above the storefront we had passed earlier. It was stifling in the stairwell, so I was relieved when we finally arrived at an upper floor. We were led through a small hallway and into a broad room with darkly patterned rugs on the gleaming wood floor. I saw at last that we were being led by a small girl who wore loose cotton pants and a tunic. She stopped and bowed before two women who were seated at a round table carved in dark wood. The chairs they sat in were also of dark wood but inlaid with mother-of-pearl.

As Miss Howe and Dr. Kahn bowed and spoke to them in

Chinese, I couldn't help but stare. They were young—I guessed less than twenty years of age. They had round faces with entirely serene expressions. Their dark hair was pulled back severely and decorated with delicate blossoms that trembled when they moved. Drop earrings of small pearls dangled from their ears. Their gowns were of a light-colored silk, heavily embroidered in flowers and geometric patterns. The fabric covered them from neck to ankles, and the sleeves were so long the tips of their fingers could barely be seen. When I saw their small feet poking from under the hems of their gowns, I remembered Mary telling me about how Chinese women bound their feet. One wore silk slippers smaller than my fist, while the other had her stubs of feet balanced on little porcelain platforms. Each woman had a teacup with a cover and no handle perched beside her. A vase with a tall spray of blossoms sat between them on the table and there was a faint scent of incense in the air.

Suddenly I realized they had all turned to me. "Mrs. Chapman, we are introducing you," Miss Howe explained. "These are the Mrs. Moys. Mr. Dong Chew Moy's wife's name is Chin Guy, and Mr. Dong Yee Moy's wife's name is Luk Shee. Mr. Dong Chew Moy is more commonly known as Hip Lung. He is the oldest of three brothers who are very prominent in Chinatown. His wife is a friend of ours." I bowed in acknowledgement. Meanwhile, the little girl had moved an additional chair so that the three of us could sit facing the young women. Ida continued to converse with them while the girl scurried around placing a small table in front of us and bringing a tray with a teapot and cups.

Miss Howe murmured to me in a low voice. "These are the wives of two of the three brothers who run the Hip Lung Yee Kee Company. It's most unusual for Chinese women to emigrate. Only the wealthiest merchants can afford to bring their families over. Most of them marry and leave their wives behind in China when they come and make their fortunes here. They call it coming to the Gold Mountain and the women left behind are sometimes called Gold Mountain widows. It can be years before the husband returns. Of course he sends money back to his wife all along. But it's unusual to see women in Chinatown. There are only about twenty in the whole city. That's not including prostitutes, of course. Those poor women are often sold into the trade. Many of our missions try to offer girls in that situation a place to go."

"It must be lonely for them...the wives, I mean," I commented.

"Indeed, that is one reason Ida and Mary were welcomed here. When the wives of Hip Lung and his brother heard there were two Chinese women doctors in the city they sent word begging them to visit. The girls have been here once a week during our stay this summer."

"They speak no English?"

"None. But, even if they did, they would never go out of the house. No upper-class woman would, even if they were back in China. They are actually merchant class but here that is virtually the highest class of Chinese you would meet. A few scholars come to study but they would never remain long." She seemed to open a door a tiny bit, to give me a sliver of a view into the very different world which she and the two women doctors had come from. I was intrigued.

Ida turned to me. "They say they are honored to meet a woman scholar such as yourself," she told me. "Learning is highly prized in our country and for a woman to excel in studies is unusual."

"It is not uncommon here. You must tell them they would be welcome to study at the university. I could introduce them to Dean Talbot. She is the dean of women."

Ida smiled and turned back to relay my message. The ladies looked startled and I could tell that they politely demurred. Miss Howe stirred restlessly beside me. Her impatience was impossible to ignore, even for the determinedly impassive young women before us. Ida took a breath and began to speak with animation. I saw Hip Lung's wife respond with accents of concern.

"At last," Miss Howe whispered, "she is telling them about

Mary." She followed their exchange closely, translating for me. "They are shocked. They cannot believe anyone would accuse Mary of such a thing. They both knew the herbalist. That is odd. Luk Shee made an allusion that makes me think the herbalist had other businesses, or had secrets. We'll never get any more out of her, just a hint. Ida is pleading with them to get their husbands to help Mary. And now they are doing the Chinese 'I'm an unworthy woman with no influence,' nonsense. Of course they can pressure the men. Women can always do that if they want to. Drive them mad if they put their minds to it, but naturally they can never admit to it. Well, I think we've done as much as we can here, Ida. Tell them we'll go to the King Yen Lo restaurant. They can send someone for us there if they want us."

We stood and bowed formally to take our leave, with me imitating the actions of Miss Howe and Ida. When they spoke in Chinese it felt like I was looking through a somewhat transparent curtain, with the sounds muffled and the actions blurred. It was a strange feeling to be the only person in the room who could not understand what was going on. That must be what it felt like to be deaf and dumb.

# SEVEN

S oon we were back on Clark Street, with Miss Howe striding ahead while Ida and I hurried to keep pace. We went a block, passing several saloons, stores, and a laundry. We arrived at the glass storefront of a saloon, on which florid gold letters announced *M. Kenna's Workingmen's Exchange*, when Miss Howe abruptly turned into a nearby doorway.

I was used to passing by such establishments in the area of Hull House but I never stopped. While it was a necessary evil to have to walk past such places, I would certainly never enter one. I hesitated, but there was a banner over the door covered in Chinese characters and I realized it was not the door to the saloon. The other two women had already entered and were mounting the steep stairway, so I gathered my skirts and followed. The heat of the day was oppressive and I felt clammy and uncomfortable as I made my way upwards.

At the top, we entered the large open room of a restaurant. The ceiling was high and the wall on the left had large uncurtained windows that let in light but no air. While it was not cool, it still felt less oppressively hot than the outside. The room was filled with round wooden tables that had mother-of-pearl inlays around the edge and patterned marble tops. Teapots and menus in holders sat in the middle of each, and chairs of dark carved wood were placed around them. From the ceiling hung four or five brass chandeliers with flower-shaped glass ornaments in a modern style. Interspersed between them were Oriental-looking boxy paper lanterns with fringes in red and gold. There must have been more than a dozen tables, yet only a few were occupied—one by a pair of Chinese men in business suits, and another by two American women, who could have been from Hull House, in summer hats, shirtwaists, and skirts. Alone in a corner, a Chinese man in a Western-style suit stared at us, and I thought a glance was exchanged between him and Ida.

Miss Howe marched up to a large table in the middle of the room and sat down. Ida and I followed. Almost immediately a short Chinese man with a pigtail down his back and a skull cap, and wearing a loose black cotton shirt with a mandarin collar and wide trousers of the same material, brought a tray with a hot pot of tea and small round cups without handles. I was glad to sink onto one of the hard wooden chairs. It was unexpectedly comfortable. Sipping tea, I listened while Ida talked to the man in Chinese. I was behind the veil again. Their discussion was animated, and soon over. Miss Howe drank down a full cup of tea and sighed as she poured herself another.

Meanwhile, the man who had been sitting alone in the corner stood up and approached us. As the waiter left, he stepped up and bowed, speaking in Chinese to the two women. Miss Howe frowned, but Ida introduced him in English. "Mrs. Chapman, this is Wong Chin Foo. His English name is Mr. Philip Wong. Mr. Wong, this is Mrs. Chapman. Her husband, Dr. Stephen Chapman, has been helping us to visit the medical community during our stay here." She turned to me. "Mr. Wong is a journalist. He had a newspaper, *The Chinese American*, in New York and has recently begun a paper here in Chicago. He also started the Chinese Equal Rights League. Dr. Chapman told us that his wife worked at Hull House, Mr. Wong. I'm sure that will be of interest to you."

Small and dapper, Mr. Wong had no pigtail. His hair was cut short and his suit was of fine linen. I could not tell his age, it might have been anywhere from thirty to fifty, but there was no gray in his hair. A smile remained on his round face as he unexpectedly offered his hand to me. "Wonderful. Delighted to meet you, Mrs. Chapman. Of course I have heard of Hull House. I am a great admirer of Miss Addams and her work there." I shook his outstretched hand. "And so nice to see you again, Miss Howe."

Miss Howe ignored his hand and poured herself another cup of tea. Ida did not flinch, but I sensed that the encounter was uncomfortable.

"Come now, you must not stay offended," he told the older woman. Then he turned to me. "Miss Howe and her missionary friends are not happy with my views, you see, Mrs. Chapman. But I have merely suggested that rather than having them come to the Chinese to spread Christianity, perhaps we should bring Confucius to you in America!"

Miss Howe glowered, but Ida attempted to explain. "Mr. Wong wrote a very controversial article called 'Why Am I a Heathen?' He does not believe in the benefit of Christian missionary work. Unlike Mary and myself, who embrace Christianity and feel we have benefited very much from my adopted mother and her friends," she said, as she squeezed Miss Howe's arm, "Mr. Wong argues against such work. But, without them, Mary and I would never have had the opportunity to come to America to study medicine, so we cannot agree with him."

He beamed at her. "But that is not to say I do not see the worth of the work done by you and Dr. Stone. Not at all." He turned to me. "These young women represent the New Woman of China, Mrs. Chapman. I am a great admirer of them. After years of oppression and ignorance they are wiping away all that and bringing the light of science and knowledge to our race. They are the future. Only when our women become enlightened like this will they be able to inspire our children and truly change the course of civilization."

I couldn't help but notice that he had not been invited to sit with us, but he seemed to have no problem continuing this conversation while standing. The waiter returned carrying a tray full of steaming platters, which were spread in front of us. Bowls of rice with wooden sticks in them were placed in front of Miss Howe and Ida. They quickly took up the bowls and began to reach for meat and vegetables from the platters. I watched in surprise. Another man arrived with a plate of chicken, vegetables, and white rice, placed it in front of me, and laid a fork and knife down beside it.

"Chop suey," he said. This waiter wore Western dress—a white shirt and gray trousers—but he had a pigtail down his back.

"Ah," Mr. Wong said. "Chop suey! The national dish of China. Even Americans can enjoy it. And this is my friend, Mr. Chin." He clapped the man on the shoulder. "Lao Chin, you are an up-and-coming man—first a waiter, now the manager. Soon you'll own the place! You're becoming a real American. Now all you have to do is to cut off that pigtail and join my Equal Rights League, eh?"

The young man smiled at him, but moved away to serve someone else. Miss Howe put down the wooden sticks I later learned were called chopsticks and frowned at Mr. Wong. She turned to me and explained. "Chop suey is a dish that is local to Taishan. That's the area in southeast China where most of the Chinese in Chicago come from. There are different dishes further north, where we come from. This dish has become popular with Americans." She pointed to my plate. "You see, there are chicken and vegetables—celery, onion, bean sprouts—in a sauce over rice." I took a fork full and tasted it. It had a salty flavor mixed with the smooth chicken and crunchy vegetables. I thought it was very good. Miss Howe seemed satisfied with my reaction and returned to her own plate. She and Ida held their bowls of rice in their hands as they picked pieces of meat or vegetable from the three platters in front of them.

"As for the pigtails," Miss Howe continued after a couple of bites, "by cutting his off, Mr. Wong here has made it impossible for him to return to China. The Manchu emperors decreed that all men must keep their pigtails. That is why they are so prevalent. Most of the men come here to work and they have families back in China. They plan to return to visit, if not to stay for good. To do that they must not cut off their pigtails."

"But to become true Americans, they should," Wong said, still smiling. "To fight the Exclusion Act and the Geary Act, we must band together and refuse to leave. We can become Americans, too."

Miss Howe applied herself to her food while Ida picked at hers, listening skeptically. She gazed at Mr. Wong and rolled her eyes. I was familiar with the desire of those, from all parts of Europe, to make a life for themselves when they came to Chicago. The West Side, where Hull House was located, was filled with immigrants struggling to survive. But I was not at all familiar with the Chinese who had come. I knew there was controversy, especially in San Francisco and California, about the influx of Chinese that had led to an act in 1882 to try to prevent Chinese from coming in the numbers the Europeans had, but I didn't know the details.

"Speaking of people who should become Americans, I must ask you, where is your companion, Miss Stone, today?" Wong was smiling at Ida. She looked unsure of how to respond but Miss Howe was not.

"Mary has been arrested for the murder of Lo Sung Chi. We are here to ask Hip Lung for assistance in getting her released. Apparently they sent witnesses to the police to accuse her falsely of having something to do with it." Her glare might have turned a lesser man to stone.

The smile on Mr. Wong's face did not change, yet I had the impression that the rest of his body deflated, like a balloon stuck by a pin. Still, his smile remained firmly in place and his speech did not betray his shock at the news. Ida had stopped eating and was staring into the distance. I saw him look at her with concern. "Surely there has been a mistake in this. Perhaps I can be of some assistance."

At that moment two men entered the restaurant and strode across to our table. I was startled to recognize the first man as Mr. Peter Francis Fitzgibbons. I hadn't seen him for several years. He was tall and broad shouldered, with hazel eyes, mutton chop sideburns, and a mustache. His auburn hair was long enough to reach his collar and had more gray strands than when I had seen him last. He was a big man, with big expressions, and I could see that he recognized me as well. He hesitated halfway to the table, causing the smaller, narrow-eyed, balding man behind him to jerk to a stop. But Fitz swallowed and continued until he reached us.

"Fitz!" Mr. Wong greeted him. "What are you doing here? And Hinky."

Fitzgibbons clapped him on the shoulder and addressed us. "I'm looking for a Miss Howe and a Miss Kahn." He turned to me. "Miss…I mean Mrs.…Chapman, we haven't seen you in the Fourth Ward lately." He cleared his throat, fingering the bowler hat in his hand. "Congratulations on your wedding. How is the doctor?"

I felt warmth rise from my neck to my scalp. It was such a different time and circumstance from the last time I'd seen him. Once I had pleaded with him to help me save Stephen from hanging. Once I had scared him into believing he might get smallpox. And once he had taken me to a brothel, when I sought the truth about my father's death. It was a shock to see him here. "Thank you. My husband is not with us. This is Miss Howe, and Dr. Ida Kahn. Miss Howe, Ida, this is Mr. Fitzgibbons. He is a ward boss in the area of the city where Hull House is located."

Fitz seemed distracted by the meeting as well, but he turned to his companion. "And this is Mr. Kenna, Alderman Kenna. He owns the saloon downstairs." I recognized the name of the infamous politician known in the newspapers as "Hinky Dink Kenna." Fitz continued, "Uh…Hip Lung asked us to meet with these ladies." He approached Mr. Wong and put his arm around his shoulder, turning him away from the table and towards the door. "As for you, Wong, nice to see you, but if you will just leave us, we have some private matters to discuss. I'm sure you will excuse us, yes?"

Mr. Wong strained to look back at us. "Hip Lung sent you? Is it about Dr. Stone?"

"Now, now, that's between us and the ladies, so if you will just be on your way." Fitz began walking him towards the entrance, but Mr. Wong shook him off and turned towards us to make a formal bow, the same smile still on his face.

"Goodbye, ladies. I hope you will achieve good fortune. And please give my regards to Dr. Stone." With that he walked away.

Fitz heaved a sigh and came back. He and Mr. Kenna sat down opposite us, without asking for permission to do so. Suddenly, plates and glasses of beer were thrust in front of them. It was apparent that they were frequent customers, as Fitz was given a plate of chop suey like mine, with Western utensils and Mr. Kenna was given a plate with meat, fried onions, and peppers, and a small plate with a bread roll on the side. As we watched, he crammed the meat and vegetables into the bread to make a sandwich, slurping a mouthful of the beer afterwards, and wiping his mouth with his hand. Fitz ignored him.

"Mr. Hip Lung asked us to talk to you about this situation with Miss Mary Stone," Fitz told us. "I understand the police have arrested her for the death of Mr. Lo, the herbalist."

At last Miss Howe had found an adversary and she let loose a salvo. "Hip Lung paid a man to go to the police to lie about it. And he sent an interpreter to make sure the man told the right lie. He claimed that the man said Dr. Stone poisoned the herbalist because she wanted to steal his practice. That accusation is ridiculous, and the fact he was being paid to say it is outrageous." She pounded her hand on the table.

Fitz hunched over his plate, uncomfortable with the anger

she directed at him. I saw him glance at me, as if calculating how close I was to the other women.

"We were at the police station when the man was being questioned by Detective Whitbread," I explained. "The man and his interpreter were speaking Chinese, but Miss Howe could understand what they were saying."

"He lied!" she repeated.

"I see. Well, now, Mr. Hip Lung is an important man in this community and this has come to his attention, so he would like to be of assistance."

"Hip Lung is the one who sent them down there to lie," Miss Howe told him. "It's only because we went to his wife, who is a friend of ours, that he is reconsidering."

Fitz looked down at his plate, turning his fork in the food. "I see." Mr. Kenna appeared to be paying no attention to the conversation. He was relishing his sandwich and beer. Fitz was in charge of the discussion. "Now, ladies, I think we are all very sorry there has been such a misunderstanding. What we are here to tell you is that Hip Lung has an arrangement with Mr. Kenna, so we'll do what we can to help Miss Stone out of these problems."

He held up a hand to forestall Miss Howe. Ida was watching with concern in her expression. "Now, we have some attorneys on commission, you see. And we'd like to offer the services of Robert Cantwell, one of the best attorneys in Chicago, to help Miss Stone. He knows his way around the police stations and courthouses in this city, so we're sure he'll be able to get this young lady released, don't you see, even if the police continue the investigation."

I could see anger bubbling up in Miss Howe. Ida saw it too and put a hand on her arm, but it was to no avail. "Well," the older woman proclaimed, "I must say that would be most considerate of Mr. Hip Lung. Especially since he was the one who sent those men to lie about Mary. And it is *Dr.* Mary Stone for your information."

I saw Fitz take a big breath, in preparation for another attempt to placate her, but at that moment we became aware of two women who had entered the restaurant quietly and were now hovering just beyond Fitz and Mr. Kenna's shoulders. Miss Howe gestured to them.

"Mrs. Appleby, Miss Erickson, please join us." Waiters brought more chairs and we all shifted to make room for them. Before she made introductions, Miss Howe told them the distressing news. "I have to tell you we are here because Mary has been arrested."

"Oh, no. How is that possible?"

"She has been arrested for the murder of Mr. Lo, the herbalist. You knew him."

"Certainly, certainly. In fact, Charlotte and I were just there. Mr. Lo's son served us. We asked after his father and he told us he had passed away. But murder? How can it be?"

Fitz was listening with an expression of discomfort.

"It *cannot* be, it's a lie," Miss Howe proclaimed, glaring across at him. "Hip Lung sent a man to swear to the police that, last week...when Mary went to visit Lo...she poured poison in his ear and it killed him."

"But that is untrue. She did put medication in his ear but he was fine. It was a treatment they had agreed on. He was fine when we left."

"Wait...you were there?" Fitz asked.

"Yes, surely. I was there, and so was Charlotte."

# EIGHT

Laura Appleby continued. "Yes, Charlotte and I went with Dr. Stone that day. I was searching for an herb to help one of my patients who had a stomach malady. Nothing else she has tried has worked for her."

"Mrs. Appleby is skilled in herbal remedies," Miss Howe explained.

"My late husband was an invalid for many years," Mrs. Appleby added.

"He was a very eminent physician," Miss Erickson said softly.

Laura Appleby patted her hand. "It is true. Marcus continued his work despite his health problems. When he became blind as a symptom, he came to depend on me to continue his work. For him not to continue would have been a form of death. So I became his eyes and I made it a study to search out treatments that might relieve the pain. He resisted, as so many physicians do. As men of science, they disparage the age-old remedies, despite the evidence that they remain in use because they are effective.

"My late husband was as skeptical as Charlotte's father." She shook her head. "So stubborn. But in the end Marcus could not deny the relief he felt. My searches led me to Mr. Lo. The Chinese herbalists have certain remedies that are passed on from generation to generation, from one family member to another. Lo had one that gave Marcus great respite and he had another that eased the pain for Charlotte's dear mother in her final days."

She patted the young woman's hand again. "Dr. Erickson still disdains it. He won't hear of it. Actually Mary...Dr. Stone...was attempting to convert Lo to the use of Western medicines as well as herbal remedies. So, of course she knew Mr. Lo. She often met with him. The herbal recipes are closely guarded secrets, you know. The exact proportions are known only to the initiated. Mary was studying with him. She introduced him to certain Western medicines in return for learning herb lore from him." Mrs. Appleby looked around at all of us, as a waiter filled small cups of tea for her and Miss Erickson. "Mr. Lo had been suffering from an infection of the ear. After much discussion, Dr. Stone convinced him to try a soothing wash of some sort. He submitted willingly enough. We had finished our purchases for the day, so we left them together. I cannot imagine that the treatment could have done him any harm."

Fitz cleared his throat. "Lo died that night. He went into a fit and foamed at the mouth. There were others who witnessed Dr. Stone's treatment. They went to Hip Lung the next day and accused her of poisoning him."

"Outrageous," Miss Howe sputtered. "She was helping the man."

"Certainly there were others in the shop who witnessed it," Mrs. Appleby told him. "But there was no subterfuge. He willingly submitted to the treatment. They had some back and forth in the Chinese language but I took it to be a kind of banter."

Ida spoke up then. "It is perhaps due to superstition. The other customers must have heard what they thought was a dispute between Old Lo and Mary. They are ignorant. They did not understand that it was merely two scholars debating. They are suspicious of Western medicine, especially from a woman who claims to be a doctor. So when the man died, they thought she had cursed him and caused his death."

"But that is absurd," Miss Howe insisted. "Why would she harm him?"

"They were friends," Mrs. Appleby agreed. "She was always respectful of him."

"But these other men do not understand that," Ida suggested.

"Besides," I commented, "if Dr. Stone was not to blame and this Mr. Lo died suspiciously, then they might worry that one of them would be suspected."

Fitz put down his fork and pushed his plate away. "Now there you have a point, Mrs. Chapman." He seemed to roll my name around his tongue as if to get used to it. "It's a sensitive topic, you see. That's why Hip Lung has asked for our help." He gestured towards himself and Mr. Kenna, who was pouring the last of his beer down his throat.

"Exactly what do you have to do with this, Mr. Fitzgibbons?" I demanded. Fitz was a politician and I had come up against him in the past. He had his own ideas about what was right. I had come to the conclusion that, while he usually had the interest of his constituents at heart, he could be unscrupulous in fulfilling goals he determined were necessary.

He frowned at me. "Our friends Hip Lung and Sam Moy are careful men. They know the customs of their countrymen are not the same as those of Americans and they are anxious to avoid misunderstandings. So they cultivate friends in the community to help keep things smooth. They want peace in their neighborhoods, same as anybody else. And, well, a lot of their men don't speak the language, see, so Hip and Sam, they make sure things don't get messed up in translation, if you see what I mean." Fitz's Irish brogue reminded me that he was no more a native than the Chinese he was discussing. "So, now you see, when something like this happens they wouldn't like the authorities to take it against their community. What with the exclusion laws and the Geary Act, it's a very sensitive topic, don't you know."

"So they jump on the opportunity to blame an outsider like Dr. Stone?" I asked bluntly.

"It's outrageous," Miss Howe repeated.

"How awful!" Mrs. Appleby added.

"Now, now." Fitz put his large hands up, as if to ward off blows. "Perhaps it's naught but a misunderstanding, ladies. Hip Lung asked us to see if we couldn't help the authorities to talk to the right people. He wants to do the right thing now."

"Hmph," Miss Howe grumbled. "Only because we went to the wives and got them on our side."

Fitz raised his bushy eyebrows, gazing at her with respect as he lowered his hands. "It never does to underestimate the influence of the ladies. We know that for a fact now, don't we, Hink?"

The bowler-hatted little man beside him just grinned. Finished with his sandwich, he was chomping on a pickle.

Before Miss Howe could start another tirade, Fitz rose. "Ladies, what do you say we go and visit Lo's shop? Perhaps his son can set us straight and give us something we can take to the authorities to free Dr. Stone."

There was a bustle of activity as we paid the bill, gathered our belongings, and bade Mrs. Appleby and Miss Erickson goodbye. I noticed that Mr. Chin approached Ida with a worried look on his face and she talked with him in a low voice. I thought he looked somewhat lost as we all hurried out of the dining room and it made me wonder what Ida had told him. We made our way down the steep stairway to the street where Mr. Kenna ducked back into his saloon as Fitz led us to a doorway half a block down the street. I marveled at what a strange mixture of saloons, laundries, restaurants, and less savory establishments made up this part of town. From doorway to doorway you passed to different worlds— Irish, Polish, Chinese, and others I was not sure I could identify.

A bell jingled merrily as Fitz held the door for us and we entered a tiny shop. It was clean but with a dusty feel to the air and a hint of strange-smelling powders. We made our way through a deep, narrow space with crates and barrels stacked along the sides and shelves filled to the ceiling with wooden drawers, rolls of paper, and glass vials. About halfway down on the left three Chinese men in ill-fitting Western suits and hats sat around a small round table. They hunched over tiny cups of tea and had their feet on battered suitcases, marking them as travelers. We passed them single file to reach the counter at the back, where a tall young Chinese man in cotton pants and jacket, which were worn but clean, was measuring herbs on a weighted scale. His face was square and flat with a very high forehead. He wore a queue down his back and had a small black cap perched on his head.

The man stopped what he was doing and bowed from the waist as we formed a semicircle in front of him. Little paper-wrapped packages, each marked with Chinese characters, were lined up along the counter. A mortar, pestle, and other tools were on a shelf behind him. Ida spoke to him in Chinese. He nodded as he answered her.

"He says he is Lo Zhong Di, son of Herbalist Lo," she told us. Then she turned back and questioned him, with Miss Howe occasionally injecting a word or two.

I looked around, suddenly uneasy. Fitz was staring at me as we waited for them to interpret. I felt a catch of my breath as if discovering a loss. I felt bereft. I was missing something valuable, then I realized my arms felt heavy with emptiness. With a flash of panic I thought of Lizzie and longed to feel her in my arms. What was I doing here, when my children were at home without me? Logic told me that Delia was well able to care for them in my absence. But what if something happened to her? What if she fell sick? What if something happened to Lizzie and Jack because I was not with them? I felt a visceral fear as if I were at the edge of a pit.

I took a deep breath, aware that Fitz was still looking at me. Realizing it had been a very long time since I had been out of the presence of my children for so many hours, I struggled to calm down. I had to force myself not to run from the shop and find a way home immediately. If I went home the children would be there, but Stephen would not. I reminded myself that I was uniquely qualified to help sort out this misunderstanding. I had an obligation to help Mary. Until she was released, I couldn't stop.

"Mrs. Chapman, are you unwell?" Fitz reached out and took my arm to steady me. Ida and Miss Howe looked up with concern.

"I'm fine. What is he saying?"

They exchanged a glance. They were not satisfied with his testimony. "He says he was not here when Mary treated Herbalist Lo. He was out delivering medicines to regular customers, including Mrs. Moy. When he returned, his father was not well and he went to the back to rest. The son, here, was left to take care of the shop. That was when the other customers told him of what had happened. They said Herbalist Lo and Mary Stone disagreed. She put medicine into his ear and left. They thought she did something bad to him. The son went to check on his father, found him having convulsions and quickly he was gone. The son was very afraid. He sent to Hip Lung for help. They are all afraid to deal with American authorities. They always go to Hip Lung. Hip Lung helped him to tell the police what had happened. The police came and took the body away. He waits for the body to be returned for funeral rites. He knows nothing else."

Just as Fitz took a step forward to ask a question the doorbell jangled violently. I turned to see Detective Whitbread stride into the room, followed by two other men in suits and four uniformed policemen.

"Stay where you are!" he shouted. "You are under arrest for being in the United States unlawfully!"

The three Chinese men at the table sprang to their feet. But it was too late. They were surrounded.

# NINE

The three men backed towards the wall, surprise and alarm in their eyes. The uniformed officers following Whitbread parted to allow a shorter man to enter. He stepped through their ranks with an air of privilege. By a slight hunch of his shoulders, I perceived a certain irritation from Detective Whitbread.

The small man kept his eyes on the three scared Chinese men until he reached the table. Stopping, he took off his bowler hat and brought out a white handkerchief with which he wiped first his face and then his bald crown. He had a fringe of sparse salt-and-pepper hair, a brush of a mustache under his nose, and tiny deep-set eyes. There was an unhealthy grayish cast to his skin, and his face was mapped with wrinkles, yet he moved with a physical ease.

He sighed. "I am Officer Lewis of the Bureau of Immigration of the United States government. Your papers." He held out a hand. "Papers, now."

The three men suddenly understood. They dug in their suit coats and each brought out a carefully folded sheaf of papers. "I son of Wang," announced the first, placing his packet in Lewis's outstretched hand.

"I son of Chou." "I son of Yang." The others proffered their papers and Lewis spread them on the table, where he began perusing them.

"Chou," he snapped. "I see you're from Jiujiang. What's the name of the mayor?"

"Mao Lin-chu," the man responded.

Lewis stared at him. "You are well coached. We shall see exactly how well." He turned to the uniformed officers. "Put them in the wagon."

The policemen herded the men out the door but, before Officer Lewis and Detective Whitbread could follow them, I stepped forward. "Detective, what is going on here? Where are you taking those men?" I had worked with many immigrants, from many places, in my time at Hull House but I had never seen people treated like this before.

The small man turned and squinted at those of us in the back of the room. Before Whitbread could respond, Lewis pointed a finger in our direction. "Just a minute. Who is that woman? I want to see her papers." He kept pointing rudely at Ida as he strode towards us.

Miss Howe stepped forward. "How dare you? This is Dr. Ida Kahn who has recently received a medical degree from the University of Michigan and she is *my* adopted daughter." She loomed over Lewis before he could reach Ida, who continued to smile politely while tilting her head away from the onslaught.

"Is that so?"

"Lewis, mind your manners," Detective Whitbread intervened. "This is Miss Howe and Miss Ida Kahn, they are accompanied by Mrs. Chapman and Mr. Fitzgibbons, who are well-known local citizens and can vouch for Miss...I mean Dr. Kahn. Ladies, Officer Lewis is here from the immigration authorities. He had a tip that these men entered the country illegally."

"But why are you arresting those men, when they have papers?" I demanded. Miss Howe appeared to be simmering towards an outburst at my side. I put a calming hand on her arm.

"We are upholding the law of the land," Lewis announced. He was a pompous little prig. "It's the law of the Congress of the United States that forbids entry of Chinese laborers, in order to stem the tide of yellow peril that threatens to overwhelm the Western states. Recently, they've been trying to enter illegally through Canada into this area, and I've been sent here to stop them."

"Yellow peril!" Miss Howe scoffed. "What rubbish. And, despite the Geary Act, scholars, merchant classes, and relatives of residents *are* allowed to enter. These men said they are sons come to join their fathers. That is allowed."

"Hah! And have you heard of 'paper sons'?" I noticed Whitbread and Fitz both rolled their eyes at this exclamation, but Lewis was just hitting his stride. "There's a lucrative business in illegal documentation. Because your laws only allow a man to enter the country if he is sponsored by a close relative—a father or uncle—many men who want to get into the country arrange to be sponsored by someone already here who is not really a relative. They pay well for the privilege. They're given information to memorize about the town or village, and the family. The young man pretends to be related. He stays working for the man who sponsored him for some months and then starts a business or gets a job of his own. In eighty-five percent of the cases, extended interrogation will force them to trip up. You'll see, these ones will break."

"Break!" I said, glancing at Whitbread. "How long do you keep them until they 'trip up,' as you say?"

"As long as it takes." He pursed his lips.

Shocked at the idea that this little despot could keep the men for as long as he wanted, I was about to object when there was a commotion at the door. A large Chinese man in a long black silk gown and a square hat moved slowly into the room. Wide sleeves with beautiful embroidery hung down to cover his hands. He had a graying, thinning queue down his back and a mustache with ends trailing down to a long, sparse beard. His face was plump with round cheeks that nearly hid small black eyes beneath wiry eyebrows.

"Hip Lung," Fitz said, stepping forward. "It's good to see you."

So, this was the famous Hip Lung, oldest of the Moy brothers who were so powerful in the city. He looked to be nearing sixty. I thought of his young bride in the quiet room scented with blossoms. What must her life be like?

Charlie Kee stepped out from behind Hip Lung and Lewis greeted him. "Charlie, where have you been? I've got some paper sons needing translations."

"Sure thing, boss."

"He works for you?" I asked in disbelief. "But he was just helping some men with the police."

"Charlie Kee acts as a translator in all sorts of situations," Detective Whitbread told us.

"Well, his translations are pretty poor," Miss Howe announced. "We caught him lying back at the police station."

Hip Lung folded his hands carefully in front of him. Charlie Kee glanced at him and said, "Misunderstanding. All a misunderstanding. Hip Lung will make it right."

Lewis looked around the room as if to be sure he didn't miss anyone. "What about this woman?" he asked, pointing at Ida again. "What do you know about her?"

At this point, Hip Lung stepped forward and spoke to Ida in Chinese. The words rolled out over the heads of all of the Westerners except Miss Howe. He finished with a formal bow to the ladies. They responded in kind, bowing from the waist, eyes on the floor, as they spoke a stream of Chinese.

Charlie Kee interpreted in his own way. "Hip Lung says he is very honored to meet scholarly lady of many accomplishments. She is very fine lady."

"Huh." Lewis was unimpressed. "You'd better be right about that, Whitbread. The only Chinese women who get smuggled into the country are prostitutes. Everyone knows that."

There was a gasp from several people, including me.

"That is quite enough," Miss Howe began, but Detective Whitbread stopped the argument by taking Officer Lewis by the arm and forcing him down the length of the room to the door.

"Come on. You have your men. Go interrogate them." He shoved the little man towards the door. Lewis exited unwillingly, looking back over his shoulder at us, but Whitbread closed the door firmly and strode back. "I apologize for his behavior, madam. The man is overly conscientious."

"The man is a bigoted, petty tyrant!" Miss Howe responded.

"Will they really keep those men indefinitely?" I asked.

Whitbread grimaced. "He is within his rights. He is working under the provisions of the Exclusion Act of 1882, which restricts Chinese immigration to only those who are *not* laborers. It was extended and made even stricter by the Geary Act of 1892. Any Chinese who are now in the country legally must present a certificate of identity and answer any questions as to its authenticity. Practically speaking, he'll ask repeatedly about their supposed home villages, families, and all of that. If they are in fact 'paper sons' he'll probably prove it. However, that's no reason to be insulting to Miss Kahn."

"*Dr.* Kahn," Miss Howe corrected him.

Ida was deep in conversation with Hip Lung during this exchange. Now the man turned to Fitz and spoke in English. "Has Dr. Stone been released?"

Fitz's ruddy face turned even redder. "She has not, at the moment, but Hinky was contacting the lawyers. Cantwell should be at the courthouse now."

Whitbread groaned.

"Hip Lung," Miss Howe attacked, "it was your man who told the detective here that Mary Stone had an argument with Mr. Lo. It's not true, but you paid the man to lie. I suggest you get him to withdraw his false testimony."

Hip Lung's eyes narrowed as he turned towards Miss Howe. Ida said something in Chinese, which made him pause. By her gestures I understood that Ida was introducing her adoptive mother. Hip Lung frowned. "There was a mistake. My wife has told me about it. The man in question will never speak against Miss Stone again." He was a man used to being obeyed.

I was surprised to realize that, like Wong Chin Foo, his English was extremely fluent. This was in contrast to the English of Charlie Kee, despite the fact that he acted as an interpreter. I supposed it was necessary for an important businessman like Hip Lung to be able to communicate well, especially since he seemed to act as the chief contact between the Chinese and the rest of the city. I was impressed with his ability to speak English with an educated accent as he did.

Detective Whitbread responded. "If you are so convinced, now, that Dr. Stone did not cause the man's death, how do you think it happened? There are other witnesses who saw the same thing, including his son here."

The man behind the counter glanced at Hip Lung and quickly looked away again.

"Here, now, Whitey," Fitz intervened. "Mr. Hip Lung is an upstanding citizen, as you well know. He's known to the deputy mayor, the aldermen, and even judges. I'm sure he was only trying to do his duty as a community leader."

"I'm aware of his connections and pull with local politicians," Whitbread said. "That will not prevent me from questioning him in an attempt to find the truth of what happened."

Before Fitz could try to placate the incorruptible detective, Hip Lung spoke up. "Herbalist Lo was a longtime member of our community but, lately, he had become distant. There was something very strange, something new, in his manner." Hip Lung's voice was deep and slightly hoarse. "Possibly he suffered some disease for which he was seeking a cure from your medicine. He had business with many more of those outside our community this past year. Your Western medical men. On the other hand, he also had visitors from China not known to us. Men whose backgrounds were misted over. For the most part, we know all our people and where they are from at home. But he entertained men we did not know. He had met some of them through Wong Chin Foo. That I do know. These men today," he gestured towards the door, "they were not known to us." I had the impression that men like the three who had been taken away might well be known to Hip Lung and his associates. I suspected that he would be fully capable of arranging for a "paper son" to get the help he needed, for a price. I wondered if the dead man had been starting a rival organization, and if Hip Lung had even been the one to tip the authorities to the presence of the three who had just been taken away.

Whitbread stared at the plump Chinese man with speculation, as if he shared my suspicions. "We will certainly look into whether Lo was involved with smuggling men illegally. You wouldn't go in for that yourself, now, would you, Hip Lung?"

"Now, now," Fitz interrupted. "Enough of that. You've heard the man has retracted his accusations about Dr. Stone. You'll have to release her now and look elsewhere. There's no need to be rude to Hip Lung."

Hip Lung turned to leave, but stopped to bow and speak to Ida and Miss Howe and they responded in kind. Then he stopped beside Whitbread. "You would be wise to investigate Lo's association with the Western doctors." Having had his say, he continued towards the door.

Whitbread did not appreciate being instructed by a man he suspected of being involved in criminal activities. He moved restlessly, as if to shake off the influences. It was not until the bell jangled at the door, confirming the man's exit, that he spoke. "He is right about one thing. With that statement withdrawn, we'll have to release Dr. Stone." Miss Howe and Ida smiled at him. "But, let me be very clear, she is not to leave the city until all of this is straightened out."

# TEN

The news that Mary would be released, freed me as well. I had done what I could, although, in truth, it was Hip Lung and Fitz who had managed to get the charges dropped. But Stephen could no longer hold me accountable.

Suddenly, I felt the need to return to my children. I said a hurried goodbye and found that Fitz insisted on escorting me to the train. He said little in the cab that appeared miraculously at the curb. I was too overcome by guilt at having been absent from my children for so long to comment. He seemed to understand that and he asked me about them. Telling him their names and ages conjured them up before me and I blathered on about their personalities and habits. At the back of my mind I remembered how pathetic I had found women whose only conversation concerned their children and realized I had joined their ranks.

But Fitz listened to how Lizzie loved to watch the shadows of leaves above her, as she lay in my arms in the garden, and how Jack refused to even try to climb to his feet, preferring to scoot along on his backside when he was chasing the kitten. Fitz sank back in the corner of the cab, his large hands clasping his knees while his eyes glittered in the gloom. He seemed disappointed when I insisted he leave me at the station gates as I rushed off to catch the four o'clock train. I brushed aside thoughts of him as I hurried off, still vaguely worried about the children.

My fears were groundless. Delia had the children well in hand

and I even allowed supper to be served at the wooden table in the kitchen. I had some hope that Stephen would have heard of Mary Stone's release and make an appearance. I felt good about my concessions to his preference for an informal meal but, when he still had not appeared by the time we put the children to bed, I was angry. I told myself he might not know of the change in Mary's status, or that he might well have gotten caught up in some experiment, to the exclusion of every other care in the world, but it didn't help.

When the doorbell rang the next morning, I was primed to pour out recriminations on my thoughtless husband but it was not him. Of course, he had a key. Why would he ring? It was Ida Kahn whom Delia led into the parlor.

Jack saw her and promptly piled up his blocks as she had taught him to do, so he remembered her. She gave me a slight bow and then turned to greet and praise him. I was disconcerted.

"Good morning, Dr. Kahn. Of course, it is a pleasure to see you."

"Mrs. Chapman, I wonder if I might speak to you of a matter of some importance." She wore a suit of pale gray with fashionably big sleeves and a pinched waist. Her face was perfectly round above the high-necked collar of a white shirtwaist. It was different from the shape of Mary Stone's face, which I remembered as more heart shaped. The rimless spectacles hid her almond-shaped eyes and her dark hair was parted in the middle and pulled back severely. The tiny pearls still dangled from her ears.

At my wave, Delia gathered Lizzie into one arm while she scooped up Jack with the other. He was easily distracted by the promise of cake. I sighed. My offspring seemed determined to spend more time in the kitchen than the parlor.

I turned back to Ida. "Please, sit down. What's the matter? Was Dr. Stone not released as promised?"

She perched on the edge of the sofa and I felt captured by her unblinking gaze. "Mary was returned to us last evening. We are very grateful to you for your assistance. Mr. Fitzgibbons brought her home himself."

"I fear I am not the one to thank. I'm sure it was the ladies you sought out in Chinatown who deserve your thanks. Mr. Hip Lung appears to be most influential. I doubt my efforts accomplished anything though, so I am not sure what you want from me now." I had hoped to be done with the Chinese ladies and with the strange world of Chinatown to which I had been introduced the day before. As a wife and mother it had nothing to do with me now, surely.

"The police insist that Mary may not leave the city."

"Well, yes, that will be the case until they're sure of what caused the death of the herbalist. But surely that will not present any problems?" I began to wonder if she was looking for a place for them to stay. I shivered at the thought of offering our hospitality. We had barely enough room for ourselves. It was inconceivable. To my relief, that was not her intention at all.

"We must leave," she said and my spirits rose. I wanted to cheer her on. "We must return to our province before the end of next month. We have booked passage on a ship leaving San Francisco in three weeks. We must be on it."

I was relieved. "Detective Whitbread is very competent," I told her. "I'm sure he'll do everything he can to conclude his investigation as quickly as possible. Surely, if it's not done in time, you can book passage on a later ship?"

She leaned forward earnestly, her hands clasped to her waist. "You do not understand. When we return to Jiujiang we have been offered a building, for a clinic. It was arranged last year. The local officials have seen to it. But we were expected to return in the summer. We were delayed due to the opportunity to visit the medical community here. Mary was most anxious to learn about local hospitals, and the Woman's Medical School. She wants to train Chinese women in medicine. My mother also wished to solicit funds, both for her missions and for our clinic.

We should have returned already." She shook her head gloomily. "In my country, things are very difficult nowadays."

I felt her burning gaze again. She was very intense. Where Mary Stone had seemed like a gentle breeze, with a hint of cooling rain, Ida Kahn was hot and dry like a crackling blaze.

"My country has been pushed cruelly by the Western powers. They force their way in and demand more and more concessions. The imperial court is very weak. They demand much of the Chinese people but they give away so much to the foreigners." I was puzzled by the lecture, but I listened patiently. Somehow this was not what I expected. "You see, there is a great need for new ideas in China." This reminded me of Mr. Wong Chin Foo, the journalist we had met at the restaurant. "The young people go away to Europe or to Japan seeking new ideas. And some come to America, the Gold Mountain. But, you see, too many never return. For Mary and me, the whole reason to come and study medicine was so that we could return to our home province to share what we have learned. We can change our country by bringing back new ideas."

She stood abruptly, and paced across the room several times, before continuing. "Many do not believe in Western ideas and, if we don't return, they will turn back to the old ways. They will not believe in change. The officials offered the building for the clinic, but they doubt that we will really return and they will use our failure to say that all foreigners only take away from China, even the young people. There are those who would throw all foreigners out and, with them, all the new ideas, all the hope for change and modernization."

"I see. You're worried that Dr. Stone won't be able to leave? Perhaps you and Miss Howe might have to return ahead of her, in order to make sure you're there in time." I did not much like the thought of Mary Stone alone in Chicago, so in need of protection. For some reason, the idea stung me like a wasp. There was something about the comparison between myself and these young women doctors that seemed to leave me lacking, at least in the eyes of my husband. I would be happy for them to return to China.

"It's not right," Ida said. "Mary's parents wait for her return. They have sacrificed much to allow her to become a woman medical doctor. For me, I was adopted by Miss Howe. My Chinese family did not support me, they abandoned me long ago." She said it simply, but it was a fearsome thing to contemplate. I thought of Lizzie and could not imagine giving her away, as Ida had been by her family.

"It is my adopted mother who supported me. As such, I am a sort of stranger in my home province. But Mary is a daughter of true Chinese parents. They chose to become Christians. They chose to bring up their daughter without binding her feet. They chose to encourage her to become a medical doctor. You must see…for her to fail to return would not be possible."

"But surely she *will* return. The delay will only be temporary. I am sure Detective Whitbread will discover the truth or, if he does not, he won't hinder her return. It's just a question of time for him to complete the investigation."

She shook her head. "What if he accuses her again? Mary looks always for the best in people. She does not see that there are those who wish her ill. She has enemies but refuses to see them. She has friends who are not true friends and I fear her heart may be engaged where it cannot be."

Her heart? My heart skipped a beat. Was Ida aware of a connection between Mary and my husband? Stephen had expressed admiration for them both, but not in that way, surely? "Just what are you asking me to do?" It was blunt but she was in no way offended.

"Your husband has told us of your work with the police. Please, help us to clear Mary's name so we may return to our province at the time we are expected."

"I don't know how to do that." Stephen must have told them about the cases I'd been involved with in the past, but it was a type of thing I had not done for the past two years. It was what I had avoided since giving birth to children who depended on me.

"You must. Please come with us today. We will tour the women's hospital. Mrs. Appleby and Miss Erickson will be there. Despite the help from your husband and other medical people in the city, I fear Dr. Erickson will ruin Mary's reputation by telling people of the accusations against her. I have learned he blames his wife's death on Chinese herbal medicine. He seeks revenge by destroying Mary. He has already contacted some of the people who had offered to donate money for our clinic."

"If that's the case, I'm not sure that I can help you. Why do you want me at the tour of the women's hospital?"

"Because we are hoping that Miss Erickson will help us convince her father of Mary's innocence. She told me that she admires you. And, also, because your husband insists that you should attend."

# ELEVEN

So, Stephen *was* aware that Mary Stone had been released but he still had not returned home. Instead, he had summoned me to the city using Ida Kahn as his messenger. I was exasperated and annoyed, however, I saw no choice but to accompany Ida back to the city.

Mary, Miss Howe, and Mrs. Appleby met us at the Twelfth Street Station. Mary appeared to have survived her incarceration without suffering any great harm but, when I congratulated her on her release, she seemed not to want to discuss it. She reassured me that she did not hold me responsible for the fact that her arrest had taken place at our home. Nor did she seem to see any connection between my friendship with Detective Whitbread and his actions. In fact, she insisted that she was grateful for my efforts on her behalf. I protested that Hip Lung's influence was the true reason for her release.

The plan had been for Miss Erickson to accompany us to the hospital but, when we stopped at her house, we were refused admittance. The butler informed us that Dr. Erickson had forbidden Charlotte to go with us on the tour and that we were not to be allowed to relay any messages to her. As if that was not enough, he left instructions to summon the police if we caused any difficulties.

Mrs. Appleby shook her head with disappointment as the carriage pulled away from the curb. "I am so sorry for that scene."

"What an exceedingly rude man," Miss Howe added. If she had been present in the operating theater at the Rush Hospital her opinion of Dr. Erickson would certainly have been even worse, considering how he had treated Mary. Apparently the young women doctors had not complained to her of that treatment. I suspected they had long experience of having to soothe the forthright Miss Howe when she became angry.

Rather than anger, Mrs. Appleby appeared to feel pity for the physician, despite his continued bad behavior towards her. "Poor Isaac. He has been unable to recover from the deep sorrow he felt after his wife passed away last winter. He was not at all like this when she was alive. He misses her influence in so many ways and poor Charlotte suffers for it."

I wondered about his shocking accusation that the young woman had poisoned her mother, but Mrs. Appleby did not address that issue, dismissing all of his behavior as the result of an inconsolable grief.

Meanwhile, Miss Howe had started a different topic. She was advising Mary and Ida that, when they returned to China, they should spend some time at a hospital in one of the cities before establishing their own clinic. It seemed it was an ongoing argument between them. Mary was gently adamant in her disagreement. "To spend time under the tutelage of other doctors after receiving our degrees would only raise doubts about our abilities," she insisted. "We have studied and trained. We must not give the impression that we require the guidance of male doctors or we will never succeed in our goals. No, we must open the clinic and train our own women to be nurses."

Miss Howe appeared stubbornly intent on continuing the discussion but Ida distracted her with something she saw out the window. As they started a separate conversation, Mary turned quietly to me. "Mr. Grubbé appears to benefit greatly from the support and encouragement of Dr. Chapman," she said.

I felt surprised and at a disadvantage. Usually Stephen confided in me about his scientific enthusiasms but this new interest in the Roentgen rays was totally unexpected. Our relations had been so strained of late he had never even mentioned it to me. This omission was something I did not wish to share with Mary. "My husband is frequently interested in the latest advances in his areas of study," I said, rather inadequately.

"There is, perhaps, a more personal interest for him?" She sat back in the leather seat, making herself small and still in the jogging vehicle. I shifted uncomfortably.

"I don't know what you mean," I admitted.

She was quiet for a moment, as Miss Howe and Ida continued their exclamations concerning the local homes we passed. "It is only that I thought perhaps his own condition might be improved. He was injured by a shotgun blast some years ago, is that not so? It has made him lose the use of one arm, has it not?"

The memory suddenly came to me of the crowded tenement sweatshop, the jittery little tailor, the explosion, and the smell of smoke. I could almost hear the scream I let out, as Stephen fell bleeding on a pile of cloth. Remembering my frantic ride through the city to find him at the hospital, I gasped at the memory, but quickly shook myself. "Yes, he was crippled by an accident. It was some years ago now." I looked at her. What was she saying?

"Perhaps Dr. Chapman believes that with the use of the Roentgen rays there might be hope to repair some or all of the damage that was done."

"Oh, no. He was long ago resigned to it." I thought of the operating room we had visited. "He was a surgeon, in Baltimore, before he came here to study. But he had no regrets when he could no longer do that. He had given it up for research even before being shot. No, no, you are wrong about that. I'm sure he's fascinated by the advances presented by Mr. Grubbé's work, but it is nothing personal, I assure you."

"Perhaps not…if you say so." Mary lapsed into silence again and I struggled to sit more upright in the jostling carriage. I was appalled at the thought that she might see Stephen's interest as an attempt to correct the lameness of his arm. It was not something he ever spoke of and I thought it presumptuous of her to mention it. His damaged arm was so much a part of him now, I never thought of it. He found ways to compensate for any lack of strength and dexterity and even accepted assistance with a self-effacing irony. He certainly never complained of his injury. Mary Stone had somehow inserted herself once again into my family and it made me very uncomfortable. She knew nothing about us or our past together. How dare she presume like that?

Before I could become indignant, we reached the Mary Thompson Hospital for Women and Children. It was an impressive five-story brick building on the corner of Adams and Paulina Streets. Mrs. Appleby explained that Dr. Thompson had been one of the few women physicians in the city for several decades and had established, not only the hospital itself, but also the Chicago Woman's Hospital Medical College, since women were not admitted to the all-male medical colleges in the city.

I found myself beside Mrs. Appleby as we stood in the main hallway. On the opposite wall were two large portraits. The one on the left was of Dr. Thompson, and was a typical, rather stiff, portrait of a middle-aged woman. On the right was a striking, full-length portrait of a handsome woman in a very fine gown trimmed with lace. She stood in a stance used by some of the best portrait artists, her body partly turned, as if she were just walking away from the viewer. She had a face that beamed with a smile filled with kindness. Mrs. Appleby saw me staring at it. "That is Katherine Erickson. She was a great friend and patron of Dr. Thompson's," she said, nodding to the other portrait. "Her husband was as well, you know. It was at her instigation that he consulted here and helped to train the women doctors. We lost both her and Dr. Thompson last year. Mary had a sudden stroke and was gone in days. Katherine had a long illness that made her weaker and weaker. It was difficult to watch, impossible for poor Charlotte to bear."

"You were close to both of them, then?"

She sighed. "Closer than to anyone but my own husband. It was hard for me to lose them." She turned to me and bit her lip. "You must not believe anything Isaac says about his daughter poisoning her mother. It was my fault...but at Katherine's behest. As I mentioned yesterday, my husband was a physician and a colleague of Isaac's. As his illness he got worse, the pain was exhausting. While *he* would grit his teeth, *I* could not endure it. I began a search for anything that might provide relief. Of course, there are drugs that may be used, but he was all too aware of the way they could sap the intelligence and undermine the brain. He refused to administer to himself anything that might affect him in that way.

"The Chinese herbalist was able to recommend several treatments that have been passed down through the ages. Not opium, nor any harsh drug, but other combinations of herbs. I found a few that provided some relief to my husband, for various of his pains. He resisted at first, but I was learning so much about Western medicine, through assisting him, that I was eventually able to convince him. It could not stop the deterioration, but it made it more bearable. Katherine was aware of my work and my interest in both herbs and homeopathy. You may be aware that the local medical men look down on the homeopathic branch but it has its own supporters and institutions. Hahnemann Medical College, where Mr. Grubbé is training, is one of them."

She glanced around. The others were all safely occupied, so she moved a little closer and spoke in a low voice. "When Katherine was suffering so badly at the end of her disease, my husband had already passed away. But I continued to explore the possibilities of herbal medications—especially with some of the patients with debilitating diseases whom I had helped him to treat in his last years. They trusted me and I wished to bring them relief where possible. Charlotte came to me in distress over the pain her mother was enduring. That was when we went to the Chinese herbalist together. We experimented and found a combination that brought Katherine some relief. Isaac only found out about our treatments after she passed away. It is not true that the herbs in any way hastened her passing. There was nothing he could do to extend her life. In truth, he knows this, but he cannot bear it. His harsh reaction is not at all logical, it is only his way of refusing to accept her death." She shook her head and glanced at the handsome woman in the portrait. "Katherine would be so disappointed in him. He has practically stopped all of his work. Certainly he has stopped his connection here, which she would have wanted him to continue. That is what would honor her, not this retreat from his work and his friends. I only wish I could find a way to get him out of his sorry state." She shook her head in sorrow and I could find nothing to say.

We were summoned to a private dining room where the luncheon proceeded, followed by a tour of the hospital. It was a fine modern building that had opened in 1885. Mrs. Appleby acted as our guide and I sensed that she had taken over the duties of her deceased friends in describing the work of the hospital. It was begun when Dr. Thompson moved to the city after the Civil War. At that time it was a small endeavor and Dr. Thompson was the only woman medical doctor in the city. When the great fire burned down much of Chicago, the doctor found her services called upon and she began to receive the support and recognition that resulted in this five-story building.

Mrs. Appleby took us to the top floor where there were broad and airy wards. "The hospital has sixty beds comfortably and eighty when crowded. Patients are gynecological, obstetrical, medical, and surgical. We have ten free beds supported by subscriptions from patrons like Mrs. Erickson and one free bed in the children's ward."

Mary and Ida were very interested in the details of funding for the hospital and—as we proceeded through the children's ward and surgical areas—on the details of surgical cleanliness and diet, methods of treating wounds, and stopping hemorrhaging. They were particularly interested in the training in these methods given to the nursing students.

"It is a training we would like to provide to Chinese women in our clinic," Mary said.

"Yes, Dr. Thompson was very keen on that," Mrs. Appleby told her as we passed through a classroom. "There are at any time from twenty to twenty-five women enrolled here in a two-year course." The two young Chinese doctors were excited by the prospect. I could see that Mary thought of it as a way to allow young women of her own background to escape some of the constraints of their lives in China.

Mrs. Appleby introduced us to Dr. Jane Williams, who was one of several postgraduate medical students. "On graduation from those medical schools that will accept women," she told us, "it can be very difficult to find a position in a hospital as most will only employ men. I was lucky to get this appointment."

Mary asked for details of the program and Dr. Williams obliged. "The first four months are spent in the drug room, the second four months are spent as house physician, and for the last four months the physician is fully responsible for her patients including home visits. Dr. Thompson knew what was needed to complete a medical education and the experience is invaluable. I can't tell you how grateful I am to have had the chance to work with her. She was an inspiration."

Mrs. Appleby thanked her and led us to the ground floor. "We have trained women physicians from thirteen states, Korea, and Japan. Dr. Thompson's legacy is huge."

All the while, I was thinking about what Laura Appleby had told me about Dr. Erickson and his daughter. His wife had supported Dr. Thompson's efforts to forge a place for women in the medical world and she had even enlisted his help to train the nurses and women doctors. But it had not been enough to save her life when she was struck down. I began to wonder if his rage against the world had taken some criminal form. What if he'd discovered that the Chinese herbalist provided the concoction that he insisted had poisoned his beloved wife? What would he do? Certainly he had the know-how necessary to poison the man in return. I also believed that he was capable of purposefully conducting the murder in such a way that suspicion would fall on either Mary Stone, the woman physician he disdained, or Laura Appleby, the woman he hated for compromising his daughter. Mrs. Appleby pitied his state. But what if he was more to be feared than pitied? I couldn't help wondering.

# TWELVE

Before I excused myself to catch a train home, I managed to get directions to Dr. Erickson's house from Mrs. Appleby. It was very near the train station, so I had a cab take me there to pay a short visit. I still had plenty of time to catch the next scheduled train to Hyde Park.

It was a fine stone row house within a few blocks of the Prairie Avenue mansions of George Pullman and Marshall Field. I noticed that black crepe marked the door as a house of mourning, although, from what Laura Appleby had told me, it seemed long past when the signs of mourning should have been put away. My knock was answered by a maid, who left me in a small parlor while she took my card to Charlotte.

The young woman looked pale when she joined me. She wore black, in deference to the loss of her mother, her father's grief, or perhaps her own grief. She showed no surprise or curiosity about my visit. I suppose any relief from the unending sorrow her father appeared to demand must be enough for her. I felt some sympathy.

"Miss Erickson, thank you for seeing me. We were all sorry you were unable to join us at the hospital. Mrs. Appleby explained it was a favorite charity of your mother's and we saw the wonderful portrait of her in the main hall."

"My mother spent a lot of time there, with Dr. Thompson. She might have preferred to spend her last days there but my father would not agree to it."

"I am so sorry for your loss. I lost my own mother a few years ago and I still miss her. I did not have a father left to console me, as he had passed away long before."

"My father grieves for my mother still. I don't believe he will ever recover from it. And he blames me. You heard him. He blames me for her passing." She huddled in her chair as if waiting for a blow.

"Mrs. Appleby explained. She said you had provided your mother with some herbs to help with the pain of her last days, but that your father did not approve. Men can be unreasonable, sometimes even—or especially—men who consider themselves scientists," I said, in an attempt to console her. "Actually, that is why I wished to speak to you. You know the herbalist, Lo, who died a few days ago? Dr. Stone was accused of poisoning him. It turned out to be a false accusation…that has been resolved. But there is still a cloud hanging over her, and she's been forbidden to leave the city. I know that you and Mrs. Appleby visited the man shortly before he fell ill. I wonder if you've remembered anything that might help us clear her name. Did you see him take anything, for instance?"

She looked up at that, giving me a long stare. Then she clasped her hands until her knuckles showed white in her lap. "You could have asked Laura about that, couldn't you? Why are you really here? You heard how bitterly my father hated the idea that my mother took herbs before her death. You're hoping I'll implicate him, aren't you?"

I think my mouth dropped open in amazement. I'd thought that I might gently explore a suspicion that had been growing in my mind since Dr. Erickson's display of anger. But I never thought the girl would jump to the conclusion that I was looking to implicate her father. I protested, but she waved off my denials and stood up, pacing to the ornate mantelpiece, which she grasped with one hand.

"He did hate Mr. Lo. I heard him revile the man many times. He hates Laura for taking me to his shop. He hates the college of homeopathy where Laura studied. He hates many things since my mother's passing." She gulped. "And I am nothing but a pawn. My mother wanted me to study at Dr. Thompson's school. My father wants me to remain at home to take my mother's place. Laura Appleby wants me to follow her into the study of herbs and homeopathy." She turned towards me, her eyes overflowing with tears.

"But no one cares what I want. Why can't I have a normal life like other girls of my age? Why do I always have to care for someone? For years my mother suffered and I was at her side to do her bidding. Now my father demands even more, and Laura attempts to bring me out of his influence, but for what? To attend lectures and shop for herbs, to attend luncheons at the hospital. I'm sick to death of it. I want to go to parties and dinners, like other young women on Prairie Avenue. Why shouldn't I? I want to wear ball gowns, not this awful black. But when will I? Never, never. I'll be locked in this house, listening to the complaints of my father until I'm too old to do anything. I want to marry. I want my own home. I will never have that now." At that, she rushed to the sofa and collapsed in a fit of tears.

I felt exasperation rise in my throat. With all the work that women like Mary Stone and Ida Kahn, and even Miss Howe and Mrs. Appleby, were doing, this young woman could only regret ball gowns and dinners? Yet I recognized her desires. They were very like the ones that had driven my younger sister, Rose. We were so different that we had never been able to see eye to eye. I felt Rose would have understood Charlotte's desires as I never could. I moved to the sofa and patted the young woman on the shoulder. When she quieted I tried to ask again. "Charlotte, you had no reason to believe your father had any conversations with Herbalist Lo, did you?"

She sat up wiping her eyes, and I could see there was a good deal of anger behind the tears. Later, she would have a painful headache to battle, I could tell. She sniffed. "He did talk to Mr. Lo, but it was weeks ago. He threatened him. I heard about it when I went to the shop with Laura. The son was afraid to serve us and finally he admitted my father had been there and argued with them.

He blamed them for my mother's passing." She teared up. "And he blamed me. He still does."

"Miss Erickson…Charlotte…your father is overcome with grief. He will recover someday and I'm sure he'll regret the things he's said to you. Mrs. Appleby is only trying to help you. If there is anything I can do for you, I hope you'll tell me."

She sniffed again. "There is nothing." I was glad she didn't suggest I invite her to a dinner or dance. It was not the sort of thing we went in for down at the university, and I didn't believe she would be grateful if I offered to introduce her to the scholars I knew there. Her ambitions were in quite a different direction. I thanked her for her help and left as quickly as I could without hurting her feelings. I felt embarrassed, yet it did seem significant that Dr. Erickson had quarreled with the dead man. But it was too late to seek out Detective Whitbread with the news, as I needed to board my train. I walked the two blocks quickly, navigated the great vaulted spaces of the station, then sat staring out the window all the way down to Hyde Park.

I let myself into our apartment. The windows were open to a breeze in the empty sitting room and I heard noises from the kitchen. Lizzie was sound asleep in the cradle, and I checked her peaceful breathing before I followed the noise to the broad kitchen table. Stephen was sitting there with Jack in his lap, balancing our squirming son while he fed him with his good hand. I was conscious, as I had not been for quite some time, of the effort it must take to manage the child with his crippled arm. Because it *was* crippled. His right arm hung at his side, fairly useless. But usually he was so busy and full of energy I hardly noticed it. Today, because of what Mary had said in the carriage, I had to restrain myself from staring at it. Was my husband keeping something from me? Did he really have hopes and desires he hadn't shared with me? Had we grown so far apart?

# THIRTEEN

D r. Chapman wanted to eat in the kitchen," Delia told me. I could see she expected my disapproval. Jack reached out and called for me as soon as he saw me, so I took him in my arms and sat down to finish feeding him.

"That's right," Stephen rushed to her defense. "It was my idea. I told Delia it would be all right." Watching me for signs of anger, he relaxed as I picked up a fork and lifted some peas to Jack's eager mouth. "I was glad you could see the demonstration by Mr. Grubbé the other day. These rays produced by the Roentgen tubes are being called X-rays. They are revolutionizing what we know about what is going on under the surface of the skin, without using a scalpel. Isn't it amazing?"

"Yes, very impressive. Was it true what Dr. Erickson said about Mr. Grubbé's hand? Was the burn on it caused by the rays?"

"Apparently. He got that last year. But at a demonstration after the first of the year—when he showed the effects—one of the physicians pointed out that something that could cause such damage could also be used for treatment. That was how he began to use it to treat cancers."

"Dr. Erickson doesn't agree with that at all, does he?"

"The establishment takes time to believe in new treatments. But he'll see, he's wrong and Grubbé is right."

Stephen made no mention of his absence for the past two nights. I needed to talk to him about that. I decided we should stay in the kitchen where he seemed to feel more comfortable than in the parlor. I had raised no objection to Jack eating there, and I felt no need for a supper, myself. The luncheon had been more than enough to satisfy my appetite. I could see that Stephen had been eating along with Jack. I asked Delia to take our son up to his bed when he'd finished eating and I remained myself, watching Stephen finish a plate of cold meats and cheese.

"I went on the tour of the hospital," I told him, when Delia and Jack had disappeared down the hallway. "And Mary Stone has been released. But Ida is afraid she won't be able to leave the city to return to China on the ship they've booked. It leaves San Francisco in a few weeks."

Stephen finished the last bite of his supper and pushed his plate away. "Emily, it was unkind of you to let Whitbread take Mary Stone away from our home without protest. She and Ida Kahn are brave young women to come all the way here to study, so far from their home. For one of them to be arrested for murder must be a tremendous blow. Imagine how they feel, so far from all that they know and so powerless against a system that barely recognizes them, as they are not only women but Chinese women. How could you let her be taken away to a prison, so alone?"

I felt my face burn at this charge. "I couldn't stop Whitbread," I defended myself. "Perhaps I should have gone with her that night, but there was nothing I could do. In fact it was her friends in Chinatown, the wives of some of the most influential merchants there, who got her released. When Ida came to me today and requested my help, I went with her. Isn't that enough? And no matter what my faults, how could you stay away from your own family, as you've been doing? Will you stay now or do you plan to leave again?" I let the bitterness show in my tone. I couldn't help it. I knew I had truly wondered that morning whether Stephen was gone forever. It was unimaginable, and yet he came from a background so different from mine that sometimes I couldn't tell what he was thinking.

"Emily…no…of course I'm not leaving. I was just so angry the other night, I feared what I would say if I stayed." He moved to a chair beside me and took my shoulders in his hands, forcing me to face him. His right hand balanced heavily, as he could not grasp with it. I felt tears in my eyes, although I tried to stifle them. "Emily, I've tried everything I can think of, but in the last year you've become more and more unhappy." I opened my mouth to object. "No, hear me out. You say you need to stay with the children and I can see you love them. Having lost my own mother so early I envy them the attention you give them. I know you cherish them. But so do I. Don't you think I do? But you worry about the clothes and the furniture and whether they will know how to eat in a formal dining room. You complain about the lack of funds to have servants. You think the apartment too small, you constantly worry about their future. But I look at them and see happy, healthy children whose parents are so much more attentive than my father ever was. I know I come from a background different from yours. I don't even know what you expect. But I do know that I cannot earn the salary that will fulfill all of the desires you have.

"When we married, you had no such ambitions. You knew I couldn't provide you with a mansion on Prairie Avenue, or even the niceties from the income of a surgeon like Erickson. You wanted the life of the university. You had your own plans and dreams and they weren't for formal dining rooms and furniture. What has happened? How can I ever bring you what you expect? I suppose I might have once, before this." He lifted his dead-weight hand and let it fall heavily to the table in front of us. It lay there useless, and suddenly I understood what he must have felt about it every day. Perhaps Mary Stone was right. It stung me to realize it.

"Stephen." I grabbed the arm before me. "Is that why you are so interested in Grubbé's work? Is that where you've been this past month? Working with him to produce the X-ray films with the hope of fixing your arm?" He started to pull away, but I held on, leaning into his arms. I remembered the scorn Dr. Erickson had expressed about the picture of the shattered arm. Of course it had been Stephen's. I realized how mean the blunt statement of fact had been. I faced my husband. "I was only worried about the future because of the children. I never wanted to say that you couldn't support us." But I *had* said that. I had complained that the apartment was too small, the money was not enough to raise two children. He had every right to feel I was regretting my decision to marry him.

Suddenly, it occurred to me that, if we had not married, I would have few money worries with only myself to feed, yet I would not have Jack or Lizzie, and I would not have Stephen. I saw what a fool I had been about that. "I was afraid. I've been afraid of the consequences of bringing two lives into the world," I told him, realizing how very foolish it sounded. His left arm slipped away and I grabbed him by the shoulders, forcing him to look at me. "I thought I had lost your affection," I admitted. "I thought you had stopped caring for me. All your admiration was for these Chinese doctors, while I was struggling to make a home."

He looked at me with disbelief. "Emily, what are you saying? I praised Mary Stone because I thought she was a shadow of what you had been when I married you. You were so interested in what you were doing. You were so determined to do what you thought was right, no matter how the world conspired against you. I hoped that she and Ida might make you remember your own dreams. How can you be afraid? I've never known you to be afraid. How could you suddenly become so?"

"What if something happens to them? To Jack and Lizzie? What if they don't grow up to be healthy and go to good schools? To earn enough to live?" I blurted out my fears.

He reached out and smoothed the hair from my forehead. "Whatever are you thinking, my love? You've seen too many tenement children on the West Side. They won't have that fate.

Emily, think about it. They'll never lack for food and clothing. They'll be able to make of their lives what they choose to put the effort into making. A house that is a little larger or eating in the dining room will not change that. I may not be able to become a surgeon with clients up and down Prairie Avenue, but our children will never starve. I can promise you that, dear, even with a bad arm."

Of course, I sobbed in his arms then, unsure what it was all about. I hated that he had been made to feel inadequate because of his damaged arm. I hated even more that I was the cause of those feelings. Yet I knew I had managed to fall in his estimation. I would never be that fearless young woman I had been before. I had to fear now. I had to fear a world that could harm the two souls we had chosen to bring into it.

But I also finally realized that I did not have to fear the loss of Stephen's affections. Any loss would be entirely of my own making. I did feel that I had treated Mary Stone unkindly though, and as I felt Stephen's arms around me once again I was determined to right my wrongdoing. I would find out who had really killed Herbalist Lo so that Mary could return to Jiujiang, China to start her clinic. Whatever it took, I would do it.

# FOURTEEN

The next morning I was much calmer. Stephen insisted on continuing his work with Grubbé. I suppressed the memory of the burn scars on Grubbé's hand and mastered my fears of what the rays could do to my husband, allowing him to go on his way without any recriminations or hesitations from me. I left instructions for Delia, who seemed relieved to finally be caring for the children as she had always expected, and headed to the Harrison Street police station to confer with Detective Whitbread.

Just before stepping out the door, I stopped at the oval mirror from my mother's house that hung near the entryway. Straightening my straw hat with the wide brown ribbon reminded me that I had purchased it my first summer in Chicago, when my mother and brother came from Boston to attend the World's Columbian Exposition. So much had happened since then, not the least of which was the passing of my mother. I thought how much she would have loved to see Jack and Lizzie.

What would she think of the woman who looked back at me from the mirror now? I wore a shirtwaist, black leather belt, and brown skirt, as I had so often when I was a student and researcher. The brown walking jacket I wore over the shirtwaist was a little tight in the shoulders but the plain oval face was the same as it had been then. Pale brown hair swept away from my face, with a few escaping strands frizzled by the humidity. My straight nose was still sprinkled with unfashionable freckles and I suspected that my small mouth was more often pursed with annoyance than before. Would she have seen a change if she were here? Certainly I had seen much more of the world than the girl she visited back then. So much had happened, and yet I had to admit it felt right and fitting to see my own figure poised to go out the door again in my plain and businesslike outfit. I almost breathed a sigh of relief, as if I had been playing a part and could finally let down my guard. Impatient with myself, I shrugged off the feeling and hurried off to the train station.

At the Harrison Street station the desk sergeant no longer questioned my admittance. In fact he ushered me up the stone staircase, past the second floor, and on to a third floor meeting room. We were there before I realized his mistake. He assumed I had been invited to the meeting taking place there. Detective Whitbread sat with his back to us at a wide maple table, surrounded by half a dozen men, in a room with tall windows overlooking the street. I halted but, before I could excuse myself, Mr. Fitzgibbons rose from his place opposite the police detective and held out his arms in welcome.

"And here is Mrs. Chapman, a lady of our fair city who I am sure will be willing to assist with our planning."

The men stood at my entrance, except for two Chinese men, one of whom was Mr. Hip Lung. His black silk robes and square hat, which had appeared so foreign and impressive in the herb shop, were quite simple in comparison to the layers of red and black embroidered silk worn by the man beside him. He was introduced as Mr. Yang, a representative of the Chinese government. A tall and muscular guard, also dressed in black and red silk, with a long queue hanging down his back and a sword at his waist, stood behind Yang. I had obviously interrupted an important meeting but my attempts at retreat were overruled by Mr. Fitzgibbons, who seemed to regard my coming as some sort of rescue.

"Mrs. Chapman, please sit down," Detective Whitbread told me. He was impatient with my intrusion but I could see that Fitz was really in charge. "We are here to discuss the upcoming visit of Li Hung Chang, Viceroy of China. Information about his visit has not yet been released to the press, although there are rumors. First, we must agree on certain matters before the visit becomes public. Mayor Swift sent his representatives." He introduced a couple of very young-looking men. "And he has asked Mr. Fitzgibbons to take the lead with local arrangements. Mr. Hip Lung represents the Chinese community, as well as acting as interpreter for the representative of the Ching court, Mr. Yang." He did not seem overly pleased with the pecking order. Whitbread was always suspicious of Fitz's motives. I wanted to tell the detective about Dr. Erickson and his hatred of the dead herbalist, but there was no way I could approach that topic in the present company. I held my peace.

"That is correct." Fitz took over expansively. He, at least, seemed very pleased to see me and I relaxed as I took a chair and we all sat down. "Li Hung Chang is coming. They say President Grant estimated him as one of the three greatest men of our time and Mayor Swift believes it is fitting that Chicago should honor him. To that end he has asked me to form a committee of prominent citizens to plan for his visit."

So, was I suddenly promoted to be considered one of the city's most prominent citizens? It seemed unlikely, but I judged it wise to hold my tongue. The discussion returned to plans for the viceroy's visit. The Chinese official suggested the following week, which would be the summer festival for the local Oriental community.

Fitz tried to slow things down. "Well, now, I'm sure we would be most honored, but that would hardly give us time to prepare a proper reception. The entertainment of Viceroy Li will be a great affair and involve a large expenditure of money. For this reason, the mayor is anxious to have the cooperation of the city council.

I'm afraid they're not in session this week, which must, perforce, delay our invitation."

Hip Lung spoke up. "The Hip Lung Yee Kee Company will be most honored to undertake to fund all expenses for his most excellent Viceroy Li's visit. We have already many preparations underway. We have planned first a parade with a dragon dance, then a dinner for two hundred, and fireworks such as the city has never seen before, for this most auspicious occasion."

Fitz was taken aback. "Well, that is most generous of you, Hip Lung. You should know, gentlemen, that Mr. Hip Lung is a very important local person. He is well regarded by city councilors, like Mr. Coughlin and Mr. Kenna. Very well regarded. A veritable first citizen. And Mrs. Chapman can help to identify other prominent citizens. Perhaps Miss Addams would like to attend." He turned to me. "And people like Mr. Marshall Field, and Mr. Pullman. Oh, any number of local people. It will be a great affair."

There was a pause as Mr. Yang spoke in Chinese and we waited for Hip Lung's translation. "The honorable counselor says to remind you that the viceroy is aware of the Exclusion Act of the United States, and the Empire of China resents this insult. It is to address such wrongs that Viceroy Li travels to Europe and the United States to correct the relations between these peoples."

Fitz was stymied. "Yes, well, that is a federal statute. I'm sure the viceroy will visit Washington and talk to the president and the federal officials there. But Chicago will be most anxious to welcome a representative of the Ching court."

After another burst of Chinese, Hip Lung continued. "Honorable Counselor Yang is greatly concerned with the safety of the viceroy. He demands protection from the army and that all other arrangements for his safety be guaranteed."

"Yes, yes, in fact that is why we are here today. We are putting our best man on it. Detective Whitbread here is known for his integrity and he has been very successful in protecting the peace of our city." More translation ensued.

"The Honorable Counselor insists that any people who are threats to the viceroy be found and arrested before his arrival. In particular anyone associated with the traitor Sun Yat Sen must be detained."

I could see Whitbread straining to control himself at this demand. Fitz had a coughing fit.

"Is there any reason to believe someone wishes to harm the viceroy during his visit?" Whitbread asked. He had a notebook open before him and a stub of a pencil poised in his hand.

Translation of his question led to a barrage of fierce noises from the Chinese official. He pounded the table twice before he finally stopped and Hip Lung translated. "This revolutionary dog and his followers dare to threaten the Ching dynasty. America must condemn these traitors and show friendship to the Middle Kingdom by destroying its enemies. This must be done before the viceroy arrives."

Whitbread frowned. "Yes, I have heard that Viceroy Li arranged to have Mr. Sun Yat Sen arrested during his visit to England. However, I must point out that our laws do not permit us to detain a man simply on suspicion. In any case, we have no reason to believe Mr. Sun will attempt to come to Chicago at any time in the near future."

"But he has followers here." Hip Lung spoke on his own this time. "There are those who are friends to him, like Wong Chin Foo. We know he has connections to Sun."

"He is a journalist. I have no doubt he claims acquaintanceship with many people he barely knows," Whitbread countered.

"Now, now," Fitz intervened. "Wong is just full of political fire in the belly, that's all. Why, he tried to start a Chinese American party during the Democratic convention this summer. He's big at talking, is Mr. Wong, but he'd not be assassinating anyone or anything more than a reputation or two, I reckon." It seemed Fitz recognized and valued a fellow politician when he saw one.

There followed a discussion that would have been more heated were it not for the necessary pauses for translation that had the odd effect of slowing down the whole argument and tamping the passions involved. Finally, it was agreed that a great reception in honor of the viceroy, followed by a parade and fireworks display, would take place the following week when the annual summer festival was already scheduled. Whitbread refused to round up perceived enemies of the Chinese government merely on the recommendation of Hip Lung. As a matter of fact, he practically accused the man of trying to use the occasion as an excuse to eliminate his business rivals, but I was sure this accusation was never fully translated for the Chinese official.

In the end, Fitz insisted that Whitbread "have a little talk" with Wong Chin Foo and promised on his life that the viceroy would be safe. Based on the impression of restrained power represented by the guard standing behind Counselor Yang, I hoped Fitz was right. If anything happened to Viceroy Li, I feared for the Chicago politician's safety. For that matter, I feared for the relations between the two countries.

While the Chinese men were being shown out, Fitz stayed behind with me. He took out a large handkerchief and wiped his face. "My goodness, it's hot in here."

"With these stone walls and the high ceilings, it's actually not as warm as our apartment in such weather," I told him. "But you must excuse me, I came to speak to Detective Whitbread on a very important matter and I must catch him before he leaves the building."

Fitz reached out and put a large hand on my arm before I could rise. "I'm so glad you came along today," he told me. His eyes were bright and he gave me a look that I could only call beseeching. It made me a bit uncomfortable. "I really need your assistance with this committee. I know it's short notice but I—"

"I'm flattered, Mr. Fitzgibbons, but surely there are more prominent people you want to recruit. The mayor and his wife, for instance?"

"Yes, well…" He stood and removed his hand. I had a warm feeling about his obvious admiration for me and a small twinge of guilt for inspiring it. He looked a little bereft as he stood up. "To tell the truth, Mrs. Chapman, I'm afraid some of our prominent citizens are not as enthusiastic about our Oriental visitors as we might hope, if you take my meaning."

"I see." It was typical of Fitz to proclaim the mayor's great enthusiasm to the representative of the Chinese court, all the while knowing that, like many of his fellow countrymen, the man actually scorned the Chinese. There was something to be said for Fitz, in that he honestly did not give way to such feelings. He had a great sense of fellowship with all the many different types of people in his city. "I know…why don't you contact Mrs. Julia Lang at Hull House? She's been handling Miss Addams's social invitations. If anyone can gather a group of prominent city people in a hurry, she's the one. By all means, tell her I suggested you ask for her help. I'm sure she'll be willing."

"Thank you so much, Mrs. Chapman. And can we count on you and your family to attend?"

"Certainly. Oh, and you must invite Dr. Stone, Dr. Kang, and Miss Howe. They'll be able to converse with your guest of honor. But I really must go and find Detective Whitbread now."

"Thank you again, dear Mrs. Chapman."

I left him there. It had all been very distracting but I needed to tell Whitbread about the connection between the dead herbalist and Dr. Erickson and his daughter. There were so many hatreds simmering out there in the world. Erickson wanted someone to blame for the death of his wife, the Chinese had bitter feuds that could threaten the assassination of a government official, while some Americans fostered such a dislike of Chinese immigrants they wrote laws specifically designed to exclude them. What a world to bring children into. Children like my Jack and Lizzie.

# FIFTEEN

A sk him about Dr. Erickson. He's a medical doctor, tall, with white hair and a beard," I insisted. We were back in the narrow herb shop, interrogating the younger Lo as he stood behind the counter. Surrounded by bins filled with strange-looking dried and crinkly plants, he was using a mortar and pestle to grind herbs. There were all sorts of scents in the air, but they were light and scattered. Nonetheless, I felt the need to hold my breath every now and then to keep from sneezing.

I had convinced Whitbread that there might be other suspects in the death of Herbalist Lo. But he insisted on interviewing the dead man's son before accosting a local physician who was as prominent as Erickson. To my dismay, Whitbread recruited Charlie Kee as our interpreter on the way, despite my protest that the man had lied when he'd translated before.

The younger Lo, in his traditional garb, provided quite a contrast to the Western-suited, bowler-hatted Charlie Kee. Lo was also much taller, with broad shoulders, although he stooped and hung his head. On this occasion Kee had added a rather Oriental-looking embroidered silk vest to his Western suit. He shot off some questions in a gibbering of Chinese syllables, pointing one finger at Young Lo as he did so. "Damned Peking accent," he grumbled, after the man gave a brief reply. Kee was clearly annoyed with the herbalist.

The younger man stooped a little, the better to hear the interpreter, keeping his eyes lowered. Kee snapped something at him that made him abandon his work and turn towards us with his hands held stiffly at his sides. He spoke softly.

"That's more like it," Kee told us. "He does not know Erickson by name but he knows him as the Old Healer with white beard and angry eyes. He says the man came in months ago. He yelled at Old Lo. This one did not understand everything but Old Lo told him not to give women any more herbs. At least certain ones he is not to give them. Old Lo forbids it. Old Lo told Apple Woman and daughter of Old Healer he doesn't have those things. He tells Young Lo to pretend to not understand, give them other medicines when they ask. He says they still ask, now that Old Lo is gone. He still pretends not to understand. Says he doesn't know what to do. Worried about Chinese doctor ladies, too. Ladies came back, they still want Old Lo special recipe herbs. He does not give it to them. He is afraid Stone woman killed Old Lo."

"Tell him Dr. Stone has been released," Whitbread instructed. "And, unless he knows something he hasn't already told us, we have no proof she poisoned his father."

"He says he's afraid of Stone doctor lady."

"That's ridiculous," I protested. "Dr. Stone had no reason to harm his father. It's Dr. Erickson who blamed the man's herbs for the death of his wife." Charlie Kee translated and the poor young herbalist looked upset, jabbering something in return. I knew what he was worried about. "No, no, we don't think he harmed Mrs. Erickson. Nobody else believes that. The doctor is unreasonable in his grief, that's all. He blamed Herbalist Lo because he needed someone to blame. Tell him not to worry. No one thinks he or his father harmed the dead woman, but Dr. Stone did not harm his father either. What kind of concoction did they supply for Mrs. Erickson? Can he tell us that?"

Whitbread moved impatiently. I knew he wanted to be off to find Wong Chin Foo and talk to him about the viceroy's visit, but I wanted to follow up on my suspicions. If it was Dr. Erickson who had poisoned the old herbalist, Mary would be free to return to China. And I had promised Ida and Stephen to do everything I could to clear her name.

"He says it was just a combination to ease pain. Very common, nothing really special." While we talked, the young man was searching in a drawer behind him. He turned back with a small cloth bag tied with a string and he put it on the counter in front of me. "There, he says, that is it. He gives it to you. This proves they did not harm the angry old healer's wife," Kee explained. His eyebrow was raised sardonically, as if he were skeptical of the claim.

"Well, that proves nothing," Whitbread barked.

I put my hand on the bag. "Nonetheless, I'll take it and have my husband analyze it." I felt badly for the tall young man whose father had so recently been taken from him and who was now being questioned by the police. I could see that he was fearful. I didn't think Charlie Kee—whose allegiance was to Hip Lung—was a particularly reassuring presence. It occurred to me that I should return some time with my own translator to verify Kee's version. To that end, I thanked the young herbalist and indicated to Whitbread that I was ready to leave. Lo bowed from the waist as we turned away.

I followed an irritated Detective Whitbread down the length of the shop and out the door. "That proved nothing," he told me.

"But Erickson did threaten the old man," I protested.

"Months ago. It means nothing. I must find Wong Chin Foo. Kee, do you know where he would be?"

The translator grimaced. "Wong has big meeting. He invited all the newspapers." He shook his head. "He wants to build a Chinese temple in Chicago, to honor Confucius. He is man of big ideas, big plans, big mouth. Mouth is working overtime today."

"Where?" Whitbread asked.

"Down the street. I take you. Offices of Chinese Civil Rights League, 329 Clark Street." He bustled off and we followed him for a couple of blocks to a brick building. A small grocery, a laundry, and two saloons were on the ground floor but he took us up some stairs to an office on the upper floor. The door was open into a good-sized room where men with notebooks sat on chairs and stools ranged in front of a most peculiar-looking object. Wong Chin Foo stood at the front of the room wearing a long black robe and pointing as he talked. We stepped into the back of the room to listen.

"This is the altar we have borrowed from the Wong Family Association to show you the type of thing we will have in the new temple. In the center you see the tablet of Confucius. As you can see, it has dragons and inscriptions and it contains the writings of our great sage. Above it, hanging from the ceiling, are the clouds from which the genii, servants of the god, descend. Of course, neither Confucius nor his priests are considered godlike. The moral philosophy of Confucius makes no claims to divinity.

"Here, in front of the tablet, is a bowl for incense." He lit a stick and a faint scent wafted into the room. "At this end, we have the sacred drum, to call the spirits and, at the other, we have a container of flags. In front of the altar is the sacred mat where worshippers can make their bows." I stood on tiptoe to see the mat he spoke of and watched with the rest of the room as he knelt down, facing the tablet above him, and lowered his head to the ground three times in succession.

One of the newspapermen was on his feet, pointing at the altar with his pencil. "So, will an altar like that be in Kimball Hall when you have your first meeting tomorrow night?" With a shock, I recognized the voice and the back of my brother, Alden. He had returned to Chicago as a newspaperman several years previously and he was due to finally wed my friend Clara at Christmastime. I shouldn't have been surprised to see him there, nor should I have been surprised to see Detective Whitbread roll his eyes with recognition. Since his return to the city, Alden had managed to get himself into several scrapes. Just as before, he had called on Whitbread to help extract him from trouble. I could see the detective expected annoyances wherever he found my brother, and I couldn't blame him.

Meanwhile, Wong was answering. "It is probable that we will not have such an impressive structure prepared in time. As you can imagine, it takes time and skill to carve an object such as this." Wong stood with his hands clasped in front of him, covered by the long sleeves of his robe.

"So, why should the local Orientals attend a service lacking an altar when they have them elsewhere in existing places of worship?" Alden asked. I heard the other newspapermen cackle. They liked to let my brother act like a gadfly, annoying the speaker.

Wong Chin Foo was unmoved. He seized the opportunity to explain his intentions. "This temple will be open to anyone, but the hope is to convert Americans. If properly introduced, Confucianism will bring about an almost perfect civilization in the United States." There was a movement and more chuckles from the audience, but they all got their notebooks out in anticipation of something good. "No, you do not understand. In this city there are more real followers of Confucius among the Americans now than among the Chinese. While Christianity has not always been a good influence on the societies where it has been introduced, Confucianism has always had an elevating effect."

"How do you figure that?" one of the other reporters asked.

"Take China, for instance. There was no trouble, no bloodshed there until Christianity was introduced. The American people I admire greatly—they are intellectual, they are a nation of geniuses—but see what they have to fight against. They have trouble in their homes, they have trouble in public life. The officials are corrupt.

"Social life in America is all upside down. There are good things in it, but they are often done incorrectly. The United States is adopting civil service, but it is going about it all wrong. It should have begun with the men at the heads of things. Instead of examining applicants for the lowest kind of positions, those seeking high places should be put to the test. With good men directing the government, there will be good men beneath them." That pronouncement was met with a great scraping of pencils against notebooks and a bombardment of questions, as it became clear that this new temple was not meant for the eight hundred or so English-speaking Chinese in Chicago, and even less for the non-English speaking, but rather it was intended for the conversion of Americans. Wong claimed that America was ripe for a change in religion. He ended with a final appeal, "If I could find some man of good education and good standing...*and* American birth...to preach Confucianism, I am certain that the philosophy would be understood and accepted. I am now looking for such a man, but he is hard to find."

Wong remained unflinching in his sincerity until the reporters finally ran out of questions and started leaving. At that point, I noticed Mary and Ida standing nearby. I was curious to hear what Whitbread would say to Mr. Wong, but since it looked like it would take him some time to get to the front of the room, I approached the two women. Ida was shaking her head.

"Mrs. Chapman," Mary greeted me. "Mr. Wong invited us to hear his announcement. It was certainly quite startling."

Ida snorted. "He knows we are Christians. 'No bloodshed in China until the coming of Christianity,' hah! He is deluded. On the contrary, there has been no progress in China until the coming of Christianity!"

"In China," Mary explained, "Confucianism is a form of ancestor worship and it does not always encourage scientific advances."

"It is backward," Ida chimed in. "By Confucian precepts we would have bound feet and stay in a village as married women who are never let out of the house."

"There are certain aspects of ethics and moral philosophy and certain practices, like civil service, that can be adapted in the West as improvements," Mary suggested. "He is right about some things."

Ida snorted. "He is proposing burning incense and calling down geniis."

Wong worked his way through the crowd of departing reporters to greet the young women doctors he had invited. He did not appear to be the least discomposed by Ida's objections. On the contrary, it was obvious that he enjoyed the several minutes he spent sparring with her. Meanwhile, my brother had joined us and pestered me, until I finally introduced him not only to Wong but to Mary and Ida as well. Whitbread stood by the door trying to contain his impatience.

"Yes, Mr. Cabot," Wong Chin Foo said, as he gestured towards Mary and Ida, "here you meet the future of China. Here are the type of young women who will bring progress and build a new society."

"Excuse me, Mr. Wong," Ida objected. "We are Christians and proud of it."

He refused to be drawn. "And China is proud to have such accomplished women, medical doctors, to lead the way to the future."

Ida huffed at him. It seemed to me that Mr. Wong did not require consistency in his logic, certainly not where religion was concerned. The topic might have led to a fascinating discussion, but the time had come to break up this little party. Mary excused herself and Ida, saying they must leave to meet Miss Howe at the King Yen Lo restaurant. She invited me to join them but I explained that I had to remain with Detective Whitbread and promised to follow if I could. My brother's attempts to attach himself to the group were unsuccessful, so I was stuck with him when they left. Finally I could introduce Whitbread to Wong Chin Foo. The detective looked at my brother with disapproval.

"I thought I would just wait for my sister," Alden explained innocently. Neither Whitbread nor I were fooled by this.

"I have some confidential questions for Mr. Wong," the detective announced. Wong's eyebrows rose in question.

"I promise to be discreet," Alden said.

Whitbread rolled his eyes. He did not want either of us present, but he knew us well enough to know it would take a lot of effort to get rid of us. Besides, we were enough afraid of him to never disobey him about confidential issues. The three of us had been through a lot together. With a shrug, Whitbread turned to Wong Chin Foo and attempted to ignore us.

"Mr. Wong, are you acquainted with Mr. Sun Yat Sen?"

"*Dr.* Sun Yat Sen. Most certainly. Those of us who have founded the Chinese Civil Rights League look to Dr. Sun to lead a revolt that will bring down the Manchu Dynasty and establish democracy in China!"

# SIXTEEN

hitbread and I both stared at Wong with our mouths open. I'm sure we'd both assumed that Hip Lung exaggerated when he accused Wong of supporting Sun Yat Sen. It seemed we were wrong.

Wong continued enthusiastically. "The present rulers of China are unpatriotic and cowardly, and their deposition will save the empire from partition by foreign powers. I am confident that Americans will render the same sympathy to us that they have so generously extended to the struggling Cubans." By this I knew he meant the way our country had supported Cuban patriots in their rebellion against Spain. Although the public had mixed reactions to such activity, obviously it signaled to young revolutionaries like Wong Chin Foo that the United States would always support revolution against an imperial system and actions of rebels who sought to establish democracies.

Alden was busy taking all this down in his notebook, while Whitbread appeared to me to be grinding his teeth. "Now, look here, Wong, whatever conflict you have with the rulers of China, you must take it up with them in China. We will not allow that fight to spill over into the streets of Chicago. We'll have order here or we'll have arrests."

"No, no, Detective, there is no intent to wage the struggle in this country. Such a thing would be meaningless. The Chinese Empire is a rotten hulk and can be easily overthrown by a well-organized expedition against the capital city. We shall not try to involve this country in war. Our forces will rendezvous at one of the South Sea islands from which they will aim a well-directed blow."

Whitbread grimaced. It seemed Wong was just the sort of dangerous revolutionary the Chinese official had claimed after all. "Exactly when is this expedition of yours scheduled to happen?"

"That is where we here in America come in," Wong continued happily. "We hope to bring people together here to support Sun Yat Sen. He has the money but no men. We have numbers of men in this country who are willing to fight for China, but they have no money. We are hoping to form a syndicate of capitalists who will supply the cash for men of war and for the purchase of ammunition. To such a syndicate we will grant a ninety-year lease to build railroads in China, and to operate cotton factories. This would result in untold profits."

"Mr. Wong, exactly how many men have you signed up for this expedition so far?" Whitbread raised an eyebrow, indicating a certain amount of skepticism.

"Sam Yuan, Yu Long, Wong Kee, Dong Tung, Lee Lung, Yee Wah," Wong announced proudly, pointing to a poster on the wall which displayed what I guessed was a list of signatures in Chinese characters.

"I see. And how much money have you raised for these war ships and ammunition?"

"We have only begun to organize," he admitted, but with irrepressible optimism. "In fact, we are trying to persuade Dr. Sun to come on a speaking tour next spring with the intention of raising interest and money for the cause."

"Next spring? I see." Whitbread shook his head. "Let me put you on notice, Mr. Wong. It has not yet been announced, but Viceroy Li Hung Chang of the Chinese government will be visiting the city next week for the summer festival. And, no, Mr. Cabot, you may *not* print anything about those plans until we are ready to publicly announce them. The Chinese government has asked us to detain you, Mr. Wong, and your followers as a safety measure during the viceroy's visit."

"You can't do that!" Alden protested.

"Be quiet, Mr. Cabot. We have refused to do this. But you should be aware, Mr. Wong, that if there are any attempts on the life of Viceroy Li, they will be thwarted and anyone who makes such an attempt will be apprehended and prosecuted to the full extent of the law. Do you understand that?"

"Certainly. But I know the American people will sympathize with our efforts to overthrow the corrupt Manchu court."

"That is beside the point, Mr. Wong. Viceroy Li will be visiting as a guest of the American government and the mayor of Chicago. Any move to assault him or his followers will result in swift and unmerciful justice. Are you quite sure you understand what I am saying?"

"Yes, yes. We will not involve this country in our struggle. We look only for financial support. We will take our fight to the streets of Peking, not Chicago."

"You had better be telling the truth about that or, I promise you, you will regret it."

"I am telling the truth," Wong replied. He folded his arms over his chest and his eyes narrowed. "But you should know there are many who hate the representatives of the emperor and especially the dowager empress. Li is very close to her. There are those within the court itself who might wish to do him harm."

"You just keep your own men in check," Whitbread told him. "And you, Mr. Cabot, you will print nothing of this except the plain fact of Viceroy Li's visit. And you will only do that when I tell you it is all right to do so. Understood?"

"Yes, sir." Alden looked down at his notes.

"I wish these foreigners would keep all their feuds and conspiracies in their own countries and not be bringing them here like baggage." Whitbread sounded exasperated. "The mayor has invited Viceroy Li, so he will come, he'll enjoy the celebrations, and he'll leave without a hair on his head being touched, so help me God." With that, the detective stalked out of the room and down the stairs.

# SEVENTEEN

When he heard that I would be meeting Mary and Ida at the King Yen Lo restaurant, Mr. Wong was anxious to accompany me. Alden was clearly still assuming that he would be included in our party. I wanted to ask Ida to return to the herb shop to help me verify that Charlie Kee had translated Young Lo's account truthfully. But I didn't want to incite my reporter brother's curiosity. I was wary of having him take up the story of the death of the herbalist and Mary's arrest. The last thing the young women doctors needed were sensational press accounts of their plight. Nonetheless, I was forced to accept the company of both men.

The restaurant was only a block from the office where Mr. Wong's meeting had been held. When we arrived I led the way up the narrow flight of stairs, my boots echoing on the wood. Reaching the top, I was struck by an unexpected tableau. In the light from a tall window just inside the entrance, Mary was turning away, towards the dining room. She gave me the impression of a small bird about to take flight. On the opposite side of the window Mr. Chin, the waiter we had met during our earlier visit, stepped back into the shadows. Had we interrupted something?

"Mrs. Chapman," Mary greeted me. "I am so happy you could join us. And your brother, Mr. Cabot." She turned her gaze down to the floor shyly.

"Yes. I'm afraid my brother followed me. Perhaps you know

how younger brothers can be." I was trying to lighten the atmosphere, which suddenly seemed to be strained. "He is nothing if not persistent." She looked up at that with a slight smile on her lips. I continued, as Mr. Wong reached the top of the stairs. "And apparently Mr. Wong is feeling hungry as well. But perhaps Alden could keep him company. I'm sure he must want to interview Mr. Wong further after that fascinating presentation. My brother is devoted to his job," I said, with a smile plastered on my face to keep from grimacing at him. "I'm sure neither one of these gentlemen would want to impose themselves on your party."

Both men began to sputter. Of course they had every intention of inviting themselves to join Mary and Ida. But I was just as determined to prevent them from intruding. However, before I could make a sharp comment, Mary told them she had no objection to their joining us. She was much more polite to them than I would have been.

"We would be very happy to have the gentlemen join us. It is a large table, you will see. But I must beg a favor of Mr. Wong." She turned to face him, blocking the way into the dining room. "I must ask you not to distress Miss Howe, who is with us. While Ida and I are interested to hear of your plans to open a Confucian temple, I fear Miss Howe would be offended by your comments concerning Christianity. As you are aware, Miss Howe, Dr. Kahn, and I are all faithful Christians. I hope you can display respect for our beliefs, no less than we have done for yours."

Mr. Wong was uncharacteristically quiet in response to this, so I seconded Mary's request. "Can we count on you, Mr. Wong, to not provoke argument on these issues? Because you can still sit apart with my brother at another table, if you feel you cannot restrain yourself." I smiled brightly.

Alden looked puzzled but Mr. Wong rolled his eyes and sighed. "Ladies, ladies, I beg your pardon. I promise to behave and to refrain from teasing Miss Howe." He turned to Alden. "Miss Howe is a well-known Christian missionary and also the adoptive mother of Dr. Kahn." His eyes were lit with mischief, which made me wonder if Mary was being wise in allowing them to join us. "You must interview her, Mr. Cabot. She has many stories that would interest your readers." He grinned at Alden.

I think I rolled my eyes at that, and I know I shook my head as we followed Mary to a large round table where Ida sat with Miss Howe and two older women who were introduced as fellow missionaries. The men pulled over additional chairs after the introductions. I made sure I sat beside Ida, as I hoped to persuade her to accompany me back to the herb shop for another talk with the son of the dead herbalist.

I removed my jacket and hung it on the back of my chair as Mary and Ida had done. It was another very warm day. Mr. Wong was obediently avoiding the topic of religion by asking the ladies if they knew about plans for the festival in Chinatown the following week. As if on cue, my brother asked for the story behind the celebration. He even had his notebook and pencil out.

"It is known as the Double Seventh Festival—held on the seventh day of the seventh month," Wong began to lecture. "But that is according to the lunar calendar, so it is always in August. In China it is known as a holiday especially for lovers."

"Lovers?" Alden looked up. "Well, that's interesting."

"It celebrates a story about a cowherd and a weaving girl."

"It's a famous Chinese fairy tale," Mary explained. The others were attracted to the story and stopped chatting to listen.

Wong took up the tale. "You see, the weaving girl was daughter to a queen of the spirits, but she fell in love with a cowherd. They even married and had children, a boy and a girl. But when her powerful mother found out, she sent her genii to reclaim her daughter. They stole her away and brought her back to heaven."

"What about her children?" I asked.

"They were left behind with the father. They were all mortals, you see. But no matter how the queen punished her, the daughter refused to give up on the cowherd and her children. Now, as it happened, the cowherd had the help of a magic buffalo. He was able to fly up to heaven, so he took his children with him and tried to get his wife back." Wong clearly relished the attention we were all focusing on him. "But the angry mother caused a huge heavenly river to rise up and keep him away from his wife, the weaving girl."

"Good heavens. Didn't she care about her grandchildren?" I couldn't help asking.

He waved a hand. "Mere mortals. Not worth worrying about. It was only when her daughter was pining away to nothing that the queen finally gave in. She said that once a year they could cross the heavenly river to meet. And that happens on the seventh day of the seventh month. It is to celebrate that meeting once a year that we have the festival."

"What a very sad love story," I said. I couldn't imagine such a cruel mother who didn't even want to see her grandchildren. It seemed very strange to me.

"The heavenly river is in the sky," Ida told me. "It's the stars you call the Milky Way."

"Chinese love stories frequently end in disaster," Miss Howe told us. "In a society where marriages are arranged by parents, and husbands and wives are often separated by long distances for various periods during their lives, there is not much room for romantic love."

"But it *is* a romantic story," Mary insisted. "It's a story of great faithfulness and the strength of a love to remain true through such trials. That is the true story and that is why everyone thinks of the cowherd and the weaving girl as the epitome of love."

"I suppose it's like our story of Romeo and Juliet, a tragedy due to feuding between families," I said doubtfully.

Ida chimed in. "But, unlike Romeo and Juliet, the cowherd and the weaving girl did marry and have children. And they did not die. They could see each other across the river but they only met once a year."

I shivered. "That almost seems worse to me. At least Juliet woke to pain and had it over with. The weaving girl stands on the opposite shore and sees her husband and children but can't reach them? What torture that would be!"

"It demonstrates, perhaps, the value the Chinese people place on endurance," Mary suggested.

"That's true," Miss Howe told me. "There's a term in Chinese that translates roughly as eating bitterness. The Chinese refer to themselves sometimes as people who eat bitterness, and it is held to be a virtue to be able to do that and endure."

At that moment the waiter Chin swept up to the table with a large tureen of soup. Helpers placed dishes and spoons in front of him and he began to serve up steaming bowls and hand them around. It was a clear soup with a few chopped green onions and a doughy dumpling floating in each bowl. Despite the heat of the day, it tasted good as I sipped it. The broth was salty and the dumpling contained spiced meat in a tangy gravy. When I bit into it, the flavor filled my mouth.

"I see you do not appreciate the rigors of romantic love as portrayed in the most famous Chinese love story," Mr. Wong chided me. "But perhaps the new Chinese women, as represented by Dr. Stone and Dr. Kahn, will be more Western in their romances. What do you say, ladies?"

Mary ducked her head to sip her soup at this impertinence but Ida disagreed with him. "Perhaps it is not so easy to find a man as faithful as the cowherd these days," she said. "He showed great courage in pursuing his wife even to the gates of heaven. Not every man would be so worthy."

"True," Wong admitted. He accepted a bowl of soup from Chin. "And while we are on the topic of romance, we must congratulate Mr. Chin here. I heard you've recently married, is that not so, Chin?"

The young waiter smiled and bowed from the waist, then began gathering up extra utensils and wiping a spill from the table.

"Congratulations, Mr. Chin," Miss Howe said. "Is your wife here?"

"Thank you. Thank you. No, in my village. In China. We are married by proxy. Arranged by my family. I received the letter only last week."

"Married by proxy?" Alden asked, as Chin carried the soup tureen away. I glanced at Mary but her eyes were lowered, concentrated on her soup.

"That's often the custom in China," Miss Howe explained. "A man lives and works over here and sends money home to his family. They'll find a suitable woman and arrange a marriage by proxy. The young woman will go to live with his family and they'll consummate the marriage the next time he travels home. It can be several years before they meet."

Alden looked stunned, so I decided to cover the awkwardness by teasing him. "My brother is engaged to be married. The wedding will be in the winter. His fiancée is one of my good friends who has just completed her studies at the university. She received a doctorate in chemistry." In fact, their marriage plans had been postponed to allow Clara to finish her studies. They had planned to marry a few years earlier but they found the prejudice against married women at the university too much to contend with and had finally decided to wait for Clara to complete her work before having the wedding.

Ida turned to Alden with a smile. "Congratulations, Mr. Cabot. It would seem that you approve of the education of your wife. That's very enlightened of you."

"And the marriage was not arranged by your parents?" Wong asked. It occurred to me that the two of them, Wong and Ida, had managed to turn the interviewing around, so that they were asking questions of the reporter.

"Oh, goodness no. My parents...Emily's and mine...have passed away. But even if that were not the case, it would be our choice entirely, not arranged. There was some little concern from

Clara's family but she managed to convince them."

"You see," Wong said, smiling expansively, "this is the future. This is what will be available to the New Woman of China as well. Enlightened men marrying educated women. Do you not agree?" He seemed to aim the question at Ida who was watching Mary with some concern. Ida was having none of it.

"You have great hopes for the future of China, Mr. Wong. However, it would appear from your haircut that you have no intention of returning there yourself," Ida retorted.

"Ah, certainly not while the Manchu court retains power. But the number of days for that court is limited. In our lifetimes you will see a great revolution. Surely you've heard of Dr. Sun Yat Sen? We are hoping he will lead a revolution, to be funded by patriots here and in other places abroad."

"You're an optimist," Ida responded. "It won't be an easy thing to bring down a government that has been in power for so many centuries."

"But this is a new age and China must become new. I know many men in China who will welcome your arrival, Dr. Kahn, and will see you as a model for the young women of our time. I have already written to some of them in Jiujiang to expect a couple of paragons of new womanhood who will join them soon."

"You are too kind," Mary told him. "You exaggerate our abilities."

"Not at all. Those of us who want to promote change in China welcome your coming. You are indeed new Chinese women!"

"Good Christian women," Miss Howe pointed out and her missionary friends nodded in agreement. "But there's a long way to go in China and we see many old practices that will need to be revised before it becomes a modern nation."

"And I am not at all sure the kind of violent change advocated by Dr. Sun Yat Sen will not lead to great bloodshed," Ida told him.

"The result will be worth the sacrifice if we can establish a republic," Wong insisted.

"So long as the sacrifice is not your blood," Ida responded. "Dr. Stone and I are healers. We will advocate for education and improvement. Unlike you, I could never condone violence for the sake of change." I was reminded of the violence I had seen in recent years in this very city and I had to agree with Ida. Perhaps it was a particularly feminine perspective, but I feared the threat of violence that could spring from anger at injustice, no matter how righteous that anger might be. It made me wonder about the threats to the viceroy. It seemed the man from the consulate was right, there were those in the Chinese community who might attack a person like Li Hung Chang. I hoped Mr. Wong was not one of them.

He seemed to sense that Alden and I were thinking about the earlier conversation with Detective Whitbread, during which we had all promised to keep the plans for the viceroy's visit confidential. He moderated his arguments after that and returned to a discussion of the coming Double Seventh Festival. From the way he urged the women to participate in the celebrations I could not think that he expected any violence. But I still had difficulty in understanding his character. He was vibrant and intelligent. He appeared to admire Mary and Ida, although he locked horns with Miss Howe over religion. He appeared to be ardent in his beliefs about American values and yet he was frequently ironic. I liked him, but I was not sure I could entirely trust him.

I found I liked Mary and Ida as well, yet I was unsure if I quite understood them, either. Certainly I didn't feel akin to them in the same way that I did to the women who attended the university with me. I seemed to understand Miss Howe more easily. I could imagine what she would do and how she would react in any situation. But, with the young Chinese women, I foundered when I sought to understand them. There was something always just out of my reach, something elusive. Miss Howe had a better understanding of them, perhaps from long acquaintance with their countrymen, but for me it seemed as if

I saw them always through a gauze veil so that the outline was not clear, not clear at all.

I became quiet, tired from trying to keep up with the sparring between Mr. Wong and Ida. After the meal concluded I asked her to accompany me to the herbalist's, and she readily agreed. I didn't want to ask Mary to join us since she was still a suspect, and I remembered that Young Lo had seemed to believe she might have poisoned his father. I knew Ida would get at the truth for me, so I was glad she was willing to go. Mary would be going to visit Hip Lung's wife, who regularly consulted her as a personal physician. As we all stood up from the table I noticed Mr. Chin whisper something to Mary and saw her put a hand on his arm. I looked over to Ida and saw that she had observed this as well. Perhaps she was right, it would be a good thing for the two women doctors to return to take up their duties in China as soon as possible.

As I turned towards the stairs I was surprised to see a man, sitting in a booth by himself with a napkin stuffed in his collar, hungrily taking forkfuls of food from several platters arrayed in front of him. He was much too occupied to observe us, but I recognized him as the immigration officer, Lewis.

# EIGHTEEN

I followed Ida down the narrow stairs. When I reached the street, she put her arm in mine. She bent towards me to talk, completely ignoring the men we passed along the way. It was usually my practice to put my head down and rush along, avoiding contact with men on the street. It was an inbred caution that came from being a woman alone, travelling through the city. But Ida kept our gait to a stroll with her head up, paying no attention to the knots of men, and they, in turn, kept out of our way.

"You must wonder about Mary and Mr. Chin." She didn't wait for me to answer. "In the four years we have spent in this country we have sometimes missed our home very much. The people at the university in Michigan were very kind but sometimes one just misses one's home. In English you call it homesickness. In Chinese it has the meaning of longing. For us, coming here to Chicago, where there are Chinese people, customs, and food that we recognize, we feel a little closer to home. So we came here several times a year. We always went to the King Yen Lo restaurant."

"That's how you met Mr. Chin?" I was glad for the shade from my straw hat when we crossed the street into the full light of the sun. Ida wore a flat little hat decorated with a pile of velvet roses and a broad yellow ribbon that tied under her chin, emphasizing her round face and spectacles. It didn't provide much shade and she had to squint in the bright sun. We were both careful to skirt the horse droppings on the street and the garbage that overflowed containers on the walkway.

"Yes. He is from the south of China, where he was brought up to be a scholar. When his father died, he had to give up his studies to come here to make money to support his mother and younger brothers and sisters. He has an uncle whose brother-in-law owns the restaurant. Chin started as a waiter, but he is very bright, so he has moved up to become the manager." She looked quizzically at a knot of men in front of a saloon. They backed up to make room for us, so we continued arm in arm. I was impressed by her composure.

"He seems to admire Mary."

"He works very hard, but talking to us reminds him of the life he had to give up when he stopped his studies. You see, in China, if a man can complete his studies and pass the examinations he can rise in the world. He expected to have such a career while his father was alive, but now it will never be."

"Never?"

"You cannot go back. The life of a scholar requires wealth enough to have the time to study. Once a man becomes a merchant or takes some other job to earn money for his family, he does not have the time to study to take the examinations for a government post. And once he comes here, to America, the time is past for him to have that kind of career. Men from the scholarly class do not come here, they remain in China. It is merchants and laboring men who come here. The path of the scholar is gone for Chin. He can never return to it now."

"Yet he is doing well here, from what you say."

"Yes."

I wasn't sure it was a matter she wanted to confide in me but I felt compelled to ask. "It seems as if he and Mary might have feelings for each other. Surely if they care for each other something might be done." It was a new and welcome idea that Mary might have a suitor. Yet Mr. Wong had congratulated him on a marriage by proxy. How very strange.

"Oh, no. It was always impossible." Ida shook her head and patted my arm. "He has his mother and siblings to support. His mother is aging. His wife will go to live with his mother and help her. Of course a woman like Mary could never do that."

"But surely what Mary can do, being a doctor, must make up for that. No one would want her to waste all of that work and study and training."

"Of course not. But Chin's mother still needs and deserves to have a daughter-in-law to help her and to provide company for her as she gets older."

"But what about Mary and Chin? Do you mean to say there is no way for them to overcome such obstacles, even if they care for each other?"

"It would never do. Mary must return to Jiujiang. Chin must remain here to make money and send it home. So many people depend on him. And so many people depend on Mary and me to return and open our clinic. You can see how impossible it is."

I glanced at her face, but it was round and impassive as ever. I felt sad for Mary and her young man who could never be her young man. I was having a hard time understanding these young Chinese women now that I was getting to know them.

We reached the herb shop and entered, causing the little bell on the door to jangle. It was dim inside, after the bright sunshine, and it took at least a minute for me to be able to see again. I was surprised that the same three men who had been taken away by Officer Lewis were once more planted in the middle of the room around the tiny table with suitcases at their feet.

Ida proceeded down the room, ignoring the men, but they looked up and their dark eyes followed us as we walked to the counter at the far end. When we reached the area where Young Lo was working with mortar and pestle I had the nagging sensation that someone was right behind me. It made the hair on the back of my neck stand on end. Young Lo looked past me with an expression of alarm and Ida turned to face the man who stood behind me. She barked a few words in Chinese at him. I looked over my shoulder, then, just in time to see him shrug and back away, returning to his friends. When I turned towards the young herbalist, he looked relieved. I wondered if he was somehow afraid of the men who seemed to have come to roost in his shop.

I was surprised and impressed by Ida's air of authority. She looked at me now and asked, "What is it you want to ask Mr. Lo?"

I explained that I wanted to know about Dr. Erickson and his daughter, particularly their relationship to Lo's dead father.

"He says you already asked these questions earlier today," Ida reported. "You were with a policeman?"

"Yes. It was Detective Whitbread. But I didn't completely trust Mr. Kee who was translating for us."

Ida nodded and continued her conversation with the young man, translating as she went along. He told us much the same story as I had heard through Charlie Kee's translation. Young Lo said that Charlotte and Mrs. Appleby often ordered a special concoction of herbs from Herbalist Lo. But when Dr. Erickson showed up in a rage, threatening Lo with prosecution, he told his son never to give them that particular recipe again. Lo claimed his father had substituted something else, less powerful, but the women noticed and returned. Finally, the old man refused to give them anything and sent them away. He had forbidden his son from serving them as well.

It was all much the same as what I had heard in the morning but, at the end, Lo spoke quickly and vehemently and Ida stared at him with alarm.

"He says Miss Erickson came in today after you and the policeman left. He says she asked again for the herbs. He did not want to provide them. He still remembers his father's command and thinks it would be unlucky to disobey him. She left unsatisfied, but then her father, Dr. Erickson, came in very angry. He yelled at Lo and threatened him. He wanted to know where his daughter had gone. Erickson told Lo if he ever even spoke to his daughter again he would have him deported. Then he left, still very angry."

"I think I should find Detective Whitbread and tell him about this," I said. I was worried by this development. "Ask him if he knows where Dr. Erickson went when he left."

Before Ida could do that, the doorbell jangled and a young boy ran down the room to Ida. Grabbing her skirt, he poured out a torrent of Chinese. Still talking furiously, he pulled her towards the door.

"Mary sent him," Ida told me. "There's something wrong. I think she has been hurt. We have to go."

Her usually impassive face looked as if she had been struck. She hurried after the boy to the door and I followed. I still felt uncomfortable about those men in the middle of the room but I attempted to ignore them as I pushed past. The bell jangled wildly as we left.

We ran along, briefly in the blinding sun, then into shadows, as the boy ran under awnings and into the alleyway where we had gone to visit Hip Lung's wife. There was a crowd of Chinese men gathered around the doorway. They were mostly in cotton pants and jackets with queues hanging down their backs, working men. I felt uneasy following Ida as she shouted at them in sharp barks. She came to a sudden stop before the door. "Ay yah, oh no."

I stopped beside her and saw her face was contorted in fear. Looking down I saw a pool of dark liquid. There was the unnerving, slightly sweet smell of human blood in the air. Whatever had happened had been catastrophic. I fought a wave of nausea. Poor Mary.

The little girl who had led us into Hip Lung's home when we had visited before was leaning out of the doorway, beckoning. I heard Ida gulp a sob as she stepped over the blood to follow her. I felt my stomach turn at the prospect of what we would find above.

# NINETEEN

But it was not Mary who was injured. It was Charlotte Erickson who had been discovered beaten on the doorstep. We found Mary in one of the bedrooms of Hip Lung's family apartment. Ida ran to her, questioning her in Chinese. I took a huge breath, amazed at how relieved I was to see her. She was standing over a large, dark mahogany four-poster bed. Charlotte's body seemed no more than a pile of cotton rags crumpled on top of the silken bedding. There was a bloodstained cloth on the floor, and Mary was wrapping a bandage around the girl's head very carefully. The smell of blood tinged the air, sickening in the summer warmth. I recalled a dark stain on the ground right where we had turned into the doorway of the building. That must have been where they found her.

It was only then that I noticed Hip Lung's wife and her sister-in-law huddled in a corner, supported by their young maid. They tottered a bit on their bound feet, each clutching a shoulder of the girl for balance.

"What happened?" I asked.

Mary herself was white faced but calm. "I found her when I arrived at their doorstep. I don't know how long she had been there." The doorway was in an alley off of Clark Street, so I could see that she might have been there for a while without being found.

"Who did this? Did anyone see what happened?"

"I hardly know. I had her carried up here and I sent for Ida

because I knew she had gone to Lo's with you." Ida took up Charlotte's wrist and watched Mary finish the bandage.

"We must get her to the hospital," Ida said. "The bleeding will stop, but there may be other injuries."

"Was she conscious at all?" I asked. "The head wound looks severe."

"It is. I fear for her life. I cannot tell if her skull was fractured. She was unconscious when I found her and remains so." Mary's expression was grim and I saw her and Ida exchange a look.

"What is it? Will she recover?"

"We cannot tell," Mary answered. "She was hit on the back of the head." She gestured to her own skull.

"As if someone had come up from behind and hit her?"

"Yes, a very strong blow from what I could see. I think there are injuries on her arms and legs as well. The blow to the head caused bleeding but I think that was only the skin. I cannot tell if the bone of the skull itself was damaged."

"If it was?"

Ida took up the explanation. "That would be very bad. If the skull was fractured there may have been pieces that entered the brain. It could cause damage from which she would never recover. We cannot say."

"It is dangerous to move her but more dangerous to let her remain here," Mary said. "I have asked them to find transport to take her to the women's hospital. When we get her there, perhaps we will know more."

"How awful. Is there anything I can do to help?" I thought of the girl's complaints the day before, how she hated her life and longed to live differently. Surely she never imagined such a turn of events. She should have had her chance for the balls and dinner parties that she wished for. I felt sorry that I had scorned her ambitions, if only in my own mind.

"Perhaps you could notify her father?" Mary suggested.

I was about to tell her that Dr. Erickson was last seen in

Chinatown angrily searching for his daughter but Ida interrupted. "No, they can do that at the hospital. You should go and find your husband and Mr. Grubbé and ask them to bring their X-ray equipment to the hospital. At least we can find out if her skull is damaged that way."

"Yes, yes. I can do that." I stopped as some men entered with a stretcher and began to move Charlotte under Mary's directions. To my embarrassment, I realized I did not know where my husband could be found. I asked Ida. "Do you know where to find Mr. Grubbé and my husband?"

She looked at me with what I thought was pity. "Mr. Grubbé's clinic is on Pacific Avenue. I'll get one of the boys to take you." She beckoned to a young boy of perhaps twelve years of age and spoke to him in Chinese. Soon I was following him into the night as the others took Charlotte to the hospital. I wanted to tell Detective Whitbread about the attack, but finding Stephen and Grubbé and getting their help had to come first. Poor Miss Erickson. How many times had I traipsed around the city streets with no thought for my safety? I never imagined that someone would carry out such a vicious attack against a harmless young woman. How could such a thing have happened?

I followed the boy and we were soon far from the lights and noise of Clark Street, into quieter, darker alleys. I felt apprehensive, but I pushed the fear away. I trusted Ida's judgment, telling myself she knew where Grubbé's laboratory was located and it must not be far if she'd sent me with only the boy. Soon we were in a public courtyard, hurrying to the back of an office building. An open doorway spilled light out into the yard, and I could see test tubes and laboratory equipment on shelves and counters. On a large wooden placard beside the door, flowery letters announced "E. H. Grubbé, Assayer and Refiner of Rare Metals. Manufacturer of Incandescent Lamps, Geissler and Crookes Tubes." I nodded vigorously to the child to let him know this was the place, and he scampered off into the shadows.

I could hear voices coming from the back of the laboratory. Incandescent lights made the front area sharply bright, but there were shadows beyond. It was not like the laboratory at the university where Stephen spent so much of his time. There was much more in the way of mechanical equipment here, and, despite the bright light, the dark wood somehow made it seem more forbidding. I stepped inside the open door and called out, "Mr. Grubbé? It's Emily Chapman. Stephen? Are you here?"

There was a sound of movement and a muffled yell, "One moment!" from behind a door. A minute later, it was opened and my husband stood there in his shirtsleeves. "Emily, what are you doing here?"

The room beyond him looked dark and I heard other voices. "Someone has been seriously injured and I was sent to ask for Mr. Grubbé's assistance," I told him.

Grubbé appeared behind Stephen, followed by a wizened little man with a bald head, a gray mustache, and a beard. Backing away, I told them what had happened.

"Emily, that's terrible," Stephen said. "Are you all right? And Dr. Stone and Dr. Kahn? Was anyone else hurt?"

"No. Mary found Miss Erickson lying in the alley but whoever did it was gone. They've taken her to the women's hospital. They sent me to ask for your help."

"Oh, luckily we left the equipment there. We can use that. But let me bring a fully charged battery," Grubbé said. "Excuse me. Mrs. Chapman, this is Albert Schmidt. He's a glass blower and my assistant. You'll have to excuse his English as it is not very good." The man he had introduced bowed formally then followed Grubbé into the back room. While they were packing up the battery, Stephen asked me to describe Charlotte's condition. He frowned with concern and told me it sounded very serious.

While we waited for the other men, Stephen took me into the back room to show me what they had been doing. In that darkened room, a glass Crookes tube was suspended from the ceiling, facing a hatbox also hanging from the ceiling. Obviously excited by the activity, Stephen demonstrated how they would test the vacuum in the tube by putting a hand over the box, which had fluorescent crystals inside. Then they would watch until the flesh became transparent and only the bones cast a shadow in the glow of the crystals. I could see they were all wound up in perfecting their methods. Apparently this was how they could get the most vacuum in the tube in order to do X-ray work. Suddenly, I realized that this was where Stephen had been spending all his time this summer. It was hot and dark but I could sense the excitement of discovery that was animating the men.

Despite the heat, I felt myself shiver. I remembered the burn on Mr. Grubbé's hand and my eye ran over my husband's exposed arms. He was so dear to me. Could the work here be putting him in danger? It seemed to me the men were much too caught up and involved to realize that there was real danger in the work. I felt a cold chill in my heart. I promised myself I would soon talk to Professor Jamieson about the work Stephen should have been doing for him. The air of imminent discovery in the laboratory frightened me. Somehow, despite the attack on Miss Erickson, it frightened me more than the dark streets of the nighttime city.

I saw a telephone box on the wall and, with Mr. Grubbé's permission, I telephoned the Harrison Street police station and left a message for Detective Whitbread about the attack on Miss Erickson and the fact that she had been taken to the women's hospital.

The men found a carriage to transport all of us to the hospital, along with the heavy battery. Rushing through the warm night air I felt as if I had a stone in my stomach. I had a very bad feeling about the whole situation and a premonition that it could only get worse.

# TWENTY

At the hospital we found Dr. Erickson in a high rage, standing in the foyer, demanding to be taken to his daughter.

"Very soon, Isaac." Mrs. Appleby stood between him and the corridor, blocking his way. She was trying to soothe him. "Dr. Stone and Dr. Kahn are getting her settled. You must calm down now."

I halted, watching this, but Mr. Grubbé and Stephen quickly walked away to the operating theater where they had left their equipment. Albert Schmidt followed, carrying the heavy battery. I saw Mr. Grubbé summon one of the nurses. I imagined he would have her tell Mary that they had arrived. Meanwhile, I was fascinated by the sight of Dr. Erickson. I remembered vividly how the herbalist told us he had come in earlier that day, looking for his daughter in a rage. It had been nagging me at the back of my mind ever since we heard of the attack. What was she doing at the herb shop? Could it be that her father suspected an attachment between her and the young Chinese herbalist?

It seemed inconceivable, but what if Dr. Erickson was the one who had attacked Charlotte? What would he do to her now, helpless in a hospital bed? He was not only the girl's father, but he was also the most senior medical person in the building. How could they ignore him? Mrs. Appleby was the only one who seemed to feel she had some right to question his actions.

It must have been long acquaintance with the family that gave her the gumption to stand up to him. She certainly claimed to know the wishes of his dead wife, and his daughter, and to insist on supporting them, despite his anger. I wondered if he would agree to the X-ray examination that Mary had asked for, or if he would forbid it. I had no understanding of the medical issues involved. I could feel the emotions that hung in the air crackling like an electrical charge.

Even as the arguing voices were raised to a higher pitch, Detective Whitbread strode through the doors. "Mrs. Chapman, you reported an attack on a Miss Erickson. How is she? May I speak with her?"

"Who are you?" Dr. Erickson demanded.

"Dr. Erickson, this is Detective Whitbread of the Chicago police. I left him a message about the attack on your daughter. Detective Whitbread, this is Dr. Erickson. He is Charlotte's father. She was badly beaten. She was found by Dr. Stone on the doorstep of the Hip Lung family—off of Clark Street. She was so badly injured they brought her here. She received a terrible blow to the head and was not conscious. They fear for her life. But perhaps Dr. Erickson can tell you more about what she was doing in the area, Detective Whitbread. Dr. Kahn and I returned to the herb shop after our meal and Mr. Lo told us that both Miss Erickson and Dr. Erickson had been there this afternoon and that Dr. Erickson was very angry when he left."

"Why, you impertinent girl!" Dr. Erickson shouted at me. "How dare you accuse me of being at that shop? I did nothing of the kind, and neither did my daughter. I forbade her from going there."

"And why was that, Dr. Erickson?" Whitbread asked.

"That is none of your business."

"On the contrary, I am investigating the death of Herbalist Lo and your name has been mentioned as someone who had a grudge against the man."

"Grudge? No, he was an incompetent charlatan who tricked my daughter into giving her mother herbs that hastened her death."

"Oh, Isaac, he did no such thing. Detective Whitbread, I am Laura Appleby. I'm an old friend of the family. I took Miss Erickson to the Chinese herbalist to get some mixtures of herbs that are used to relieve pain."

"Poison," Erickson growled.

"By no means. The prescriptions have been used by many of my husband's patients, indeed by my husband himself in his final illness."

"I see." Whitbread turned to her. "Were you with Miss Erickson this afternoon?"

"Today, no. I have been here at the hospital all day."

"Why was she going to the herbalist today, then?"

"I have no idea," Mrs. Appleby admitted. A frown creased her forehead.

"And you, Dr. Erickson, you say you were not at the herb shop today?"

"Certainly not."

"When did you last see your daughter?"

"She was not at home for dinner. I was entertaining a few of my students and she should have been there, but she went out. Against my wishes, I might add." Erickson's face was red with anger. "I demand to see my daughter. I won't have her treated by the quacks who infest this place! I am one of the most well-known surgeons in this city and I demand to find out what they're doing to my daughter. That Dr. Stone has barely graduated from medical school. I won't have her telling me how my daughter will be treated."

"Dr. Stone?" Whitbread turned to me with a raised eyebrow. "Exactly what does Dr. Stone have to do with all this?"

*Oh, no.* This was not going as I expected. I feared Erickson had harmed his daughter, but now Whitbread had clearly been made suspicious by the mention of Mary Stone. "She found

Miss Erickson on the doorstep when she went to visit Hip Lung's
wife. She was the one who sent notice to Dr. Kahn and me about
the attack. Then they rushed her here to be treated while I went
to find my husband and Mr. Grubbé." I didn't really want to
get into explaining the plan to use the X-ray tube to see if her
skull was fractured. It sounded too outlandish for Detective
Whitbread to believe.

"I don't want my daughter touched by that woman. She's the
one who was arrested for the herbalist's death!" Erickson yelled.

"She was released," Whitbread told him.

"I don't care, I don't want her treating my daughter. Now
get out of my way, you people." With that, he plunged past
Mrs. Appleby and down the hallway.

"Perhaps you could ask Dr. Stone to come out to speak with
me?" Whitbread asked the distracted-looking Laura Appleby.

"Yes, yes, I'll see what I can do."

After that, we sat waiting in the foyer for an uncomfortable
hour. Whitbread had me repeat my description of the day after
I left him. He seemed to grit his teeth, then he sank into a
meditative silence. Finally Stephen came out to us.

"She's no better. We had just set up to do the X-ray picture
when Dr. Erickson burst in. Grubbé and I convinced him to let
us go ahead. He could see there was nothing else anyone could
do for her. At least the skull is not fractured, that's encouraging,
but there's no way to know how much internal damage there is
to the brain. Those were horrific blows that she took. She has
two broken ribs and a shattered femur as well."

"Will she live?" I asked.

Stephen shrugged. Grubbé answered, "They will have to wait
and see. She is still breathing. Her pulse is weak but her heart is
still beating. The bones will mend, but it's more a matter of how
badly her brain is injured and there is no way to tell."

We spent a few moments in silent contemplation of this.
I reached out and clutched Stephen's hand. How terrible it must

be for Dr. Erickson to contemplate his daughter in such a state. How could I think that he might have been responsible?

Yet, it seemed that almost every time I saw him he was in a rage...except in the operating room where he had so coldly tried to trip up Mary Stone. In that setting he had been contained but, faced with Laura Appleby, who must remind him of his dead wife, and with his daughter, there was always this rage.

# TWENTY-ONE

There was nothing more we could do. So, after consulting with Ida and informing Whitbread, I convinced Stephen to take me home.

In the carriage on the way to the train station I clutched his hand and eventually rested my head on his shoulder. Closing my eyes, I could hear his heart beating. His left arm circled me and I pressed myself to him. He was my husband, my refuge, and the father of my children. I could not bear to think of him parted from me or injured. I needed him, and Jack and Lizzie needed him. I could not allow him to endanger himself with invisible rays or by visiting the dark alleys of our dangerous city. I *would* not allow it. I wanted him safely back in our small, hot apartment or in Professor Jamieson's laboratory.

We were in time for a train down to Hyde Park and it was late enough when we reached home that Delia had already put the children to bed. I sent her to bed as well and prepared a plate of cold ham and cheese at the kitchen table for the two of us.

"Stephen, you must promise me you'll stop this dangerous work with Mr. Grubbé. I know you're excited by the possibilities...I could sense it at his laboratory. But you've seen how he's injured himself. You must think of Jack and Lizzie...of me. I'm afraid of these rays and what they might do to you. I understand, now, what it is that kept you away so much this summer. But it's too dangerous, Stephen...please."

He sighed and dropped the thick sandwich of ham and cheese he had assembled, as if his appetite was quite lost. Finally, he looked at me with his warm brown eyes and I knew he was feeling guilt. "Emily, you have no idea. It *is* exciting. It's such an important discovery and we're only at the beginning. There's so much still to do. Every day, every night, we've come closer to perfecting the equipment and procedures. Emil and Albert are perfectly placed to do this work. Emil has a background in chemistry and physics, and practical aspects like metal assaying, while Albert is a glass blower who worked on scientific instruments before he immigrated. They have the skills to perfect the use of the glass tubes and the electrical currents and all of the elements. And, believe me, despite what Erickson and the other surgeons say, there is a use for shrinking cancers. Do you know, as early as last spring, Grubbé began treatment of some terminal patients who had no hope at all? And he's seen improvements."

"They lived?"

"No, but they saw some improvement. And some of his current patients, while not cured, may live longer. He has offices and a clinic on Cottage Grove. Physicians send him patients with various diseases."

"Does no one suffer burns as he has?" I reached across and folded back my husband's shirt sleeve from his right wrist. What I saw there made me wince.

He captured my hand with his uninjured left hand. "Emily, I had to try. I had to see exactly what is left." He meant what was left of the splintered bone of his injured arm.

It would not do to express my anger at him about this, no matter how much I was seething underneath. I gritted my teeth and spoke between them. "And what did you find?"

He raised his head to look at the ceiling and grimaced. "Not much hope, I'm afraid. It could be broken and reset, but there's no way to reverse the nerve damage."

"But, Stephen, you don't need to. You don't need to fix your arm to continue your work with Dr. Jamieson. You said so yourself. You don't want to return to surgery, do you? You always said you didn't."

He hesitated. "No, but..."

"There are no buts. You are wrong if you think the children and I need you to return to medicine. We don't, Stephen. We don't. I promise you. Will *you* promise *me* to return to your laboratory here and stop this dangerous X-ray work?"

"But the advances and discoveries are amazing, Emily. This is worth some risk."

"Not to me. Besides, what about the work you were doing with Dr. Jamieson? Isn't that important, too? Be honest. It was to find out about your own injury that you became involved with Grubbé, wasn't it? It's not that the work you were doing before was any less important, is it?" I didn't suggest that it was to get away from me and my nagging that had also driven him to Grubbé and his dangerous experiments, but I knew that was part of it.

"No, certainly the work with Jamieson is important." He took up his sandwich then and bit into it as if to escape the need to say more. He was going to be stubborn.

"Then, you must return to it, Stephen, please. For me and the children."

He avoided looking at me directly, chewing his food and taking a drink before he replied. "I cannot just abandon Grubbé. It wouldn't be right. But I could withdraw from his work to return to the laboratory by the fall. But only if you will promise to do something for me."

I stared at him. He was bartering with me for his life. How could he?

"First, you must ensure Mary Stone is not falsely accused of killing that man. You have influence with Whitbread, Emily. You know you do. You must help to prove her innocence. You can do that. You have done it before, you know you have. You must help her."

"But you know Whitbread. He let Mary go, but he still seems

to suspect she's involved somehow. No one can influence him away from what he thinks is the truth."

"Do you believe Mary Stone poisoned Lo?"

"No. I'm sure she didn't."

"So, you must convince Whitbread, and help him find out who really did it."

"I can try."

"You can do it. And there's one more thing." I suspected what this would be. "You must accept Dean Talbot's offer of the position as lecturer for the fall. That way you can continue to work with Whitbread on criminal statistics *and* work with the reformers at Hull House. No more putting this off, Emily. Delia can care for the children when you're working. You can come back out into the world. It's not enough for you to stay here with the children. I know you want to protect them. I know you've seen how bad and dangerous the world outside can be. But you can't protect them forever. They'll have to go out into the world themselves one day. We can't lock the door and keep them safe inside for the rest of their lives."

"I haven't done that!"

"You *can't* do that, but you want to." Stephen shook his head. "It won't work, Emily. The only way to protect them is to make the world outside a safer place. You can't do that by staying trapped inside with them."

I could be stubborn, too. I stared at my plate, sweeping some crumbs into a pile. Stephen knew me too well, and obviously he had been thinking about this for some time. I felt that he wanted to push me out of the nest, whether I was ready to fly or not. But I knew he meant what he said. If I didn't agree, he would continue his work with Grubbé.

"All right. Dean Talbot expects me to start in the fall quarter anyhow." She was another strong-willed person who refused to believe her plans for me could be thwarted.

"And this time you *will* fulfill your commitment."

He made it sound as if I had broken promises in the past. I resented that, but it was not entirely wrong.

"Yes, yes. But, if I do, *you* will stop working with those dangerous rays."

"And you will help Whitbread see that Mary Stone did not kill the herbalist."

I sighed. "Yes, yes. But, in that case, it's time we got some sleep." I put the dirty plates in the sink for Delia. Before going up to bed, I left the small bag of herbs on the hall table and got Stephen to agree to have them analyzed. It was the special recipe that Dr. Erickson claimed had poisoned his wife. I mounted the stairs, uncertain of what the future would bring. I was not exactly defeated but I had not won this engagement, either, so I went up to bed relieved, but not triumphant.

# TWENTY-TWO

When I went to see Detective Whitbread the next morning he was on his way out the door. He was heading for city hall, where Fitzgibbons was planning to announce the visit of the Chinese viceroy to the press, so I accompanied him, struggling to keep pace with his long strides. The meeting took place in a large anteroom of the mayor's office, although the mayor himself was absent. Fitz explained that he was on a family vacation in Michigan.

The crowd of talkative men in rumpled linen suits filling the room represented all of the city newspapers. I spotted the dark curls of my brother in the front row. Most of the men were standing, partaking of tea and coffee, which had been laid out on a table at one side. Whitbread and I remained in the back of the room.

"So, we're grateful to the Hip Lung Yee Kee Company for sponsoring the private dinner, along with the public parade and fireworks," Fitz concluded. I noticed Charlie Kee slouching in a corner and nodding at this salute to his boss. "All of Chicago is invited to the celebration, so I hope I can count on you men to give it plenty of coverage. We want to show Li Hung Chang that Chicago knows how to welcome a foreign dignitary. Because we do, don't we, boys?"

There was a rustle of agreement from the crowd but one man called out, "What about the mayor? Is he going to be back for the festivities?"

"Well, now, as I mentioned, Mayor Swift and his family are on a long-planned vacation. You know these family things, I'm sure. Can't really get out of them without offending the in-laws, and then there's no end of it with the wife, right?" Laughter. "But, now, you'll not be printing that, will you? It's the job for me, and his head for hizzoner, if I got quoted on that." More laughter. "But we'll have a lot of prominent citizens here to welcome Viceroy Li, don't you worry."

"What about the city council? Aren't they on break too?" I recognized Alden's voice.

"That they are. But, then, I said 'prominent citizens,' don't you know?" That got more laughs.

"What about this assault of a white woman down in the Chinatown area? Who did it? Do you expect people to be scared by that and stay away? White people, anyhow?"

At least it wasn't Alden who asked that question. Fitz looked like he had bitten into a bitter lemon and I saw him frown in Whitbread's direction. "That was an unfortunate incident but our police, under the direction of Detective Henry Whitbread, are hard at work on solving that crime and I'm sure there'll be an arrest before Viceroy Li's visit next week. With Whitbread on the case now, you can be sure those miscreants will be caught in no time."

I saw Whitbread grind his teeth at that. Meanwhile, another waspish reporter took a fling at Fitz. "So, isn't it true that this Li Hung Chang is hated by some of his own people and that there have been assassination attempts during his travels in Europe?"

"Now, now. This is the United States. Whatever disagreements Viceroy Li and his government may have with his people at home, why, we would just ask them to settle that at home. No, Viceroy Li is an honored guest in our great city and we don't expect there to be any trouble at all. None at all. At least not if I get all the arrangements made on time. So, with that, I'll have to end this little gathering so I can go attend to those arrangements. But we'll expect to see you all represented at the festivities because it's going to be some party. I promise you." Having had his say, the big Irishman waved off any other questions. His lackeys herded the newspapermen from the room as he strode over to us. Alden attempted to slip through, but he was thwarted and, finally, he shuffled reluctantly out the door with the others.

Two people who had not been swept out also joined us. They were Charlie Kee and the tall silk-garbed guard to the Chinese consul. The sword at his waist seemed incongruous at city hall but he remained imperturbable.

Once the door was safely closed, the cheerful smile disappeared from Fitz's face and he turned to Whitbread with a worried frown. "What's all this about a woman being attacked at Hip Lung's place? What the hell is going on? Pardon me, Mrs. Chapman."

"It's a Miss Erickson. She was a customer of the Chinese herbalist who was poisoned."

"Was it connected to that? Because, if these papers start reporting that white women are being randomly attacked down there, that'll scare ordinary folks away and this big celebration for the Chinese viceroy will be more of a farce than it already is." Fitz turned to Charlie Kee and frowned at him, as a warning not to translate this remark to the Chinese guardsman.

"Well, if you'd let me do my job, instead of summoning me to your parties for the newspapermen, I might be able to investigate that assault."

"I didn't bring you here to listen to them. There's another problem. Kee, tell him."

Charlie Kee spoke up. "New information. Hot off the presses, only I don't tell newspaper men. We got a tip—Wong Chin Foo and his men have dynamite."

"Dynamite!" Fitz was incredulous. "You've got to be kidding. When you told me you had a tip about troublemakers I sent for Whitbread. But Wong Chin Foo? Dynamite? I don't believe it."

"True," Kee insisted. "All true. You come see. Look in their offices. They have it." He was interrupted by a flow of words from the Chinese guard, who had a low-pitched, raspy voice. "Yang's man says Chinese government mad about assassination attempt. They think you're responsible if anything happens to the viceroy." I could see Fitz eyeing the man from the Chinese consulate with a worried expression. It was his responsibility as liaison to keep the Chinese officials happy and it was clear they were not pleased with this news.

Whitbread interrupted the Chinese interpreter. "Kee, what makes you think Wong has dynamite? I was at his office yesterday, along with representatives from every newspaper in town. Why would he store dynamite there with all those people in and out?"

Kee shrugged. "Who knows? We got a spy. He saw them take dynamite in. They hid it in there somewhere."

"You sure it wasn't just firecrackers?" Whitbread asked. "You know they hide those all over the place down there."

"No firecrackers. Dynamite. At Wong's place."

"I doubt it, but we'll check it out," Whitbread told Fitz. "Is that all?"

"I guess so, I don't know though. Don't tell this one," he said, as he nodded at the big Chinese guardsman, "but I'm worried nobody's going to show up for this thing and then the Chinese will be insulted. Bad enough the mayor and the council are out of town, but now, with news of that attack, I don't know. I'm just not having much luck getting people to say they'll come. How about you, Mrs. Chapman? Can you help with that?"

"I'll come myself. I already said I would."

"And bring the family? This should be a family thing. The kids would love the dragon dance and the fireworks. Trouble is, people are suspicious of the Orientals. You know what I mean? Hip Lung and all are putting on a big spread and spending a lot of money, but I've got to tell you, I can't get these politicians and businessmen to say they'll come. Normally they'll show up to anything where you're offering free food and drink, and the chance to be written up in the newspapers, but damned if I can get them to commit.

Pardon again, Mrs. Chapman. I need at least twenty or thirty of them, including wives and kids, you know. But so far it's no dice. I'm really worried."

"I'll see what I can do, Mr. Fitzgibbons. Between Hull House and the university I think there should be people who would come."

"I can't tell you how much I would thank you for that, Mrs. Chapman." Beads of sweat rolled down his forehead. He took out a huge white handkerchief to wipe his face.

"All right. Come on, Kee, let's go see this Wong character again," Whitbread said. Kee spoke to the Chinese guardsman. It was clear that the Chinese consul demanded reassurances from the Chicago authorities, so they had sent along their witness.

"Wait," I told Whitbread, grabbing his arm before he could leave. "I must talk to you. I came to town to see you."

He cocked his head in the direction of Charlie Kee and the Chinese guardsman. "This really cannot wait. You see how demanding these foreigners are."

"But when can I talk to you?"

"Oh, very well, come along. I doubt this will amount to anything and you can help me to interview Wong. He's not going to be happy about a repeat visit and he does like to talk to the ladies."

I realized my detective friend only allowed me to come because he had a use for me but I said goodbye to Fitz and went along with them. I was anxious to discuss the death of the herbalist with Detective Whitbread and to approach him about releasing Mary to return to China. I planned to tell him about the people waiting for the young women doctors to start the clinic in Jiujiang. But I could see that he would have no time for this until the threat to the Chinese viceroy was investigated. It would be difficult to make him return his attention to the death of Lo, but I had to do it. And perhaps that was not all. I think the threats had finally roused my interest and curiosity, as in other situations in the past when I had forced myself into investigations of his that concerned my friends or family.

I didn't believe Wong Chin Foo would deal in dynamite. Dynamite! I remembered the threat of dynamite explosions that had struck fear into all of us during the turmoil of the Pullman strike. I knew only too well how very dangerous the stuff could be. The thought of luring people to a celebration like the one planned, only to wreak havoc with a bomb, was chilling. I hoped the suspicions of Hip Lung and the Chinese officials were wrong. And I felt a need to find the truth, just as I knew Whitbread did. I think it seemed natural to both of us when I followed along in his wake, much as I had done in the past.

# TWENTY-THREE

Once again we found our way to the Chinese Civil Rights League on Clark Street, above the grocery store. The Confucian altar was still there, looming at the front of the room, but this time it was covered with dust sheets. Wong Chin Foo rose from a table in the corner where he had been dictating to another young Chinese man who also wore Western-style clothes and had cut off his queue.

"Detective Whitbread, you have returned. Can I enroll you as a convert, perhaps? And you bring others." His eyebrows rose at the sight of two large uniformed policemen who followed me into the room. Last to enter were Charlie Kee and the guard from the Chinese consulate. Wong merely frowned at them with distaste but approached me with his hand extended. "Mrs. Chapman, how nice of you to visit. Please, allow me to offer you a seat." When he began to pull up a chair for me, Whitbread put out a hand to stop him.

"Mr. Wong, this is not a social visit. We have received information that you are concealing dynamite on the premises. Do you deny it?"

Wong's eyebrows shot up again, and the young man who was acting as his secretary took an aggressive step towards Whitbread. But Wong blocked him with an arm. He finished placing the chair for me and turned to the detective. "The information you received—it came from the Hip Lung Yee Kee Company,

I presume? You should know, Detective, that in the Chinese community we have our little rivalries. Last year, some of my clan provided information that shut down several gambling houses run by Hip Lung and the other Moys. I wonder if the information you received is merely retribution." I was once more impressed by Wong's grasp of the English language. He was a journalist, after all, so I suppose I shouldn't have been surprised. It gave him a definite advantage over those in his community who were less fluent.

Whitbread glowered at him. "I have no interest in your feuds, Mr. Wong. But I have every interest in maintaining order in this city. I've warned you before. There will be no violence when Viceroy Li visits next week."

Wong walked over to Charlie Kee and looked him directly in the eye. Kee remained impassive, while the consulate guard glowered over Kee's shoulder.

Wong turned back to us. "As I told you before, Detective, we have no plans for violence on these shores. It is the court in Peking that should fear our wrath."

"So, you deny that dynamite is hidden here? You'll excuse me while I ask my men to verify that." Whitbread turned to the uniformed officers.

"Wait!" Wong demanded. "Know this, Detective Whitbread, I am fully aware of my rights as a citizen. You're required to obtain a warrant from a judge." I saw Whitbread tense, as if a storm cloud were about to burst over his head. Wong forestalled that. "However, since we not only are innocent of the accusation but are enthusiastic in our desire to emulate your democracy, we raise no objection to your search." He spread his arms wide. "Search, officers. Search in every place you wish. Let us know if we can assist you in any way."

Rolling his eyes at this demonstration, Whitbread proceeded to direct his men in their search. Wong's secretary looked outraged, and then confused, but Wong waved him back to his desk. Then he pulled another chair up next to mine and sat down to converse with me while the policemen tromped around. He kept an eye on them as we talked.

"How very helpful of Mr. Kee over there to warn the authorities of such a danger," he told me.

"I believe the Hip Lung Yee Kee Company has spent a lot of money in preparation for the viceroy's visit," I told him. "I suppose they want to be vigilant in ensuring his safety."

"Ah, yes." Wong shook his head. "I'm afraid poor Hip Lung thinks he can impress the Chinese officials by such attentions. He's wrong, though. The Manchu court looks down on merchants like the Moys and they always will. Ah, excuse me, we have another visitor." He rose and walked across to greet Ida, who had just reached the top of the stairs. Leading her over, he set up another chair and sat her next to me.

Whitbread and his men returned, without having found any evidence of dynamite. Charlie Kee was looking a bit less self-satisfied, although he still wore a meaningless smile on his face as if to disguise any disappointment. When the policemen began pulling sheets off the Confucian shrine, Wong's secretary rose to protest but, once again, Wong called him back with a few words in Chinese.

"I see our information was correct," Ida said. I wondered what she meant.

"Indeed. You must thank Madam Hip Lung and Mrs. Sam Moy for me," Wong told her, bowing slightly as he sat. "I so much appreciate their interest and support."

Ida grimaced. "I wouldn't say support. They have been impressed by your charms, Mr. Wong, as so many of the ladies are."

"You flatter me, Dr. Kahn. But then you are famous for your sharp wit and high intelligence. Already there are reformers in China who are anxious to make your acquaintance." He turned to me. "Do you know, Mrs. Chapman, that Dr. Kahn is seen as the model for the New Chinese Woman, who will help to raise the next generation to be strong people who can resist the attempts by foreigners to take over and divide up our nation? Imagine how much they look forward to her return to China to begin the revolution."

"You told me that before, Mr. Wong," I reminded him, as Ida rolled her eyes at his praise.

We watched as the big policemen crawled around under the Confucian altar, Whitbread directing them to investigate every nook and cranny as they continued their search for dynamite. From the sour expression on Charlie Kee's face and the nonchalance of Wong Chin Foo, it seemed to me that more was going on below the surface than we could see. I had the merest suspicion, with no evidence whatsoever, but I couldn't keep myself from wondering if Charlie Kee and the Hip Lung faction might not have planted dynamite on the premises. Could it be their plans were thwarted when Hip Lung's wife discovered the plot? I could imagine her summoning Ida Kahn and persuading her to warn Wong. But was it just my imagination running amok to think of this scenario?

If Ida had played a part in saving Wong, she did not appear to be overly impressed by him or overly concerned for his welfare. She tended to scoff at him. "Flattery is your weapon," she told him, "not mine. You may have converted innocent men and women to your cause, but there are many who would say you are wrong to advocate for the violent overthrow of the emperor. No wonder they fear your actions during the viceroy's visit."

"We have said we will not spill blood here. We want to take our fight to Peking, to Nanking, to Shanghai. It's not in Chicago that the battle will be fought and blood spilt to establish a republic."

"But why must blood be spilt at all? It's this insistence on violence that is unnecessary."

"Unnecessary? How can you say that? Even now, China is being torn apart and the pieces given out to her enemies. Japan's concession is only the latest. The court Li represents sits holed up like animals at bay while the Western powers and Japan encroach more and more." He turned to me. "You see, Mrs. Chapman, this is the problem of China today. More and more Westerners come in with their religion, and their technologies, and they invade China. They occupy the land."

"But, Mr. Wong, don't they bring progress?" I asked. "After all, every day we ourselves are amazed by the discoveries and progress this century has brought us. You must have seen the World's Columbian Exposition and all the marvels of invention on display there. Don't you think that should be shared by all the world, including China? Don't you want China to take advantage of such discoveries, too?"

"Yes, yes, of course we do. But it's not a case of sharing these things. It's a case of using them to triumph over the Chinese people. You must understand, Mrs. Chapman, China has a culture that has existed for many centuries. We have arts that rival any production of the West. We have centuries of medical and engineering knowledge that have marveled the world in the past. We have a history that is rich with lessons. Yet, suddenly, we are overrun by Western outsiders, barbarians who have no knowledge, and no respect, for centuries of tradition and culture. They would tear it all down and eradicate it without the slightest understanding of what is being destroyed."

"Surely not," I protested.

"Oh, yes, it is true. China is being pulled apart like a lamb that is set on by a pack of wolves. If we cannot become stronger, if we cannot resist, China will be destroyed."

I had thought of Wong and Ida's homeland as one of those countries far away, where life was harder, dirtier, less healthy than it needed to be. Just as Hull House could bring improvements to the immigrant neighborhoods of Chicago, I had assumed missionaries, like Miss Howe, sought to bring improvements to China. But Mr. Wong had a way of taking one's view of something and turning it inside out. I was struck by his description of his homeland and it would require a lot of further thought before I would understand it. I found it a challenge to my imagination to even begin to see China as he did.

Ida frowned at him. "We can learn from missionaries," she told him. "You would throw out the baby with the bath water, as the saying goes. It's not enough for China to resist the forces from outside. China must grow, as we *all* must grow up. If we learn from Western cultures, it's not so that they may usurp our own, it's so that we may make improvements. There is much in Chinese herbal medicine that can be used to treat sickness. But would you have us deny the Chinese people modern Western medicine *because* it is Western? Surely, you would not."

"Of course not. You and Dr. Stone prove that the Chinese are capable of excelling, even at a Western university." Wong was clearly excited by the thought and I could sympathize, for I was part of the struggle to prove that women could succeed in academic research here in the United States. He seemed to think the Chinese needed to prove that they, too, could succeed in academia.

"But proof of adequacy is not enough," Ida told him. "It is not a competition. We have also learned the Christian virtues of faith and humility. This can allow us to bring change without bloodshed."

"Ah, Dr. Kahn, you ask much. It is not in the nature of man, I think, to have change without bloodshed."

Unfortunately, Detective Whitbread had re-joined us just in time to overhear Wong's last pronouncement. "There will be no bloodshed here, Wong. I told you that."

"No, no, Detective. I was speaking figuratively."

Whitbread huffed. "In any case, we've found no sign of dynamite." He looked harassed, as he glanced across at Charlie Kee who was standing by the door.

"Well, that's very good then, isn't it?" Wong told him. "Just as I said, we have no intention of attacking Viceroy Li."

"Yes, and what of Miss Erickson?"

"Miss Erickson?" Wong looked surprised.

"The young woman who was attacked on the doorstep of the Hip Lung household yesterday. What do you know about that?"

"Why, nothing. I mean, I heard there had been such an attack, but I don't believe I know the young lady."

"You and Hip Lung's group have a feud going, though, don't you? Was the attack on Miss Erickson part of that feud?"

"There is no feud, Detective." Wong looked across at Charlie Kee. "Or, if there is one, there is no action on our side and certainly no reason to attack a woman. Why would we?"

Whitbread growled. "I confess, sir, there is little that you do that has a plausible reason behind it, as far as I can see. Be aware, we will be keeping an eye on you, so don't cause any trouble when Hip Lung has his party next week. Because, if there is any trouble, I'll know where to look. Come on." He signaled to his men and they followed him out. I decided to stay, to see if I could learn more about Charlotte's status from Ida. Whitbread was hardly in a mood to be approached about allowing Mary to leave and I believed the attack on the young woman had something to do with the herbalist's death.

Charlie Kee and the consulate guard were the last to leave. The interpreter stopped for a final look around before he turned and ran down the stairs.

Wong Chin Foo watched him go with his eyes narrowed. "Kee looks like he lost something."

# TWENTY-FOUR

I da asked me to accompany her to visit Hip Lung's wife. As we left, Wong Chin Foo bowed us out at the top of the stairs. He seemed quite pleased with the results of the visit. I wondered a little about Whitbread's final questions. Was it possible that Wong was behind the attack on Charlotte? He claimed he was not involved, but could the attack be part of some struggle between Wong and Hip Lung, as Whitbread seemed to suggest? I had no way to tell.

Ida informed me of Mary's current plight while we walked. It was not good. Dr. Erickson continued to storm around the hospital demanding that his daughter be moved home, and that Mary be arrested for the assault on her. Whitbread had refused. It gave me some hope that he had not ruled out the doctor himself as a suspect. Meanwhile, the detective intended to detain Mary as a precaution but a compromise had been reached. Mary was staying at the hospital in a room next to Charlotte's, with a police guard in the hall. She was allowed into the presence of the unconscious woman only in the company of other hospital staff. While this appeased Dr. Erickson to some extent, as he convinced himself this meant she was under house arrest, the hospital staff were grateful for Mary's assistance in caring for the gravely ill young woman.

Ida told me there was very little hope now that Charlotte would recover. While her skull was not fractured there had been damage to her brain. It was impossible to know the extent of that damage

146

but the fact that she had not recovered consciousness was not good. Her other injuries were also quite severe and it was necessary to closely monitor her movement to prevent further damage. The fact was, they did not expect her to live out the week.

"And then what will happen?" I wondered out loud. "Will Whitbread have to arrest Mary to placate her father?"

"That is what I fear," Ida told me. "And how can my mother and I abandon her here and return to China if that is the case?"

We reached the doorstep of Hip Lung's household. Ida knocked and exchanged words with a little boy who led us upstairs to Hip Lung's wife and her sister-in-law.

The scene was much calmer than the previous day. Once again the two women sat quietly in the high-ceilinged room. I still remembered the smell of blood that had assaulted my senses when we had hurried to the bedroom where Mary tended Charlotte the night before. Today all was serene, with a scent of jasmine in the air.

The women conversed with Ida. The worry they expressed at the beginning soon gave way to smiles as Ida told them the outcome. "They asked about the police raid on Wong Chin Foo's association," she told me. I nodded. It seemed apparent that they knew about it, which made me more sure than ever that they were the ones who had warned Wong. Had he found dynamite before Whitbread's arrival? If so, what had he done with it? It was unlikely the Moy ladies or even Ida would confide in me, knowing my connection to the police. It seemed to me that none of them had any intention of harming Viceroy Li. They were more intent on their own rivalries. I was surprised the women had dared to go against the wishes of their husbands, even if they had done so secretly.

After a discussion about Charlotte and Mary, the conversation moved to more domestic topics. The women ordered their little maid to bring in the children for us to admire. Ida told me there was an infant and a toddler, one belonging to each of the wives.

While we waited, Charlie Kee suddenly appeared and spoke to the women.

Ida translated for me. "It seems the husbands have heard of our visit to the ladies. Hip Lung has sent Mr. Kee to bring us to talk to him. He is particularly anxious to talk to you."

"Me? I can't imagine why." Somehow the thought of facing the man without Whitbread made me uneasy—especially since I suspected his plot against Wong Chin Foo. I remembered the dark blood stain on the ground at the doorstep. What if it was Hip Lung and his associates who were behind the attack on Miss Erickson? "I don't think I should talk to Mr. Hip Lung without Detective Whitbread," I told her.

"I don't think you have a choice. Hip Lung is a very powerful man. If he wants to see you he will find a way to force you to come to him. I don't believe he intends you any harm. I will come with you."

"But who is he to demand anything from me?" I asked. "How very rude! Who does he think he is?"

"He is a very powerful man. As for rudeness, it would be considered a great insult to refuse his request. I know it is not the custom here for a man to be so demanding of a woman, but I'm afraid Hip Lung is acting in a way that is more in accord with Chinese customs. Please, won't you come along to meet with him? I will stay with you."

I glanced at the Moy ladies. "Isn't it rude to break off our visit so abruptly?"

"On the contrary, they would not want to disobey their husbands." And yet it seemed they had foiled a plot against Wong Chin Foo, possibly laid by their husbands.

"All right." I was not happy but there seemed no help for it. We had barely time for a glance at the children who were brought in, dressed up in embroidered silk outfits, before we followed Charlie Kee down the stairs. He led us out to busy Clark Street and only half a block down to the Hip Lung Yee Kee Company.

Through the glass door we found a very large dry goods store stacked floor to ceiling with all sorts of items. At the front of the store there were elaborately carved screens of dark wood, and silken banners hung from the ceiling. Many Chinese men congregated at the back of the store, but I only had a glimpse of them as we were led through the shelves to a stairway up to the second story.

Upstairs, there was a huge open area set up with chairs and tables for dining. It was not a restaurant, however, but a private dining area used for Moy family association gatherings. Ida explained this to me quietly as we walked across a broad expanse to a corner where Hip Lung sat behind a table littered with paper. Two younger men were writing notes for him. Standing in front of him, like a pupil explaining himself to the principal, was Mr. Fitzgibbons.

Fitz looked relieved to see me. "Mrs. Chapman, thank you for coming. Hip Lung heard you were visiting his wife and it seemed you were just the person to consult." He looked anxiously across at Hip Lung, who was ignoring us while he continued the instructions to his clerks. Finally, he turned his attention to us. He did not offer us seats, nor did he rise himself. He wore the same black boxy hat and the wide-sleeved Chinese jacket he had worn at the police station.

He regarded us with a frown. "You are the woman who would help with the invitations? Why do so many refuse? What is the matter?" he demanded.

Fitz tut-tutted. "Now there, I just asked Mrs. Chapman to help with the guest list. She is not responsible for the responses," he protested.

"Not responsible? Then who is responsible?" Hip Lung snapped. "When I came here many years ago, I found the people of Chicago to be not against our kind. They never asked me whether or not I ate rats and snakes. They seemed to believe that we also had souls to save, and these souls were worth saving. The Chicagoans found us peculiar people to be sure, but they liked to mix with us." He walked by me and out to where Charlie Kee stood, before he turned back again. "Then there was the Geary Act and all the attempts to humiliate us during the World's Fair." There was a fierce frown on his face. "You know it was Chinese merchants who put up the money to build the Chinese Village at the Exposition. The Ching government refused to contribute."

"That's right and it was a wonder," Fitz said, attempting to soothe him, but it didn't work.

"That did not prevent your officials from treating us like animals."

"There was a fear—an unfounded fear, really, from other parts of the country that scores of Chinese would be smuggled into the Fair and then disappear in the crowds."

"So they came to photograph us all and to make us all afraid!" A simmering rage was bubbling to the surface in Hip Lung. "Are we not residents here? Do we not pay taxes as property holders? We are not law breakers, yet you wanted to put all our pictures in a rogues' gallery like criminals. Does this show the advancement that this nation has attained? The ridiculousness of the provisions should have killed the Geary bill."

"Yes, yes. They did stop the photographing and the village was a big success," Fitz protested.

"These insults were not enough? Now, when the highest official of the sovereign nation of China visits, the important people of this city spurn him? Even when we agree to bear all of the costs, even then, these people refuse to attend? How dare they?"

"Let me explain," Fitz interrupted. "Mrs. Chapman, I've tried to tell Hip Lung that the summer is a time when many people leave the city on vacation. The mayor and most of the aldermen are out of town." He cocked an eye at the fuming Hip Lung, who was pacing now. "So when we sent out the first round of invitations there were many refusals."

"Not all these people are gone from the city. They flee with the arrival of the invitation!" Hip Lung shouted.

"Yes, well, I fear news of the attack on Miss Erickson did not help." Fitz gave me a pleading look.

Hip Lung stalked over to the papers on the table and pounded a fist on them. "There is no one. No one of any importance at all will come."

"There are the Chinese merchants," Fitz told him.

"It is an insult! The viceroy comes and only the Chinese attend? It is an insult."

Fitz turned back to me. "I tried to reach Miss Addams at Hull House, as you suggested, but there has been no reply."

"The plans are made. There are seats for three hundred. But no one will come," Hip Lung shouted.

"It will be a wonderful attraction with the parade and fireworks," Ida suggested. "Surely many people will want to see that."

"No one of importance!"

"Mrs. Chapman, please. Can you help?" Fitz looked quite desperate. It was true that many more well-to-do families left the city in August to go to Michigan or Wisconsin but, sadly, I believed Hip Lung was correct in assuming it was a prejudice against the Chinese as a race that had caused so many negative responses.

"I'm afraid you are right that some people would be alarmed enough by the attack on Miss Erickson to refuse an invitation," I said.

"There will be no attacks!" Hip Lung shouted. "No attacks. I will not allow it."

Fitz looked uneasy. "Please, Mrs. Chapman. If only we could get a few prominent people to agree to attend. We could announce that to the newspapers and others would be encouraged to come. Don't you agree? There are politicians and aldermen that I can convince to attend, but without some of the leaders of the city it will never be a success. You can see how important it is to Hip Lung and his community."

I felt sorry for Fitz, left by his bosses to deal with this mess, and I sensed a very deep resentment from Hip Lung over such an insult. I thought about the celebration the Chinese merchants were so eager to host. "Actually, Mr. Hip Lung, I believe it is the very hasty nature of the plans that is the problem. If it were not next week and people had time to plan to attend I think they would want to do so. Why, imagine how thrilling it will be, not just for the people of prominence, but for their families. I'm sure they'd want their children to attend the parade and fireworks. It's only that it's so soon, they haven't thought of it."

Hip Lung walked behind the table, lifted handfuls of papers and let them drop back. "They refuse," he told me.

"Yes, I see." I walked over and read several of the messages. They appeared curt to the point of rudeness. Seeing the names of people from Prairie Avenue mansions, I thought of my friends the Glessners, and of Louise DeKoven Bowen, a good friend to Hull House. I thought of people at the university—President Harper, with his brood of children, and Dean Marion Talbot, whose connections to the women's clubs of the city had helped to build the women's dormitories. For people so often soliciting money from wealthy people, here was an opportunity to reward them with an entertainment.

"Mr. Hip Lung, I am sure there are many people who would want to attend. If you will trust us to arrange it, I believe Mr. Fitzgibbons and I can help."

Hip Lung drew himself up, looking not at all convinced, but he spoke a few words to his clerks and soon Fitz and I had our hands full of beautifully printed invitations. We gathered them up and bid him goodbye.

As we retreated to Clark Street Fitz kept thanking me. I told him to delay his thanks until we had acceptances in hand.

Handing Ida a stack of invitations to distribute among her missionary friends, we parted with plans to meet the next day to review our progress. I headed for a train back down to Hyde Park, intending to solicit acceptances promptly. It was then that I remembered my promise to Stephen to formally accept the position from Dean Talbot. So I decided to complete two chores with one visit. I couldn't avoid it any longer.

# TWENTY-FIVE

It's been quite a while since we've seen you." Dean Talbot gestured me into a straight-backed chair in front of her desk. She sat across from me, leaning on her arms with a grim expression on her face. Although the university was not in session, she wore her black academic robe over her shirtwaist and skirt. Her hair was pulled back severely from her plain face. She had been my mentor since my arrival in Chicago and, today, I felt an emptiness in facing her, as if I were going to disappoint her. I had done that before, but I had always been able to make up for it. This time, I was very unsure of my ability to live up to her plans for me.

"I've been meaning to thank you personally for the new set of blocks for Jack. He plays with them all the time," I told her. It was mid-August now and I had not seen the dean since June, when she'd visited, bringing the latest educational toy as a gift for Jack. Along with the gift she brought the offer of a lectureship in the Department of Sociology and Anthropology, to start in the fall. I was embarrassed to remember I had missed several appointments with her since then. "I'm sorry I didn't come in July, but Lizzie had a summer cold, and then you were gone."

"For a week. I went on my annual trip to Boston to visit relatives. I've been back for some time now." Her gaze was steady and I dropped my eyes to look at the floor.

"How was your trip? I hope you enjoyed yourself?"

"My mother is aging, so it was good to spend time with her. My sisters were all around with their broods of children."

"How nice for you. What are their ages?"

"Emily, I assume you haven't come to talk to me about my nieces and nephews, or to compare notes on their upbringing. You know I have no children of my own and, while child care is a subject of study for our department, it is not your area. Sociology and criminal anthropology are the areas in which you have been offered a lectureship. As you know, it took a lot of effort on my part and that of others to convince President Harper and the faculty senate to recognize the need for this area of study. Incorporating aspects of sociology and political economy as part of the study of the influences of the home is crucial to our ideas. We are still in the position of needing to demonstrate our worthiness. We've been struggling, but we're making some advancement. I was able to fund a few more positions this year. We were greatly disappointed when you were unable to take up the lectureship again last year, but Miss Elbert has done a fine job. I can certainly understand your need to spend time with your children. But I have argued for, and succeeded in getting, funding for an additional lectureship and I have been counting on you to fill it. There are several reasons why it is tailor-made for you."

"Oh, I know that, and I cannot tell you how grateful I am to you for thinking of me for this position."

"But? You have doubts? You agreed to fill the position when I talked to you in June."

"Yes, yes, I know." I remembered Stephen's excitement when Dean Talbot had come bearing gifts for the children and the offer of a lectureship, which would have some teaching responsibilities but also plenty of time for research into sociological issues in the city. It had been a hot, tedious day, and the children were unusually cranky, so I'd jumped at the chance to return to my studies. It was only later that I wondered whether it would be possible, with Lizzie and Jack in my life. Who would care for them while I was at work? I also had the slightest suspicion that Stephen might have approached my old mentor about the need to get me out of the house. Ever since that thought occurred to me, I wondered if they had plotted together, and I became more and more resentful. "It's only that, on reflection, I am concerned about whether I will be able to meet my responsibilities. I would so hate to fail you by not doing the job well. And with the children..."

"The children. Yes, I understand there are duties and responsibilities you have as a mother." She sat back and clasped her hands in her lap. "Don't make the mistake of thinking it will be easy to defend your appointment, Emily. There are those who believe that, once a woman is married, she is unfit for the academic life. And once she has children her only duty is to them, and the only thing she is capable of doing is rearing them. But is that true? Do you believe that, Emily? Surely not. You know there are women who have no choice but to work to feed their families." I could not deny that. At Hull House we had sheltered children whose mothers had to work to survive. "And aren't there women who want to raise their children but also want to do more? You know, marriage is not enough for some. You also know it is a dead end for others. Yet does it have to be? There are women here—few of them, it's true—but there are those who have families, yet want to continue their work. I thought... we thought you were one of them."

She paused and the silence made me uncomfortable. I thought of what had brought me to the university and how I had escaped having no choice but to teach or marry when I was admitted to the graduate school here. I had been so excited by the possibilities. How could I have changed so much from the girl I was when I arrived at the university?

"You are in the enviable position of having a husband who supports the idea that you should continue your work. Like other married women who have managed to both work in the university and raise a family, you have a husband who understands it would be a waste of talent for you to have to give up your work."

It was true. Stephen was anxious for me to return to my studies. In marrying him I had not agreed to give up that work. On the contrary it was something that we shared, that desire to continue working and learning. No, it was the children. "I know that. It's just that I never imagined how I would feel once the children were born. It's such a responsibility, you have no idea," I confessed to her.

"No, I do not have that responsibility, Emily. What I do have is a responsibility to the women who come here to work and study. As dean of women it's my job to nurture them and to help them achieve their goals. There is a tacit expectation that a woman will retire from work at the university once she has children. It is my desire to challenge that expectation and to change it. It is my hope that we can prove this is not true for every woman, that the work she does here does not preclude her ability to also raise a family. Not every woman will want to do that, it's true. But, for those who want to, they must be allowed to do so."

I thought of Mary and Ida, and how Ida had explained that Mary could not be a wife and a doctor in her society. I had disputed that. How could I not agree with the dean now? I thought of my own daughter, Lizzie. How awful if she had been born to a society that insisted on binding her feet, like Mary and Ida's homeland. When she was grown, shouldn't she have the ability to work and study without having to give up marriage and family?

"Of course, I agree with you. There is no reason for a woman to be denied a position merely because she is married. I agree."

"Agreeing is not enough, Emily. If you are to take on this position I must present you as a candidate to the faculty committee meeting in two weeks. I will face opposition because you are married and a mother. It is a battle I am willing and anxious to engage in and to win. But, once that battle is won, there can be no question of your failing to accept, or of your failing to meet your obligations. To do so would be to set back the cause for all the other women. So, if you cannot meet this challenge, you must tell me now. Or, at least you must tell me by the end of next week, so I can decide whether to propose another candidate, or to postpone the addition of this lectureship until next year. Can you promise me you will accept this position and be wholeheartedly committed to it, Emily? Can you promise me that today?"

I looked at her and felt ashamed. The truth was, I could not answer her as she wished. She was right to doubt me. Twice before, I had seemed prepared to accept a lectureship and had refused in the end because I was with child. Could I promise now? Or would I go home and face my children and realize it was impossible to meet my obligations to them, as well as to the dean and the women of the university? I felt compelled to agree with the proposal, sitting here faced by Dean Talbot, but I knew that, when I was at home, faced by my children, I wouldn't be able to resist the draw of their needs. Stephen's face rose before me and I feared what he would do if I refused. "Please, Dean Talbot, allow me to discuss this with my husband once more." She raised an eyebrow and I knew she was already sure of Stephen's support. She didn't know how angry he would be at me, if I dared to refuse. "I know how important it is not to disappoint you. I know that, if I commit to this, I must succeed. I don't want to fail you." It was the most I could say at that moment. At least it was the truth.

She sighed. "Emily, you must do what is right for you. But I would greatly appreciate it if we could avoid proposing your name and then having you withdraw. So, it is best that you are sure of your commitment. I'll be very sorry if you refuse this opportunity, as I won't be able to promise that another position will be available when you are."

I couldn't help thinking that I might wait until the children were older, but suddenly I realized that, during the intervening years, the work at the university would continue without me and it was unlikely that I could just step back into it. I would change, the university would change, the world would change. I would have to start again from the beginning, if I even had the desire to do so at that time. I realized this could no longer be just a delay or postponement. This time, if I did not accept the position, it would be because I had chosen to take a different road. No wonder Stephen was so insistent. But sometimes you are forced to take a different road than you expected and I thought this time I might be in that situation. Perhaps it was time for me to turn aside to a different path.

There was an uneasy silence. I would not, I could not, promise what she wanted without further consideration. It would be dishonest to do so.

"I understand you have been assisting Detective Whitbread again."

She must have heard of my recent activities. Stephen again, I was sure. "Yes, and there is something about which I wanted to consult you." I told her about the plans for Viceroy Li's visit and how the Hip Lung Yee Kee Company had planned a big celebration but people were refusing the invitations. I mentioned how insulted the Chinese community was by the refusals and how angry Hip Lung was. She seemed interested and left her desk to pace back and forth beside it. It was a habit of hers when she was thinking and she always reminded me of a little bird when she would stop and lift her head indicating that she had an idea. She did that now.

"Parades and fireworks, you say? Hmmm."

"Yes. And there'll be a dragon dance as part of the parade—a group of men will wear a dragon costume and dance through the streets. I've never seen such a thing, but I've heard it's quite a sight and the fireworks display will be spectacular. The Chinese love fireworks. There's to be a big dinner at the Moy Family Association, too, with all sorts of Oriental delicacies."

"Hmm. It's true a lot of the professors and their families go away for the summer. Enrollment in the summer quarter is sparse.

But this is about the time they come back. I believe President Harper and his family have just returned from Maine. I think it's a time when the children are restless. They're not yet back in school but they've lost the freedoms of their vacation homes. The celebration you describe may be just the sort of thing the families would welcome to cheer them up. Yes, I would bet it could be very popular."

"Do you think President Harper might attend? I think that would go far towards placating Hip Lung."

"More than Hip Lung. I would bet that, if you publicize the fact that Harper and his family will attend, you'll draw more of the city people and they'll think it's the fashionable thing. And, of course, a lot of the returning academic families will want to emulate the president."

"That would be marvelous. Do you think you can convince him?"

She rolled her eyes. "I doubt you could keep him away once he hears of it. He was complaining about the excess energy of his brood this morning. He'll take it as a gift."

We arranged that she would take the invitation to President Harper and confirm his acceptance that afternoon and then let me know. She also took a large stack of invitations to distribute among the academics, with the news that the university president and his family would attend.

Grateful that I would have such good news to take to Fitz in the morning, I returned home. Sure enough, when I was surrounded by my children, and all of their toys and paraphernalia, I found it hard to imagine how I could take up the lectureship position in the fall. They were so excited to see me and were so demanding of my attention. It was true that Delia reported a happy day for them, even in my absence, but I felt how impossible it would be to leave them on a regular basis.

I steeled myself to discuss the topic with Stephen, but he did not return. I ate with the children and sent Delia to bed, then waited up, but still he did not return. Finally, I received a note from one of his students who had done an analysis of the herbs I'd gotten from Herbalist Lo. There was nothing of interest, not even a simple opiate to be found in the concoction. It seemed it was no stronger than chamomile tea. Stephen had complied with my request about the herbs, but he did not return home that evening. It was true he had only agreed to stop working with Grubbé if I made sure Mary Stone was cleared, *and* if I accepted the lectureship this time. It was true that I had been unable to do either of those things yet, but I needed to talk to him. I needed to explain. It was not just that, on returning to Jack and Lizzie, I felt how strong my need was to be with them all the time. There was another problem. There was a nagging doubt in my mind, a shadow on my heart. I was not entirely sure, but I suspected. I was almost sure that I was once again pregnant. How could I take the lectureship position if that were true? It was impossible and I could only despair.

# TWENTY-SIX

Stephen did not return that night at all. I could only assume he'd spent the night in Grubbé's laboratory. In the morning, I left the children with Delia and went to meet Fitz and Ida, as I had promised. Dean Talbot sent word that President Harper would attend with his whole family, so I was able to bring that good news with me.

We met at city hall. Fitz had the use of a small meeting room in the back, with a table and some chairs and little else. It was quite a contrast to the large corner office he'd occupied when Carter Harrison was mayor. Fitz lost his position at city hall when Harrison was assassinated and, since that time, he'd worked from ward offices in various parts of the city. I had the impression that these days he was working out of Alderman Kenna's saloon.

"Mrs. Chapman, welcome," he greeted me. He looked tired, but his greeting was warm. He always looked at me with a light in his eyes and I felt the glow of his admiration. I couldn't for the life of me imagine why he should admire me. But there it was, and I felt particularly grateful for it that day. The truth was Fitz was a confirmed bachelor who liked to disguise his contentment by imagining himself as a victim of unrequited love. I remembered the wedding picture on his desk, which was of his brother's marriage to a woman originally courted by Fitz. I suspected his admiration for me was another romantic regret that he could pretend to harbor. In any case, I appreciated his warm welcome. "We're hoping you might have good news," he said.

Ida Kahn sat across from us. I told them about Dean Talbot's idea to invite President Harper and his acceptance. I explained the dean's thoughts about how the opportunity to bring children to the entertainments would encourage more people to come. "She took invitations to distribute to others at the university and she expects many will accept when they hear President Harper is going."

Fitz smiled broadly. "That's wonderful news, Mrs. Chapman. I'll bet knowing the president of the university is coming will encourage others in the city as well."

"That's what we thought," I told him. "But please let me ask Dr. Kahn something." I turned to her. "How is Charlotte? Has there been any improvement?"

Ida shook her head. "Not yet. She remains unconscious."

"And Dr. Stone?"

"She is still confined to the hospital with a policeman outside the door. Dr. Erickson is beside himself. Mrs. Appleby says he is afraid of losing his daughter so soon after losing his wife. He doesn't sound afraid, however. He sounds very angry."

At that moment Alden appeared at the door.

"Any news?" Fitz asked him.

"Not good, I'm afraid. Hello Emily, Dr. Kahn. The rumor is that the local people are afraid of the Orientals. They fear the attack on Miss Erickson is only the beginning. They certainly won't go down to so-called 'Chinatown.' Not even for a foreign dignitary. They're saying that if the mayor believed it was safe, he would come back to town for it himself, and the fact that he won't says everything."

Charlie Kee appeared in the doorway next. I saw Fitz disguise a shiver by jumping up to greet him.

"Great news, Kee. President Harper of the University of Chicago has not only agreed to attend but he plans to bring his whole family. I told you Mrs. Chapman could help us."

Alden brightened with this news. "Say, if President Harper is coming, that should make a difference for some people. We can put that in the papers."

"Yes, yes." Fitz seized on this. "You do a story on it. How soon can you get it in?"

"Today. He's got a telephone. I can call him for some quotes." Alden pulled out his notebook and pencil.

"Dean Talbot is sure others from the university will come and bring their families as well," I told my brother. "You can call her. She was delivering more invitations today. She was sure that just knowing Harper and his children were going would be enough to draw them."

"Hip Lung received many more refusals today," Charlie Kee told Fitz. The big Irishman looked at him with something verging on despair.

"But this news about Harper will change things," Alden said. "Believe me, knowing he'll attend will make a big difference to a lot of people."

Fitz had an idea. "I tell you what to do," he said, putting an arm around Kee's shoulders and turning him towards the door. "You go back to Hip Lung. You tell him to lose those refusals, lose all of them. Throw them away. Then you have him send the invitations out again. Send out all the ones he sent before, every one of them. Have him say that he didn't get any answer before, so he's sending the invite again thinking they must not have gotten the first one. Give them another chance. Alden will get the news in the paper, they'll see it and they'll change their minds." He gave Kee a little push towards the door and waved at Alden. "Mr. Cabot, to your newspaper, please. Make your deadline. Give them a story. We're counting on you!"

Alden grinned at him and slid past Charlie Kee and out the door. Kee frowned but he followed. Fitz took out a large white handkerchief and wiped the sweat from his forehead. "Well, I thank you very much, Mrs. Chapman. At least there is some hope now. Although, I'm not confident even President Harper's presence will be enough to overcome the prejudice. No offense to you, Dr. Kahn, but our people are not very knowledgeable about our Oriental neighbors. Your people tend to keep to themselves. And I'm afraid there are some wild rumors going around suggesting strange things happen down there. The death of the herbalist, Old Lo, is the type of thing that gets them humming about secret poisons and vices, don't you know."

I was offended for Ida and the others of her race. "That's ridiculous," I protested. "I can see why Mr. Hip Lung gets angry. Secret poisons, indeed. As far as I can see, the herbalist and his son only ever provided medicines to help people. Anyway, he's the one who was poisoned, not someone else."

"If only all my constituents could be as logical as you are, my dear lady, there would be no cause for concern." Fitz looked at me with a wistful smile. "You and I know that our Oriental friends are no different from our Italian, German, or Irish friends. Only it's much harder for them to become citizens. And a lot of them really don't even speak English. Nonetheless, they all are trying hard to make a life here. They work all day, mostly in the laundries spread across town, and then on Sundays they come into the city to visit with those that are like them. They send their money home to support those they left behind. They're just trying to make their way like everybody else. Yet there's a great suspicion about them from the common man, and little knowledge of their ways, it has to be admitted."

"Well, this is an opportunity to learn something of their ways then, isn't it?" I asked. "Really, this is outrageous…this disdain for what is different. This is no way to bring up our children."

Fitz looked at me with a big warm smile. "It's beautiful you are, when you're angry like this."

I flushed with embarrassment at his admiration and looked towards Ida Kahn in dismay.

"Most people are afraid of what is unfamiliar," Ida said. Fitz coughed as if to cover his expression and nodded. Ida continued. "Actually, my countrymen tend to be suspicious of Western ways as well. Even the ones who come here do not always learn the language and the customs. They, too, are guilty of some measure of prejudice. But perhaps the viceroy's trip will be an opportunity for better understanding."

"Yes. Were you able to get any of the missionaries to accept invitations?" I asked. I was glad for the diversion.

"I was able to recruit several. I have also taken the opportunity to invite some of the medical staff from the women's hospital. I hope that's all right?" We murmured agreement. "I'm sure some of them will want to bring their children when they hear President Harper and the others will come."

"Children? What children?" Detective Whitbread had come in the door while we were talking.

I explained how Dean Talbot had come up with the idea of attracting parents with restless children to the festivities. I knew that Whitbread himself had several young children at his own house. They were the younger siblings of the widow he had married. I suggested he bring them.

"Very well. I'm sure Gracie will agree," he admitted. "But I must warn you, Mrs. Chapman, there are still rumors that violence is planned during the viceroy's visit. Hip Lung continues to send me people who have heard there may be trouble, but none of them have been able to give me specifics."

"But you checked Mr. Wong's place. Don't you think that Hip Lung is just trying to get his rivals in trouble?"

"I wish I could believe that was the only thing going on," Whitbread said. Fitz looked annoyed at the suggestion of further difficulties. He had just begun to hope the festival might have a chance of coming off. He didn't want to hear about more problems.

"There are many, even in China, who might threaten violence against Viceroy Li," Ida told us. We all looked at her. "I'm afraid it's true. There are those, like Mr. Wong, who support Sun Yat Sen and others who advocate the overthrow of the Manchu court. But there are others, also. There are those, who are the old guard, who believe Li is too moderate. They are reactionaries who want to attack foreigners in China and throw them out, even though they don't have the strength to do so. They refuse to recognize that such aggression would cause retaliation and lead to an even more humiliating defeat. Li has opposed them for years, so they would like to get rid of him as well."

Whitbread shook his head. "For the love of God, why can't these people keep their power struggles in their own country? What makes you think they would send people here?"

"I don't know, but it is a possibility. I only meant to warn you that it is not only the people with whom Wong Chin Foo sympathizes who are a threat to Viceroy Li. Even at home he is constantly threatened by attempts to assassinate him."

"A gloomy thought," Fitz said. "But we do not want to plan for assassinations here, we want to plan for a celebration. We can't let these maniacs ruin everything."

"Besides, those enemies are in China," I said. "How could they be over here?"

"It's only too possible they could send assassins," Whitbread said.

"But aren't they only allowed to come to the United States if they already have relatives here?" I asked. "Like those men Officer Lewis took away to interrogate about their home villages."

Whitbread and Fitz exchanged a glance. Fitz set me straight. "Strictly speaking, that is true. But I'm afraid it's not uncommon for men to come and claim to be related to someone here just to get in."

"And they pass the interrogations?"

"Or they pay a bribe," Whitbread stated.

Fitz shrugged his shoulders. "I'm afraid that's true, as well. There are unscrupulous immigration officers who can be bribed."

"Like Officer Lewis?" I asked. "Is that how those men he took from the herb shop got out again so soon? I saw them there yesterday."

"Difficult to prove," Fitz said, and I thought he was uncomfortable with the topic. It seemed likely to me that Fitz himself might help Hip Lung bribe officials to look the other way, when he had men trying to get into the country. It was the type of thing Fitz would do and I had the impression it might be the kind of thing Hip Lung and his brothers would do as well. They might even make a profit from it. There had been some hint of that at the raid on the herb shop. Perhaps the dead herbalist had set himself up in competition with the Moy brothers for smuggling people into the country. But would either of them smuggle assassins?

"We cannot allow the celebration to be disturbed by an attack on Li," Whitbread told us. "We must all be on our guard. Clearly, the viceroy's visit must go on. And it will, as long as I have no reason to suspect anyone specifically. But, if there is even a hint of a plot, you must tell me." He looked significantly at Fitz, Ida, and me. "You're inviting all of these local people. It will be on your heads if anything happens to them. Remember that." With that warning, he left us.

I, for one, was uneasy after listening to him. What if something happened to President Harper or his family? But I wasn't going to let the mere specter of danger stop us. "We'll be there," I told Fitz. "My daughter is too small, but my son and his nursemaid will certainly come. And Dr. Chapman, too," I promised boldly, hoping that was true. I was not quite as confident as I sounded. Fitz almost flinched at the mention of Stephen. I thought I was right in suspecting that he was harboring romantic feelings for me. But I knew I was correct in assuming they were nothing more than a romantic fantasy for him. A brush with this kind of male imaginings made me impatient. "I'll stop at Hull House this afternoon to see if we can get more people there to attend," I promised.

"And I'll make sure there are preparations to entertain the children," Fitz said. "I do believe your dean has an idea there. It's true that parents are looking for entertainments for the children, after they return from summer vacation and before they begin again at school. Dean Talbot is a canny woman." This was strong praise from Fitz, who could recognize political acumen in others because he had so much of it himself. It was a talent I certainly lacked, and so did Stephen. And, for that matter, so did Detective Whitbread. It required knowledge of the strengths and weaknesses of others. I was never as sharp at distinguishing other people's needs. It also required a sense of when to take a stand, like Dean Talbot was planning to do about married women working in academia, and when to bend with the wind, like Fitz seemed to be doing by making excuses for the mayor. Subtlety and compromise were not talents at my disposal. I was always a little too blunt and uncompromising. It made me more determined than ever to make sure Fitz and Hip Lung had a good turnout for the festival. At least I could help with that.

After we said our goodbyes to Fitz and accepted his intense thanks, I decided to accompany Ida back to the hospital. I wanted to see with my own eyes how Charlotte was doing and whether she had recovered enough to identify her attacker. I also wanted to see how her father was reacting and whether I could sense any guilt in him. And, finally, I needed to see Dr. Stone. She was how I had gotten into all of this, and I wanted to see how she was accepting her current situation.

# TWENTY-SEVEN

"Mr. Fitzgibbons is very fond of you," Ida commented as we rode in a carriage towards the hospital.

"He is an old friend," I said, trying to explain. "I've known him for almost as long as I've been in the city. He was of great help to me several times." It was all too complicated to explain on a short ride, so I didn't try. "How is Mary doing?"

"She refuses to worry. She tends Miss Erickson, although there is little hope that she will ever wake up." Ida shook her head. "I fear she will die. And, when that happens, her father will insist that Mary be arrested."

"But she was with us just before we found out that Charlotte was attacked...we left her talking to Mr. Chin. Surely there was not time enough for her to attack Charlotte. They must know that."

"The father is unreasonable in his grief, and Mary wishes to leave Mr. Chin out of the discussion. She fears it would look bad for both him and her, if people thought they were alone together."

"Were they?"

"Only at the table where we saw them as we left."

"Is there no chance Charlotte will revive enough to identify her attacker?" I asked.

"Very little. Here we are."

I paid the driver and we got out of the hot summer sun and into the cool shadows of the brick building as quickly as we could. I glanced at the huge portraits as we passed through the foyer. How would Charlotte's mother feel, if she could see her daughter lying helplessly in a hospital bed? Would she be glad that at least it was at *this* hospital, which she had helped to build and had supported for so long?

Ida led me to a stairway and up two flights. Hospital staff appeared to know her. We tiptoed past a nurses' station. Beyond it, I could just see a waiting room where Dr. Erickson sat slumped in a chair. Nearby, Laura Appleby sat knitting. At the door to Charlotte's room stood a uniformed policeman. He grimaced at us but waved us by and Ida ushered me in.

It was cool and shaded in the room. Sheer curtains let in a breeze but filtered the light. It was on a side of the building that was mercifully cast in shadow. Charlotte lay on the white sheets, her head bandaged and her leg set with splints. There were bandages on her arms as well, and a sort of barrier of pillows near her ribs. She moaned a bit and I heard a murmur as Mary Stone bent over her and moved the cushioning by her ribs a little. I saw she had a cup in her hand with a bit of steam drifting up from it. She held it to Charlotte's mouth, coaxing a sip now and then. Hearing our entry, she carefully removed the cup, wiped the lips of the unconscious girl and set the cup on a side table. "No change," she said in answer to Ida's questioning look.

We set up three chairs near the window, as far from the bed as possible so we could talk.

"It's very bad, isn't it?" I asked. I hadn't seen Charlotte since we were at Hip Lung's apartment. She had been a bloody mess there, but now I was shocked at how lifeless she looked lying on the bed. Her occasional moans sounded like they came from an animal, not a human being.

Mary brushed a hand across her own forehead. "She was very badly injured. Her broken bones could mend, given time. But there is no way to know whether or not her brain will heal."

"What were you giving her to drink?" I asked.

"Chinese herbs. It's a strong concoction. It may not help, but there seems little hope, so it's unlikely to hurt her in any way."

"Don't let her father see you doing that," Ida warned.

"I cannot fail to try anything that might help," Mary told her. "Besides, he is in despair. It's not as it was before with him. He won't leave, but most of the time he just sits and stares. Mrs. Appleby has made him her charge. She sits with him."

I exchanged a glance with Ida. "We saw them. But he insisted the herbs given to his wife brought on her death. You must be careful he doesn't accuse you of poisoning his daughter. He's not rational," I told her.

She sighed. "The herbs cannot hurt. They may soothe her enough that she might rest and her body may have time to heal itself. It's the most we can hope for."

"But you take a terrible chance," Ida told her.

"My husband had the herbs analyzed and they said there was nothing unusual or poisonous in them," I said. The two young doctors looked at me in surprise. "The young herbalist gave me a sample of the herbs that his father had forbidden him to give to Charlotte. Stephen took it to his laboratory and some of his students analyzed it." When they continued to look at me in silence I went on. "I thought there might be an opiate or something in it. I just wanted to make sure."

They exchanged a few words in Chinese. Ida looked upset, but Mary turned to me. "What Young Lo gave you would not have been his father's mixture. What I have *is*. I obtained it from Old Lo before he died. But he would not have given it to Young Lo. It is the type of secret recipe only passed on to family members."

"But Young Lo is his son," I protested.

"Paper son," Ida said. I looked at her, confused. "You have heard of a 'paper son,' haven't you?"

"Yes, I have. But I thought the young man at the herb shop really was Old Lo's son."

"No," Mary told me. "Old Lo took in another paper son

every few months. In the three years we've known him there have been many 'sons.' But this kind of special secret recipe for medicine is something that is passed down only within a real family. Old Lo may have sons back in China who learned it, but he wouldn't teach it to one who was only passing through, like the young man there now."

"But he's running the shop. Didn't he inherit it?"

Ida explained. "They all want to keep the immigration authorities out of their community, so even though they all know he is only a paper son they would not say so openly. Yet the shop belongs to Old Lo and his real family. Eventually, the shop will be sold and the money will be sent back to his relatives in China."

I looked across at the young woman lying in the bed. "Then why did he give me those herbs and say they were what Charlotte wanted? And what is in the real herbs she gave to her mother?"

"Probably he just wanted to make you and the policeman go away," Mary told me. "He's probably afraid he'll be exposed as a paper son and deported. I suppose he thought if he gave you something he knew was harmless, and you found out what was in it, you would stop asking. As for what is in the real herbal medicine, I, too, would like to know that. It has worked for me on some critical patients. I believe there is an opiate among other things. But I don't know all the ingredients."

"You're sure it won't harm her?" I asked, looking over at the bed.

"Does she look like there is much that will hurt her now?" Ida snapped. It was true. She was so lost in a deep sleep there seemed little that could disturb her.

At that moment the door flew open and Dr. Erickson staggered in. His tall form was doubled over, as if from a pain in his abdomen. His clothes were stained and in disarray, his beard ragged. His eyes were sunken in his large forehead. He reached the foot of the bed and clutched the railing, staring down at his daughter.

"Isaac, come away. Let her rest." A soft voice spoke from the doorway. Laura Appleby stood there quietly, all her attention on the man who stood shuddering at the end of the bed.

Ida, Mary, and I rose quietly but held our breath, willing the man not to break out into one of his rampages. His breath came in harsh rasps. We heard him mumbling. I slid a little closer to see if I could hear what he was saying.

"Charlotte, Charlotte. No, no, no. Not you, too. You cannot leave me, too." He repeated it over and over again, softly. It was heartbreaking to hear, and all of us women were at a loss as to how to comfort him. We were also apprehensive that any move to help him might only lead to an outbreak. Then he began weeping in a whiny, gulping way.

Laura Appleby slid across to catch him just as he began to crumple towards the floor. Mary and Ida pushed a chair under him, and brought forward one for Mrs. Appleby. The guard on the door poked his head in, but she waved him away. Erickson laid his head on her shoulder and wept.

"It's my fault," he said. His voice was muffled by her dress. She pushed him away and held him by the shoulders to look at him.

"It's not, Isaac. It's not your fault."

But I wondered if he was trying to confess. Had he lost his temper so badly that, when he saw his daughter come out of the herb shop, he followed her and beat her? Perhaps he had not intended to hurt her the way he had, but that temper of his might have gotten away from him.

"I did," he murmured, sinking away from her. "I did it. It was my fault. I drove her away. But I was so angry when Katherine left me. I couldn't bear the pain. How could she leave me?"

"She didn't leave you, Isaac. You know that. She was taken from you...by disease. It was not her desire to leave you, she had no choice."

He sobbed into his hands. "I only wanted to keep her." He looked at the figure in the bed. "I wanted her to stay. I couldn't lose her like I lost her mother." His hand reached out and clawed at the blanket at the foot of the bed.

"Of course you did." Laura put an arm around his shoulder and pulled him to her. "She knew that, really. She knew all your rages were about losing Katherine. She loved Katherine, too, you know. We all did. You weren't the only one to lose her."

"I can't lose Charlotte, too," he moaned. "I can't lose her, too." He sniveled and flinched, as if something had hit a nerve in him. He looked at the lifeless body of his daughter, and then his eye moved to the table. He saw the cup. Suddenly, he stood up and staggered over to the table. He took up the cup, smelled it, looked around. He spotted Mary. Ida moved protectively in front of her. But Dr. Erickson just looked back and forth between the liquid in the cup and Mary. Laura Appleby sighed but she stood still, not making a move towards him. Finally, he spoke in a cracked voice. "Will it help?" he asked. "Will it help her?" He was beseeching Mary.

She took a step forward, gently pushing past Ida. "There is no way to know. It might at least give her some peace, so her body can try to heal. That's all it can do." She looked down at the girl on the bed. "There is nothing to do but wait."

Dr. Erickson stared at her, as if mesmerized, but to my relief there was no outburst from him. Mary and Laura pulled over a chair, close to the head of the bed, and settled him in it. Then Laura found another for herself, which she placed by his side so that she could keep an eye on him. Mary returned to the chair she had occupied in the corner.

I looked at Ida, feeling my racing heart returning to a more normal beat. The man by the bed looked defeated. I no longer feared he would attack Mary and I found it hard to believe he might have attacked his daughter. Laura and Mary seemed to have him well in hand, so Ida and I slipped out the door, into the corridor.

I sat in the waiting room, to think about what I had learned.

It seemed unlikely the herbs had poisoned anyone. Except Old Lo. Something had poisoned him. Or had he been ill? And, if someone had attacked Charlotte—but it had nothing to do with the herbs she had gotten for her mother—why had she been attacked? Or did it still have to do with the herbs from the store? And what did all of this have to do with the rumors of an assassination attempt on Viceroy Li? Or did they have nothing to do with it? Could it really be Mary's unsuccessful romance with Chin that had caused her to be accused of murder? Was it really Mary who was in danger? From whom?

I thought hard about the strange world of Chinatown, hidden among the saloons and brothels of Clark Street, and all that I had seen there—Wong's Confucian altar, the Moy family dining area and their huge dry goods store, the sinister-looking laboratory where Grubbé experimented with Crookes tubes glowing in the dark, the King Yen Lo restaurant with the strange smells in the air and the mixture of Western and Chinese ornaments hanging from the ceiling. It seemed to me that I had stumbled on a secret place where there may have been smiles on all of the faces, but they covered sinister intentions. Most of the time I had listened to a language I could not interpret, like seeing the world through gauze curtains. Was it even possible to discern the patterns? My mind wheeled with images from the last few days.

In the end, I thought I could discern a pattern. But, if I was right, there was no way to prove it, or at least none I could see. I saw great danger ahead, but was it fair for the whole community to suffer insult for the suspicions I had? It was not a choice I could make alone.

On my way home I needed to keep my promise to Fitz. I would stop at Hull House to convince those fearless reformers to attend the Double Seventh Festival. And I would take my husband and son to the celebration, joining others from the university. I would not be part of the insult to Hip Lung and his community.

But first I had to see Whitbread, to tell him of my suspicions.

# TWENTY-EIGHT

The Double Seventh Festival was held on the twenty-first of August that year, a Friday. There was a late afternoon start planned for the parade, which, it was hoped, would draw people just leaving for their homes after a long week of work. Once we'd secured President Harper's attendance with his family, other academics and businessmen had eagerly joined in. Hull House residents had rounded up a flock of West Side children as well. Besides that, they had reached out to their wealthy supporters and I recognized more than one of the women from the Hull House board, including Louise DeKoven Bowen, who had just returned from a trip to Europe with her husband and children. It was nice to see her sons and daughters mingling with the children of Hull House neighbors as they lined up on the sidewalks to wait for the parade. But it was the arrival of Jane Addams herself that had Fitz beaming with joy. He took her hand and led her and her companions to a special viewing area where they could sit in the stands. He was too far away to speak to me, but he motioned his thanks. One thing I knew about Fitz was that he remembered past assistance. If I ever needed his help in the future, I was sure he would do anything I asked.

Just as the music started, with bells jangling and drums thumping, I turned to be sure my family was in position. Delia held Jack in her arms. He was staring around wildly. Never had he seen so many people, or felt such a surge of excitement. I smiled up at Stephen, who had come from Grubbé's lab to join us. I'd told him about Dr. Erickson's change of heart concerning Mary. He was happy to hear it, but pointed out that she had not yet been released to return to China.

Because he knew Whitbread was too tied up in the arrangements for the safety of Viceroy Li to turn his attention back to the death of Old Lo, Stephen continued to work with Grubbé on the X-rays. I couldn't get him to tell me when his part in that would be finished. I had told him of my talk with Dean Talbot. He agreed that it would be impossible for me to accept the position and then withdraw. I must be able to fully commit to it.

When I confided in him my belief that I might be pregnant once again, he listened to my fears but told me that, in the end, I would have to be the one to decide what to do. There had been no more promises to stop working with Grubbé, neither had there been threats. He only said that I must bear the responsibility for the decision. I'd decided to put off my decision until after the festival, but I knew in my heart that it would be very difficult to bear another child *and* continue my work at the university. I was afraid that, if I didn't take up the lectureship, he would insist on continuing his work with Grubbé. I was unsure, but I hoped I could still persuade him of the danger.

Mary and Ida joined us, bringing the wonderful news that Charlotte had regained consciousness. It seemed a miracle to all concerned. It was after they had lost all hope, but apparently she had healed enough to open her eyes and to move her hand. She was not yet speaking, and she had a long recovery ahead, but it was a great relief, especially to her father. She had squeezed his hand, which he was able to interpret as a sign of forgiveness and he had broken down in tears of joy. Laura Appleby suggested that the young doctors should attend the festivities and had gotten Whitbread to agree to let Mary leave the hospital. She was not yet free to return to China, but it was a first step. I saw that Wong Chin Foo accompanied them. I looked around to see if the waiter, Chin, was also in their party but, if he was there, I did not see him.

"Mrs. Chapman." Wong greeted me, and I introduced Stephen, Delia, and Jack. Jack was fascinated with Mr. Wong, who gestured towards Mary and Ida. "Mr. Fitzgibbons offered the ladies viewing chairs in the stands, but, alas, I was not included in the invitation. I have told them they should avail themselves of the opportunity, but they refuse. Help me to convince them there is no need to stay here on the street with me."

"I was also offered a seat," I told him. "But I thought it would be more fun for Delia and Jack to be down here with all the other children. Look!"

There were oohs and aahs from the crowd as the dragon came into sight. It was a brightly painted cloth tunnel, held up by a line of about twenty men doubled over at the waist. They carried the body and danced along in a form that caused the long snakelike body to writhe back and forth along the street. There was a massive head that rose up high and must have required several men to hold it up. Huge glassy eyes, upright ears, and a snout with sharp white teeth made quite an impression.

On the sides of the weaving body were wings in a red gossamer material, which were particularly fascinating to Jack. He and the other children screamed with delight when the dragon head nodded in their direction. The body swayed to the music of a loud drum, accompanied by cymbals and a stringed instrument that played a high, almost sorrowful, tune. The music was supplemented by the noise of the crowd, cheering the dragon on. Delia's eyes were wide with amazement and I remembered she was little more than a child herself. Looking around, I was glad I had left Lizzie in the care of my friend Clara Shea. She was too young and would have been frightened by all the noise, but Jack and Delia were thrilled.

The dragon was followed by a troop of men in pajama-like outfits who did somersaults and handstands and other acrobatic moves that thrilled the children. Ida and Wong explained they were part of a martial arts school. They seemed triple jointed in the way they could move their bodies. Stephen winced as one man wound himself up and walked like a turtle upside down in a knot. I squeezed his arm. More men ran by with sparklers throwing out little bits of fire. The real fireworks would not be until dark, but men in the parade swung strings of burning fuses and there were explosions that startled us. Ida explained that these were considered joyful noises and all the children around us seemed to enjoy the way the sounds made them jump, after which they would giggle with joy. I confess I was not so comfortable with them. I remembered the unsuccessful search for dynamite in Wong's building and was uneasy.

Eventually, Fitz made his way over to us. "A wonderful day, isn't it, Mrs. Chapman? And we have you to thank for it. I can tell you, Hip Lung is going to be more than satisfied by the turnout."

"What about the viceroy?" I asked.

He turned and pointed to the viewing stands. "See that palanquin? The sort of covered little tent thing up top? He's inside it. Seems he gets carried around in it, and he can sit all comfortable and see out, but no one can see in. But don't worry, he'll be joining us for the dinner."

"Ah, yes, in the Moy hall, right?"

"That's right, it's all prepared. We also have a place for the children. While the grownups eat dinner, the children get cake and ice cream. Isn't it wonderful to see all the children?" He looked around with satisfaction. "What a wonderful idea that was! And this must be your boy." He looked at Jack, who was hugging Delia's shoulder, his thumb in his mouth. Jack looked at him with the suspicion any child has of a grownup they have never seen before. He was frowning. But Fitz looked out from under his bushy eyebrows and stuck out his big hand. "Jack, isn't it?" Jack cocked his head, looked at me and then Stephen and, finding no objections, he smiled and put his little hand in Fitz's. Then they both broke down in laughter. Delia laughed, too, so the rest of us joined in.

By that time the crowd was breaking up. We saw the palanquin pass by, carried by four strong men who all looked like the silk-robed consulate guard who had been following Charlie Kee. I glanced around but there was no sign of Detective Whitbread. As we followed Fitz to the King Yen Lo restaurant, which had been reserved for the entertainment of the children, I noticed a few uniformed policemen along the street but they were far outnumbered by the Chinese men in Western suits who looked alert and on guard. I assumed they had been posted by Hip Lung to keep the peace.

I was a little reluctant to leave Jack with Delia at the restaurant, but I knew he would be safer there than where I was going. I had managed to convince Whitbread of the danger I saw coming and there were plans afoot to deal with it, but until it was played out, there would be the potential for danger. I'd known that, when I decided to bring Jack, and had confided all of it to Stephen. There was no real reason to fear for the safety of the children but, nonetheless, I couldn't be totally sanguine. Even Fitz was not told about the suspected plot.

Stephen squeezed my hand as we took a last look at our son and turned to leave. I nodded to one of the Hull House women I knew who was helping to take care of the children.

"Oh, right, come along then," Fitz said to a grinning Wong Chin Foo as we came out on to Clark Street. "It's Wong, Mrs. Chapman. Hip Lung didn't send an invite but I know he's a friend of these ladies here."

I looked over at Ida, who was shaking her head.

Fitz continued, "As I'm not expecting any trouble from him, I think we can let him come. Just no arguing with our guest of honor now, you hear me?"

"It's all right, Mr. Fitzgibbons," Mary told him. "In China

Mr. Wong would be invited to the viceroy's table and he would know enough not to show bad manners by arguing."

"Yes, well, we'll keep him from the viceroy's table so there's no temptation, but I reckon he'll be all right with you ladies. I know Dr. Kahn will keep him in line, won't you?"

"I will attempt to do so," Ida said dryly. "I cannot promise anything."

"You wound me!" Wong told her, clutching his chest dramatically, but no one paid any attention as we were now maneuvering through the crowds entering the Hip Lung Yee Kee store and up the stairs to the banquet hall. When we got there, Fitz got us all settled at a large round table and left, saying it would be another half hour or so before the viceroy would arrive and the banquet could begin. While we awaited his arrival tea and savory appetizers were set before us.

We had been waiting only a few minutes, amusing ourselves by picking out well-known people, when a young boy came up to me and handed me a folded piece of paper. It was a handwritten note asking me to come back to the King Yen Lo restaurant, as my son was upset. It said, "Please do not disturb the festivities. Come alone, as it is probably a very insignificant thing. We are very sorry to trouble you." I looked around and saw the rest of my companions were still occupied with looking about the room. Only Stephen was paying attention. I explained the note and we agreed that I would be the one to go comfort Jack. We were expecting a confrontation at the dinner and we both wanted to be present, but I knew Stephen would never leave me there alone. He wanted me out of harm's way.

I hurried back the few blocks to the restaurant and up the stairs. But when I got there, none of the women in charge knew anything about the note. I felt my heart stop for a moment, then began frantically moving about the room looking for Delia and Jack. They weren't there. The women were terribly apologetic and hurried off to check the water closets and kitchen in case Delia had just wandered off. I was near to scratching my own skin in frustration waiting for them to return when I saw the herbalist's paper son, Young Lo, coming across the room towards me. I bent over, suddenly unable to catch my breath, and felt my vision narrow to a pinpoint, but I forced myself to resist the urge to faint. I was not the fainting type. I was Jack's mother, and I had to find him.

# TWENTY-NINE

I stood up straight again before Young Lo reached me. "Where is my son?" I asked. I think I could have clawed his eyes out at that moment.

"Yes, please come with me. I think I can help you." He clutched my elbow firmly and whispered in my ear. "If you want to see your son again you will not make any trouble."

I glanced around and saw the other women in the room looking at me curiously. At the back of the room I noticed two Chinese men in Western suits. For a moment I thought they might be Hip Lung's men but then I recognized them from the herbalist's shop. They were the men who sat around with their feet on their suitcases. They had been taken away by Officer Lewis but then were quickly released. So, they were Lo's men, not Hip Lung's. My skin prickled with danger and revulsion. There was a third, I remembered. He must be the one who had Jack and Delia.

"It's all right," I told the women who were watching us. "I think this man saw them in the street. Delia must have decided to go find me because Jack was frightened." They looked at me with doubt. I feared what the men would do to them if they didn't believe me. "Really, it's all right. I told Delia to come and get me if Jack started acting up. I'm sure she's waiting for me downstairs. I'm so sorry to have bothered you. I'll come back if I don't find them, but I think Delia sent this man, you see, and he'll take me to them." I gritted my teeth, willing myself not to scream out for help. There was no reason to endanger these women and the rest of the children in the room. I had every reason to believe that Lo and the other men were very dangerous.

The two men in Western suits followed us down the stairs. Once outside, I became stubborn. "Where is my son? Where did you take him?"

"He is fine and he will remain fine as long as you do what I tell you." Suddenly Lo spoke English very well indeed. He had been pretending not to understand English all this time. He sounded quite well educated.

"Who are you? What do you want?" I had a good idea what they wanted. It was as I had suspected. But I kicked myself for thinking myself so bright. It never occurred to me they would take my child to make me do something. "What do you want from me?"

He twisted my arm till I cringed in pain. "Your cooperation."

"For what? To assassinate Li?" I was being too clever for my own good again. I knew it, but couldn't stop myself. I was in too much shock to pretend to be ignorant.

"Assassinate Li? Us? Oh, no, smart lady, it is Sun Yat Sen and his followers who want to assassinate Li and topple the emperor. It is Wong Chin Foo."

They wanted to make it look like Wong and his group had done the killing, that was it. But why would he tell me that? Only if he knew I would not be around to tell anyone. *Oh, Jack, my beautiful son. What have I done?* "What? You work for Wong? Are you the ones working for him? You got the dynamite away before the police came, is that it?" I thought it was worth a try to pretend I believed Wong was behind it. Maybe he would leave me alive to testify to Wong's involvement. I saw him look at me with disdain and then exchange a look with one of the others.

"Enough. You do as I say or your son dies. You understand?" He shook me roughly.

"Stop. I'll do what you say, I'll do anything. Please, don't harm my son. He's only a child. He's not even two years old." I choked up with tears and had no need to pretend the desperation I felt.

"Listen to me. You will escort us into the banquet. You understand?"

"Yes, yes, certainly. I will." Of course, they knew of my connection with Fitz. They knew I could get them in. We had expected they would just come under Hip Lung's general invitation. But perhaps Young Lo was not important enough, even though I had insisted he be invited. Or maybe only *he* could get in and they needed me in order to get his men in. Or maybe they just wanted to be in a more prominent place and they expected me to have a front table. Whatever the reason, our calculations were off. And what would this alteration do to the rest of Whitbread's plan? If only I could reach him, but it was impossible. I wasn't even sure exactly what his plan entailed. I knew he expected Lo, but not like this.

I struggled to keep from panicking as we returned through the dry goods store and up the stairs to the banquet hall. Lo was right to expect that his entrance would be ensured with me leading the way. All of Hip Lung's men knew me and, when I insisted the men were with me, they probably thought it was part of some special arrangement to honor Li. They were on the lookout for trouble, but not from someone like me, who had special status as a friend of Hip Lung and his wife.

I was barely able to speak when I reached the table. Stephen asked me how Jack was, but I could not reply. I feared his actions would provoke Lo to attack him so I tried to act normally but couldn't speak. My throat had closed up from the anxiety. As the others, looking a little puzzled, pulled up a chair for Lo, his men drifted away into the crowd. I saw Wong Chin Foo lift an eyebrow at the placement of the lowly herbalist at a head table but Ida nudged him and reminded him that he was only there himself on sufferance. He attempted to make a joke of it with Lo but the other man ignored him. Wong looked thoughtful.

Further explanation was interrupted by the pounding of drums heralding the coming of the palanquin carrying Viceroy Li. Fitz and Hip Lung stood only a few feet from us, waiting to greet the man. I looked around but saw no sign of Whitbread. I knew he had men disguised as dignitaries at the adjoining tables but what would trigger their reactions? I felt the pounding of a pulse in my right temple. They were going to kill the viceroy right here, before my eyes. Probably they would follow that by setting off dynamite to blow the place up. I felt the need to scream a warning but my throat was still closed and I felt a vicious twist of my arm, which was Lo reminding me of his threat to kill Jack and Delia. I couldn't do it. No matter what happened I couldn't endanger my son. There was nothing I could do. Stephen sensed my agitation and suddenly swept his good arm around me, pulling me to him.

"What is it, Emily? What's wrong?"

The palanquin was set down on the ground, right before Fitz and Hip Lung. Suddenly, I saw the gold curtain swing open, as Lo sprang from his seat and rushed towards it. Then came the deafening retort of a pistol. Two pistols, smoke. Screams, more shots on the other side of the room. I jumped up. Stephen tried to grab me and force me behind him. But before he covered my head with his arms, I saw Whitbread. He stood over Lo, clutching his side. He must have been hit, but Lo was not moving at all. I began to scream.

# THIRTY

I wasn't the only one screaming, of course. The room was ringing with noise, but at least those who were close to me knew there was something wrong. Even Whitbread—bleeding from his injury and anxious to verify that the other men who'd come with Lo were caught—even he knew something was very wrong.

"They have Jack. They have Jack, They have Jack," I screamed. "Get them. Don't let them get away or they'll tell the other one and he'll kill Jack. They have Jack. They have Delia. Let me go, let me go!" Stephen clutched me to him, finally forcing me to sit down while he squatted by my side. Mary poured water and forced me to drink a little. My throat was freezing up again but I had to tell them before they killed Jack. "They have him. Lo took Jack and Delia." A sob interrupted me but I didn't have time for that. I had to find Jack and Delia before they killed them.

Whitbread waved away someone who was trying to staunch the blood from his wound and grabbed Fitz, forcing him to help him over to the table. "Mrs. Chapman, stop that. Calm down and tell us what's going on." His voice was stern and it acted like cold water thrown at me.

I straightened up. "Lo sent a message, so I went back to the restaurant…because there was a problem with Jack." I felt Stephen's hand on my shoulder. "When I got there, no one knew anything, then Lo showed up. He told me he had them…he had

Jack and Delia. He said that, if I said anything, he'd kill them. There were three of them. The men in the shop. Two of them were with Lo. The other one must have Jack and Delia." I tried to rise and looked around wildly. "Did they get them? Did they get away? If they got away, they'll tell the other one to kill my son. We have to stop them." I was pulled back down into my chair but heard Whitbread yell to one of his men.

"How many? You sure? Well, keep a hold on him."

"Oh," I moaned. "You only got one…the other one got away. They're going to kill them…Jack and Delia."

"Neither one got away. One's dead. My man shot him," Whitbread told me. "The other one is injured badly. Get me over there, we need to find out where they have the children." He was physically feeble but Fitz held him up. When I tried to follow, he snapped at me. "You stay there." I sank back into Stephen's arms but he handed me over to Mary and Ida and followed Whitbread.

They were back in a few minutes, with Hip Lung and some of his men clustered round them. Fitz deposited Whitbread in a chair.

"They got the location," Stephen told me. He was pale. I thought he would hate me if anything happened to Jack, his son. Why had I done it? I knew they expected an assassination attempt. At least I had told Stephen about it. Knowing that, how could we have brought our child? And Delia, poor little Delia, cousin to Whitbread's wife Gracie, who had been given a job with me with the idea that she would be fed and taken care of. What kind of care had I shown? I was appalled to the very core of my being, knowing I had allowed this to happen.

"Hip Lung has people checking out the location where we suspect they are, but they won't approach it." Whitbread wheezed a bit. He was in poor shape. I saw Mary bend over to look at his wound. He made a move to resist but then gave himself over to her ministrations. "Listen, we can't just plunge in there. He'll be scared to death and he'll kill the young ones out of panic, or for spite. But we need to move now, before he hears what happened."

He took a deep breath. "Hip Lung's people will make sure no one gets near enough to tell him, but pretty soon he'll know something's wrong, if he doesn't hear from the others. Probably his orders are to kill them if anything goes wrong." I sobbed but caught myself. "I could send some of my men but they're not subtle. I'd like to do it myself." He tried an experimental move, but quickly sank back down. Mary regarded him with disapproval and placed one hand on his chest to prevent him from moving.

"You cannot do it," she told him.

"I have to go," I almost yelled.

"No, they know you. Obviously they've seen you and been watching you. You can't go," Whitbread told me.

"They don't know me. I can go," Stephen said.

Whitbread nodded. "But, if you have to fight him for the gun, you're at a disadvantage." We all knew he was referring to Stephen's crippled arm.

"I'll go with him," Fitz said.

"Too many and he'll suspect something," Whitbread warned.

"I'll go myself," Fitz offered. But Whitbread looked at him without any confidence, for Fitz was not known for his skills with guns or fighting.

"We'll all go." It was Wong Chin Foo. "Here's what we'll do... we'll be three men who have been at the party. We've had too much to drink. We're staggering down the road, looking for a place to sleep it off. We knock on a few doors, then, when we get to the one we want, we get it open...but he still thinks we're just lost drunks. Meanwhile, we're talking about what happened at the banquet, how Li got shot and the men got away but everybody is out looking for them. He'll be so interested to hear what we say, he won't think to shoot us." He looked around at the stunned faces. Well, not all were stunned. Whitbread listened critically and Stephen just looked determined. "We fall through the door, Dr. Chapman grabs the children, Fitz and I jump on this lout, and Hip Lung's men follow us in and finish him." He cocked an eye at us. "What do you think? Don't worry, Mrs. Chapman. We can do this. Fitz and I are used to public performances, aren't we, Fitz?"

The big Irishman looked at him with admiration. "You bet we are. Come on, then. What are we waiting for?"

There was no further discussion and Hip Lung led the way. When Whitbread insisted that he needed to go with them, they put him back in the palanquin and carried him along. Mary and Ida stayed at my side as we rushed after the men. Hip Lung snapped orders to his men and they kept everyone else back.

Suddenly my brother, Alden, was by my side and I nearly fainted.

"It's all right, Emily. I was here, in the back rows with the rest of the press. I just heard what happened. They have Jack and Delia?"

"Oh, why did I bring them? Why, oh, why? How could I do this?"

"It's all right, Em." I felt his arm around my waist as we hurried down the street after the incongruous silk-covered palanquin. Ida told Alden about the plan. "Don't worry, Emily, Stephen and Fitz can do this. And that Wong Chin Foo is a smart cookie. They'll do it all right."

When we reached the end of the street, it was blocked by Hip Lung's men. Stephen and the rest were already beyond the barrier. I began to follow but Ida put a hand on my arm. "You don't want to slow them. They need to do this fast before the man can suspect anything."

Frustrated, I tried to see what was happening. Alden slipped off somewhere for a better view. I thought I would choke with exasperation and grief, as more and more people surrounded us but, suddenly, Ida put a hand on my arm and pulled me away. Before I could protest, she put a finger to her lips and motioned towards a small boy standing with Mary on the sidelines. She beckoned. When we reached them, Ida whispered in my ear that the boy had been sent by Hip Lung's wife and that he knew a place where we could watch without being seen, if we were quiet. Desperate, I followed them through a dark alley into an empty building and up the stairs to the second floor, where he took us to a broken window. It looked down on the street. The boy motioned towards the door of a building directly opposite.

"He says that's where they are," Ida told me.

I caught my breath. I felt paralyzed, sitting there unable to do anything. My pulse pounded in my ears so loud that, at first, I didn't hear them. The three men clung to each other and staggered down the street singing a song. They stopped for a moment then moved on.

"Oh, what a mess…oh, what a mess it was!" I heard Fitz exclaim in his Irish brogue.

"Well, friend, there's nothing you can do about it, it's over now." Wong's voice rang out, only slightly slurred. "Nothing to do but drown your sorrows. Isn't that what you say? Drown your sorrows?" They were getting closer.

"Ay, and my friend here's had a snoot full already." It was Stephen hanging between the two men like an inebriate. "Listen, he's getting heavy. We've got to find a place to let him sleep it off. I'm not taking him home to his lady like this. She'd never forgive me." I was touched by the reference to me, even in this horrid situation. Fitz was mad.

"One of these will do. My cousin told me they're empty. Owned by Hip Lung but he doesn't use 'em and hasn't sold 'em to anyone else yet. Here, over here." They were at the building next to the one we were watching and tried the door. I was anxious. Why didn't they just go in and get Jack and Delia before that madman shot them? I bit my lip and tasted blood. Suddenly Wong's voice rose in a shriek. "Ay, did you see that? A rat! Come on then, I'm not going near that one, no sir."

"Don't be such a priss," Fitz said, but I thought I sensed tension in his voice. The sooner they got this over with the better.

I pictured Jack playing with his educational blocks and Delia rocking with Lizzie in her arms and I couldn't hold back a sob. Mary patted my back.

"This is the one." Wong was at the door. "Say, what do you think about that shooting anyhow?" he said, as he rooted around in the dirt. I could see that he had a crow bar in his hand and planned to use it to open the door. He was doing his bit, trying to keep the gunman interested before they went in. Stephen hung off Fitz's shoulder in such a way that I wondered if he really had passed out.

Fitz grunted.

"I say it's that Hip Lung," Wong Chin Foo said, as he began to lever the lock off the door. "I'll bet that bastard will try to blame it on me." There was a loud crack and something broke, letting them in the door. Wong continued talking as if he had just gotten started on a long-winded story. The sound of his voice, sounding so casual, just grated across my spirit. *Jack, oh, Jack, please still be there, still be alive. I promise I'll never put you in such danger again.* I tried to hold off my panic. "Now, let me tell you a thing about Hip Lung…"

Suddenly, there were noises of thrashing. A gunshot and a flash of light. Another, and another. More men appeared from the shadows. They opened lanterns and raced in. More noise and another shot. Then I saw Stephen. He staggered out with a tiny crying form in his arms. Thank God. And Delia followed along behind him, clutching at his jacket.

We got up and ran down the stairs. Our guide led us out to the street and I ran to my husband and child and poor Delia. I wept and hugged them and found them all in one piece. Mary and Ida spoke to some of Hip Lung's men and followed them into the house to help anyone who was injured but they came back out quickly, leading Fitz and Wong. They sat the men down on the curb and took a lantern to help examine them. Both men looked worn out but relieved.

I went over to them. "I don't know how to thank you."

They looked at each other. "Thank your man, there," Fitz told me, pointing to Stephen. "He flew in there and covered the kiddies. The guy tried to shoot him. Wong got him with the crowbar, and I distracted him, but it took one of Hip Lung's men to shoot him. What happened to him?" he asked Ida.

"He's dead."

"Good." For once Wong Chin Foo was speechless and I realized that, unlike Whitbread, these men were not prepared to be fired at by pistols and I was terribly grateful for them. Stephen brought Jack and Delia over to sit with the men on the curb.

Mary and Ida took me by the arms and walked me down to the palanquin in order to tell Detective Whitbread all was well and to insist he go to the hospital to be treated for his wounds. Mary spoke in Chinese to some of the men and in a few minutes a carriage was provided. She took charge and carried Whitbread off. I wondered what he would think when he woke up in the women's hospital. As long as he recovered it would be fine. And I had complete confidence that Mary would make sure he did. They agreed that Ida should stay to take care of any injuries that might have been missed so far.

I was wobbly on my feet and feeling drained of energy as we walked back to the others. I was so relieved to see Stephen with Jack in his lap and Delia clinging to his arm. How could I ever be unhappy about anything as long as I had them…and Lizzie… with me?

Stephen, Fitz, and Wong all looked up at me, anxiety showing in their eyes. They seemed to feel guilty about something. But I was so tremendously grateful to all of them, I couldn't imagine what it could be. Then I noticed Hip Lung in his long-skirted tunic and silk-embroidered jacket standing before them. "Fireworks," he said. "Now we will have the fireworks!"

# THIRTY-ONE

You didn't bring your children today, Mrs. Chapman?" Miss Howe sat across from me at one of the large round tables in the King Yen Lo restaurant, where we had gathered for a party to wish her, Mary, and Ida a bon voyage. They were about to head back to the West Coast, where they would board the boat that would finally take them home to China. "Your son looked so happy at the fireworks last week," she added innocently. The huge fireworks display that ended that terrifying night had been enough to fill the minds of Jack and Delia, even after their kidnapping. I had been so much in shock I barely noticed the explosions in the skies. For the remainder of the night, I couldn't take my eyes off my son as he lay in my husband's arms.

"The children are safely at home with Delia," I explained. I shivered at the thought of Jack being present today. I knew he would try to crawl across the table just to prove he could do it, and I was sure Lizzie would only have shrieked her displeasure at being taken away from home. No, it was a good thing to leave them at home with Delia. And they were not alone there. Somehow, the experience had convinced Stephen (in a way that I never could) that he needed to spend more time with his children. Since the night of the banquet, not only had he returned to Dr. Jamieson's laboratory, where they were preparing for the fall quarter, but he also made a point to return home at least once a day to check on the children and Delia. I was amazed at how much that had satisfied me. "And my husband is busy preparing for fall classes, otherwise he would have come." I remembered my fears that Stephen's affection for me and the children had somehow diminished and felt how very, very foolish I'd been.

"Dr. Chapman is a brave man," Fitz announced. He joined our party, followed by Wong Chin Foo and Hip Lung. The women had visited Hip Lung's wife and her sister-in-law earlier in the day, to thank them for their help and to part from them. Mary and Ida had promised to send them delicacies from China. I thought the two young women locked away in that apartment were rather homesick for their country and I promised to visit them in the future.

"Mr. Fitzgibbons, exactly who were those men at the banquet? And why did they kill Old Lo and try to blame it on Mary?" Miss Howe asked.

"They were assassins sent by some in the Manchu court who thought Li was too liberal, as I understand it," Fitz replied.

"Young Lo was not really a son of the herbalist who was poisoned," I explained. "He was a 'paper son.' He was an assassin who needed to get into the United States. But he couldn't buy his way in through the normal channels because the people who controlled them, like Hip Lung, wouldn't approve of the plot to assassinate Li. Young Lo found out that some of the old herbalist's relatives were about to come to the United States under the current rules. He must have paid one of them off, in order to take their place. Since Old Lo had not seen that particular relative in many years he was not suspicious when Young Lo arrived. Mary and Ida told me that Old Lo had sponsored a number of men in the past few years. But it was only relatives or people from his village. It was not a business for him, right?" I looked at Hip Lung.

"That's correct," he said. "Once Young Lo got here, he sent for the other three men. They also claimed to be related and they had papers. But Old Lo got suspicious about so many 'relatives' arriving who he didn't recognize."

"He would have known that you would not approve of this, as usually men who come over needed to make arrangements through your family, isn't that the case?" I asked.

Hip Lung ignored my question and applied his chopsticks to a steaming plate of meat and vegetables that had been placed before him. As the rest of our plates were delivered, Fitz answered for him. "It's the case that most new arrivals work out an arrangement with the Moys to find employment and get started. They get all kinds of help with the authorities, loans to tide them over, help finding work. Hip Lung and his brothers have helped many a man get a start here." For which I had no doubt there was a fee, but it didn't seem worth bringing that into the discussion.

"In any case," I continued, "when Old Lo objected to the arrival of the three men who were part of the assassination plot, the man we know as Young Lo had to get rid of him. He was aware that Dr. Erickson had complained to the herbalist about the concoctions his daughter had used when his wife died, and that Old Lo had often argued with Dr. Stone, so he arranged to poison the old man and to accuse Dr. Stone of the murder. He played on my ignorance, encouraging me to believe he was the true son of Old Lo. Of course, everyone in the local community knew that was not the case, but I didn't. It didn't matter to Young Lo. He had no intention of trying to inherit the old man's property. He only needed to get his co-conspirators into the country in time for Viceroy Li's visit. They planned to assassinate the official and then disappear."

A large bowl of rice was circulated to the Chinese in the group, who ate from small bowls and chose meat and vegetables from shared platters, while we Westerners concentrated on the individual plates placed in front of us.

"He very nearly lost his men to the immigration authorities," Ida pointed out.

"That's right," I continued. "That was due to the fact that Hip Lung reported them. Anyone trying to smuggle people in—who didn't have his approval—would meet with the same treatment. But, when the men appeared again almost immediately, we were all surprised. Detective Whitbread smelled a rat. It turns out Officer Lewis was open to bribes, so the imposter Lo bought their freedom."

"I hear Lewis is in handcuffs himself now," Fitz told us. Hip Lung grunted.

"But who was this man who called himself Lo's son?" Miss Howe asked.

Wong explained. "There is a faction in the Ching court that is against Viceroy Li. They believe he is too intent on change. They are old Manchu families who want to throw all the foreigners out of China and strengthen the emperor and keep to the old ways. They are against the dowager empress and her nephew, the child emperor, who rely on Li Hung Chang's advice. Being old Manchu families they believe they are in line to succeed the emperor and that they might be able to take over and replace him. But they are the very ones who were unable to keep the Japanese from invading. If they tried to throw out the Westerners they would fail and China would be forced to relinquish even more territory. They hired these men to be assassins and to make sure Sun Yat Sen was blamed."

"What happened to Viceroy Li?" Miss Howe asked.

I took over the story. "When I learned that Young Lo was not really related to the old herbalist who had died, I realized that was a secret that was important enough to kill for. I went to Detective Whitbread. We suspected that an assassination attempt would be made by Lo, but he and his men had disappeared by that point and Whitbread needed to catch them in the act. Whitbread convinced the Chinese consulate that Viceroy Li was in danger and should change his travel plans. Indeed, there were so many threats against his life that he cancelled all of his plans and has returned to China."

"But who was in the palanquin?" Miss Howe asked.

"That was just a decoy to fool the assassins into thinking the viceroy was here," Wong explained.

"Then why was Miss Erickson attacked?" Mary asked. "Was it all about the herbs and the fact that the pretend son of Lo could not deliver the real recipe?"

"I don't think so," I said, after swallowing a tasty morsel from my dish. Once again I could not quite identify all the flavors, but I enjoyed it. "I believe she went to the herbalist again just to defy her father. I suspect she saw something there that she wasn't meant to see. They had the dynamite in those suitcases that were always under their feet. Perhaps she came upon them while they had the materials out. I suspect she left quickly and was going to Hip Lung's wife to get help. The men had to act quickly, so they followed and beat her, before she could tell anyone. They left her for dead and, if Mary hadn't come along just when she did, and if she had not treated her so quickly and so well, Charlotte would never have lived. How is she recovering now? Is she still getting better?"

Ida responded. "She's better every day. She still can't speak in full sentences but I believe eventually she will be able to tell you what happened. It's a wonder that she survived and her father agrees that, without Mary's help, she would not have. He is so grateful he has given us a generous donation to build a hospital in China. It's amazing."

"He wishes to have a hospital named for his dead wife," Mary told us. "The near death of his daughter has brought a great change in his spirit. He no longer blames his daughter, or anyone else, for the death of his wife."

"Mrs. Appleby helped him to change," Ida told us. "She explained to him that the herbs they used were harmless. Nothing could have cured his wife, and he has finally come to accept that. He saw that herbs helped his daughter, but Mary explained that they only provided her with a respite that allowed her body to heal itself. It was really her own body that healed her, not so much the herbs. He regrets his harsh treatment of his daughter. He even vowed to honor his dead wife's commitments to support the women's hospital here...in addition to the hospital in China."

I thought of Charlotte and her hatred for the life forced upon her by her father. With such a serious injury I doubted that she would ever have a life of dances and dinner parties. She would have to struggle to regain her powers just to lead an ordinary life. But at least she would do it with the support of her father, and under the kindly eye of Laura Appleby. Despite her awful injuries I hoped she would see some improvement in her life.

"So Viceroy Li has returned to China, Dr. Erickson and his daughter are reconciled, and we are finally free to return to Jiujiang," Miss Howe summed up.

"That won't be the end of it for Li," Wong told us. "If you think there are plots laid here, there are even more in China. And it's not a single faction involved, either. There are many."

Fitz looked up from his plate of chop suey. "We've no end of factions here, now, in our country, but they've no need of dynamite to make their arguments. Those men had a dozen sticks of it. They were going to blow up the whole building."

"It's just this kind of intrigue that is tearing China apart," Wong told him. "Between the internal feuds, and the incursions by foreign powers, China is in danger of destruction. That's why we must have change." He slammed a fist against the table. "We must have revolution."

Since we were all aware of Wong Chin Foo's support for the rebels, his announcement came as no surprise, but the ladies who were so soon to depart for China were not inclined to pursue an argument with him. Miss Howe started a separate conversation with the two missionary ladies who sat beside her and Mary excused herself, taking a rolled-up piece of paper with her. Ida stopped eating to watch her go, and Wong watched Ida.

"She goes to say goodbye to Chin," Ida told me quietly.

"Ah, star-crossed lovers." Wong rolled his eyes. I wondered

again at how educated young women, like Mary and Ida, could bring medical advances back home with them, yet they still would have to live under the constraints of a society with traditions that could oppress people until they could barely breathe. If feelings were so strong between Mary and Chin, how could she turn away from him?

"What would you have them do?" Ida asked. She directed her question to Wong, but I felt as if she were reading my mind.

"Throw caution to the wind and marry him!" Wong told her. "Wouldn't you? If you loved a man, couldn't you do it? Won't you?" To my amazement, and to any who were paying attention, he crossed his hands on his heart and spoke to Ida. "Won't you leave behind two thousand years of oppression and bound feet to marry me? To have and to hold, to revolt and to finally bring change to traditions that cripple a people who could be great? Don't you have the courage to do that? Will you?"

Ida did not blush. Her face was stony, as if it would crack if she tried to move it. She said nothing for some moments, which allowed the feeling of embarrassment for Wong's half-silly, half-serious proposal to grow like a thundercloud. "You flirt and joke, but the rebellion you incite can only lead to bloodshed. People will die to follow your lead."

"I take that as a refusal, then?" He picked up his chopsticks without blinking an eye. Really, Wong Chin Foo was close to the outer boundaries of civility. "There will be bloodshed but there will also be change," he told her, more seriously now. "Won't you lend your healing hands to the struggle? Isn't it you women, above all, who we need to carry us through the struggle?"

"Mr. Wong, as women, we will need to mop up the blood that is spilled. Of that you can be sure. But to incite the violence, that is beyond my power and against my principles."

Wong seemed to have lost his appetite. He pushed away his bowl, balancing his chopsticks across it, and sat folding and unfolding his napkin in the space before him. It made me wonder if there was some small truth of feeling at the core of his attempts to bait Ida. I applied myself to my food, since I could think of nothing more to say. Mary returned to her seat and took out another roll of paper.

She handed it to me. "Mrs. Chapman, we are so grateful to you and your husband for all of your help this summer. We wanted to leave you with a token of our thanks. This is not very expertly done, but I hope it will remind you of us."

I rolled open the sheet, on which were written Chinese characters in black ink. A smaller, typewritten sheet fell out. Wong looked over my shoulder and murmured his approval of the calligraphy.

"It is my writing," Mary told me. "Ida did the translation."

Wong took it from my hands, spreading it out on the table. I took up the typewritten sheet and read it out loud.

> I built my hut in a zone of human habitation
> Yet near me there sounds no noise of horse or coach.
> Would you know how that is possible?
> A heart that is distant creates a wilderness round it.
> I pluck chrysanthemums under the eastern hedge,
> Then gaze long at the distant summer hills.
> The mountain air is fresh at the dusk of day:
> The flying birds two by two return.
> In these things there lies a deep meaning;
> Yet when we would express it, words suddenly fail us.

"It is the same poet who wrote the other poem," Ida told me.

"Tao Chien," Wong added. He was staring at the calligraphy.

"'A heart that is distant creates a wilderness round it,'" I repeated. "What a wonderful line."

Mary seemed pleased that I liked the poem.

I noticed Fitz watching me from his place across the table. "And how is it with you and your family now, Mrs. Chapman?

I hope they are all recovered from the experiences at the banquet. I'd never have forgiven myself if anything had happened to your little one. I'm so sorry for what took place." He did look very sorry and I remembered Detective Whitbread telling Fitz and me that it was on our shoulders if anyone was hurt. In the end it was the detective who had suffered.

"Jack and Delia are doing well, and Stephen and I are in your debt for helping to save them. Detective Whitbread is the one who suffered the most, but I understand he is recovering well at the women's hospital and his wife has told me it's the best place he's ever been for treatment. She should know, as he has a tendency to put himself in danger and to suffer for it." I remembered how he had barely recovered, after throwing himself in front of the woman he would later marry, in order to save her from a bullet he took himself. There was no restraining Whitbread when he was bent on doing something or saving someone. I knew that from experience.

"And you yourself, now, I hope you are recovered," Fitz told me. "I expect that was enough excitement for a lifetime, that was, and you must be glad now to just stay home with the young ones, to keep them safe and sound." He looked regretful, as if he felt guilty for causing me to retreat from the danger I had found in Chinatown, in the city, and out there in the world. It made me realize that he was yet another person who knew me and expected me to want to go out and challenge the world. It seemed that I would greatly disappoint the people around me, if I chose to retreat.

"You will be surprised to hear that I will be returning to my work at the university," I told him. "I'll be employed as a lecturer but I'll also be directing research into certain aspects of crime in the city." His eyes opened wide with surprise. But then, I had surprised myself with my decision. After our experience at the banquet I found I did not want to take Jack and Lizzie and retreat from the world. Calling on Dean Talbot, I had confessed my suspicion that I was again with child but

# AFTERWORD

I first learned about Mary Stone and Ida Kahn a few years ago, when I saw them mentioned on the website of the Chinese-American Museum of Chicago (http://www.ccamuseum. org/). The two young Chinese women, who came to America to study medicine, seemed to be just the sort of women Emily Cabot Chapman might meet.

As usual, the wonderful collections of the University of Chicago Library provided a valuable starting point for my research. Later, Connie Shemo's book, *The Chinese Medical Ministries of Kang Cheng and Shi Meiyu, 1872–1937* (Lehigh University Press, 2011), provided a detailed account of Mary and Ida's lives. But their actions in *this* book are entirely fictional. While they were indeed in Chicago during the summer of 1896, there is no documentation about precisely what they were doing while there. They returned to China in September 1896 to establish a clinic and later to build a hospital, named for the wife of a generous Chicago donor named Dr. Isaac Newton Danforth.

The two young women doctors did indeed become famous in China for their medical work. Neither of them married, but Mary adopted children with another woman missionary. After many years of work, she left China in 1937—during the Japanese invasion—and died in California in 1954. At one point, Ida returned to Chicago to study literature at Northwestern University and wrote a short story titled "An Amazon in Cathay."

It is about two cousins, one a nurse and the other a member of a women's army unit during the 1911 revolution, a turbulent era of Chinese history. In my novel, Ida's rebukes to Wong Chin Foo about violence are based on the sentiments expressed in that story. She died in China in 1931. Gertrude Howe was also a very real person, who raised Ida and other adopted Chinese children, despite prejudice from the missionary community.

Chicago's Chinatown did not move to its current location until 1912. At the time of this story it was located in the Loop, near Clark and Harrison Streets. The book *Chinese in Chicago, 1870–1945* (Arcadia, 2005) provides wonderful pictures of the early years, and *Chinese Chicago* (Stanford University Press, 2012) by Huping Ling provided much useful information.

Paul Siu's famous sociological study, *The Chinese Laundryman: A Study in Social Isolation* (New York University Press, 1987) outlines the realities of immigration for Chinese men at the turn of the century. I also had access to Tin-chiu Fan's 1926 thesis, *Chinese Residents in Chicago* (University of Chicago), which provided a rich mine of information, including interviews with longtime residents such as Hip Lung.

There are many descendants of the Moy family still living in Chicago and I had the pleasure of meeting a member of the family through mutual friends. When I told her that my next novel included some of her ancestors, she recommended Clara Judson's young adult novel, *The Green Ginger Jar* (Houghton Mifflin, 1949). It gives a nice flavor of a later generation of Chinese Americans growing up in Chicago. Exhibits and presentations of the previously mentioned Chinese-American Museum of Chicago also give a view into the history of Chicago's Chinatown.

For a general depiction of life for Chinese Americans at the turn of the century I found Lisa See's family history, *On Gold Mountain* (St. Martin's, 1995), very helpful, even though her family lived on the West Coast.

As I write this series, I frequently discover people I've never heard of, who did amazing things in their time and who deserve to be remembered. In addition to Mary Stone and Ida Kahn, Wong Chin Foo is certainly one of these. A very real person, he was a Chinese-American journalist and political activist. Articulate and well educated, his own writings are available in journals of the time. His famous essay "Why Am I a Heathen?" is available in a number of places, including the Internet Archive (archive.org/stream/jstor-25101276/25101276_djvu.txt). There are wonderful newspaper articles written by and about him. He really did try to introduce a Confucian temple to Chicago. My scene regarding that event is inspired by an article in the *Chicago Daily Tribune* (December 13, 1896, p. 45). In an interview, he spoke of Sun Yat Sen in the same way I portray him doing so to Emily and Detective Whitbread (*Chicago Daily Tribune*, December 30, 1896, p. 1). The Chinese Viceroy Li Hung Chang really did visit Europe and America in 1896, and cut short his trip due to security issues, but the plot as depicted in this novel is entirely fictional.

At a time when American legislators are attempting to reform our immigration laws, perhaps it would be well to remember the very harsh Exclusion and Geary Acts, which were directed against Chinese immigrants, and were only repealed in 1943. There is much more that could be written about those practices and the underlying racism they represented. Wong Chin Foo took on these issues and had an ongoing feud with a prominent opponent. He was eloquent and outspoken and, even now, his writings can illuminate misunderstandings between the East and West. It was only as I was completing this book that Scott D. Seligman published his biography of Wong Chin Foo, *The First Chinese American: The Remarkable Life of Wong Chin Foo* (Hong Kong University Press, 2013).

Hip Lung, whose actual name was Moy Dong Chew, was also a real person and a prominent community leader. He and his two brothers established the Hip Lung Yee Kee Company. A picture of the two young brides of Hip Lung and one of his brothers inspired the Moy ladies in this story. I have taken some literary license, however, as that published picture is dated 1910, which is somewhat later than this story. Some of the words I attribute to Hip Lung are paraphrased from actual quotes of his, as he was frequently interviewed as a representative of the Chinese community. Charlie Kee was a real relative of the Moys and acted as an interpreter, although his actions in this book are entirely fictional.

Another very real person who appears in this book, and is well worth remembering, is Emil Grubbé. As I researched late nineteenth-century medicine in Chicago, I found that medical education, as we know it, did not come into being until the early twentieth century. Before that time there were a proliferation of institutions offering medical training, without any oversight or certification. Grubbé himself was a student at a medical college that specialized in homeopathy. Medical education at the time of this book may have been unregulated, but medical advances that would become so important in the twentieth century were just beginning to appear. At the International Museum of Surgical Science in Chicago (www.imss.org) I found a whole room devoted to Grubbé's work. When I discovered the fact that Roentgen rays, later called X-rays, were only discovered in 1895, but had spread to actual use by the time of this novel, it seemed too interesting a detail to leave out. Grubbé was a founder of radiological science and spent his entire life working in that field. His own book, *X-ray Treatment: Its Origin, Birth and Early History* (Bruce Pub. Co., 1949) provided much of the information I used. While I read later works that disputed some of his accounts, as a writer of fiction, I felt free to rely on him and even to include Albert Schmidt, whose existence was questioned by at least one author. Every year there is a meeting of radiologists in Chicago and they still present an award named for Emil Grubbé.

On the other hand, Dr. Erickson and his daughter, Charlotte; Mrs. Laura Appleby; the waiter, Chin; and the herbalist, Lo, and his paper son, are all fictional. And the activities I describe involving Emily Cabot and the real historical figures are wholly products of my imagination.

In my years of studying the Chinese language I have been able to read numerous works of that country's literature. At the turn of the century, writers such as Lu Xun turned away from classical Chinese and began to write in language closer to that spoken by everyday people. The stories they wrote reveal a world on the brink of change, just as the people Emily meets in the Gilded Age challenged the existing social structures and introduced ideas that helped to shape what the twentieth century became. At a time when China has become prominent in the world, we should remember the turbulence and strife that accompanied the final downfall of the imperial system that governed that country for thousands of years. At the same time that Emily and her friends were excited about new discoveries in science and technology, young people in China were also excited about the future.

I purposely included some poetry in this book, as it seems to me that there is a rich vein of Chinese stories and culture that need to be appreciated to truly taste the flavor of that society. I have always been amazed to learn that, during the upheavals of the last century, especially those of the Cultural Revolution, most Chinese people seem to have retained knowledge of their traditional poetry and literature. Despite being repudiated as decadent, Chinese stories are too much at the core of that culture to be lost.

The first poem I included, by the Daoist Tao Chien, is one that a college friend wrote out for me in calligraphy, and that I still have hanging in my home. The final poem is by the same poet, but its excellent English translation is by the British writer Arthur Waley. The story of the cowherd and the weaving girl is one I have read in several forms, including an illustrated children's book in Chinese that is on my shelves.

I also very much enjoy the mystery stories of Xiaolong Qiu, whose contemporary Shanghai police detective is a poet (much like P.D. James's Dalgliesh). He weaves poetry into his novels, and provides literary influences for his characters.

As always, I hope the story in this book leads the reader to more interesting information about the real historical figures that appear within it. I apologize for any inaccuracies the reader may uncover.

# ALSO PUBLISHED BY

# ALLIUM PRESS
# OF CHICAGO

Visit our website for more information:
www.alliumpress.com

# THE EMILY CABOT MYSTERIES
## Frances McNamara

### *Death at the Fair*

The 1893 World's Columbian Exposition provides a vibrant backdrop for the first book in the series. Emily Cabot, one of the first women graduate students at the University of Chicago, is eager to prove herself in the emerging field of sociology. While she is busy exploring the Exposition with her family and friends, her colleague, Dr. Stephen Chapman, is accused of murder. Emily sets out to search for the truth behind the crime, but is thwarted by the gamblers, thieves, and corrupt politicians who are ever-present in Chicago. A lynching that occurred in the dead man's past leads Emily to seek the assistance of the black activist Ida B. Wells.

◆

### *Death at Hull House*

After Emily Cabot is expelled from the University of Chicago, she finds work at Hull House, the famous settlement established by Jane Addams. There she quickly becomes involved in the political and social problems of the immigrant community. But when a man who works for a sweatshop owner is murdered in the Hull House parlor, Emily must determine whether one of her colleagues is responsible, or whether the real reason for the murder is revenge for a past tragedy in her own family. As a smallpox epidemic spreads through the impoverished west side of Chicago, the very existence of the settlement is threatened and Emily finds herself in jeopardy from both the deadly disease and a killer.

## Death at Pullman

A model town at war with itself . . . George Pullman created an ideal community for his railroad car workers, complete with every amenity they could want or need. But when hard economic times hit in 1894, lay-offs follow and the workers can no longer pay their rent or buy food at the company store. Starving and desperate, they turn against their once benevolent employer. Emily Cabot and her friend Dr. Stephen Chapman bring much needed food and medical supplies to the town, hoping they can meet the immediate needs of the workers and keep them from resorting to violence. But when one young worker—suspected of being a spy—is murdered, and a bomb plot comes to light, Emily must race to discover the truth behind a tangled web of family and company alliances.

◆

## Death at Woods Hole

Exhausted after the tumult of the Pullman Strike of 1894, Emily Cabot is looking forward to a restful summer visit to Cape Cod. She has plans to collect "beasties" for the Marine Biological Laboratory, alongside other visiting scientists from the University of Chicago. She also hopes to enjoy romantic clambakes with Dr. Stephen Chapman, although they must keep an important secret from their friends. But her summer takes a dramatic turn when she finds a dead man floating in a fish tank. In order to solve his murder she must first deal with dueling scientists, a testy local sheriff, the theft of a fortune, and uncooperative weather.

❖   ❖   ❖

## *Set the Night on Fire*
## Libby Fischer Hellmann

Someone is trying to kill Lila Hilliard. During the Christmas holidays she returns from running errands to find her family home in flames, her father and brother trapped inside. Later, she is attacked by a mysterious man on a motorcycle. . . and the threats don't end there. As Lila desperately tries to piece together who is after her and why, she uncovers information about her father's past in Chicago during the volatile days of the late 1960s . . . information he never shared with her, but now threatens to destroy her. Part thriller, part historical novel, and part love story, *Set the Night on Fire* paints an unforgettable portrait of Chicago during a turbulent time: the riots at the Democratic Convention . . . the struggle for power between the Black Panthers and SDS . . . and a group of young idealists who tried to change the world.

◆

## *A Bitter Veil*
## Libby Fischer Hellmann

It all began with a line of Persian poetry . . . Anna and Nouri, both studying in Chicago, fall in love despite their very different backgrounds. Anna, who has never been close to her parents, is more than happy to return with Nouri to his native Iran, to be embraced by his wealthy family. Beginning their married life together in 1978, their world is abruptly turned upside down by the overthrow of the Shah and the rise of the Islamic Republic. Under the Ayatollah Khomeini and the Republican Guard, life becomes increasingly restricted and Anna must learn to exist in a transformed world, where none of the familiar Western rules apply. Random arrests and torture become the norm, women are required to wear hijab, and Anna discovers that she is no longer free to leave the country. As events reach a fevered pitch, Anna realizes that nothing is as she thought, and no one can be trusted. . .not even her husband.

## *Beautiful Dreamer*
## Joan Naper

Chicago in 1900 is bursting with opportunity, and Kitty Coakley is determined to make the most of it. The youngest of seven children born to Irish immigrants, she has little interest in becoming simply a housewife. Inspired by her entrepreneurial Aunt Mabel, who runs a millinery boutique at Marshall Field's, Kitty aspires to become an independent, modern woman. After her music teacher dashes her hopes of becoming a professional singer, she refuses to give up her dreams of a career. But when she is courted by not one, but two young men, her resolve is tested. Irish-Catholic Brian is familiar and has the approval of her traditional, working-class family. But wealthy, Protestant Henry, who is a young architect in Daniel Burnham's office, provides an entrée for Kitty into another, more exciting world. Will she sacrifice her ambitions and choose a life with one of these men?

◆

## *Company Orders*
## David J. Walker

Even a good man may feel driven to sign on with the devil. Paul Clark is a Catholic priest who's been on the fast track to becoming a bishop. But he suddenly faces a heart-wrenching problem, when choices he made as a young man come roaring back into his life. A mysterious woman, who claims to be with "an agency of the federal government," offers to solve his problem. But there's a price to pay—Father Clark must undertake some very un-priestly actions. An attack in a Chicago alley...a daring escape from a Mexican jail...and a fight to the death in a Guyanese jungle...all these, and more, must be survived in order to protect someone he loves. This priest is about to learn how much easier it is to preach love than to live it.

*Bright and Yellow, Hard and Cold*
Tim Chapman

The search for elusive goals consumes three men…

McKinney, a forensic scientist, struggles with his deep, personal need to find the truth behind the evidence he investigates, even while the system shuts him out. Can he get justice for a wrongfully accused man while juggling life with a new girlfriend and a precocious teenage daughter?

Delroy gives up the hard-scrabble life on his family's Kentucky farm and ventures to the rough-and-tumble world of 1930s Chicago. Unable to find work, he reluctantly throws his hat in with the bank-robbing gangsters Alvin Karpis and Freddie Barker. Can he provide for his fiery young wife without risking his own life?

Gilbert is obsessed with the search for a cache of gold, hidden for nearly eighty years. As his hunt escalates he finds himself willing to use ever more extreme measures to attain his goal…including kidnapping, torture, and murder. Can he find the one person still left who will lead him to the glittering treasure? And will the trail of corpses he leaves behind include McKinney?

Part contemporary thriller, part historical novel, and part love story, *Bright and Yellow, Hard and Cold* masterfully weaves a tale of conflicted scientific ethics, economic hardship, and criminal frenzy, tempered with the redemption of family love.

## *Shall We Not Revenge*
## D. M. Pirrone

In the harsh early winter months of 1872, while Chicago is still smoldering from the Great Fire, Irish Catholic detective Frank Hanley is assigned the case of a murdered Orthodox Jewish rabbi. His investigation proves difficult when the neighborhood's Yiddish-speaking residents, wary of outsiders, are reluctant to talk. But when the rabbi's headstrong daughter, Rivka, unexpectedly offers to help Hanley find her father's killer, the detective receives much more than the break he was looking for.

Their pursuit of the truth draws Rivka and Hanley closer together and leads them to a relief organization run by the city's wealthy movers and shakers. Along the way, they uncover a web of political corruption, crooked cops, and well-buried ties to two notorious Irish thugs from Hanley's checkered past. Even after he is kicked off the case, stripped of his badge, and thrown in jail, Hanley refuses to quit. With a personal vendetta to settle for an innocent life lost, he is determined to expose a complicated criminal scheme, not only for his own sake, but for Rivka's as well.

*Her Mother's Secret*
Barbara Garland Polikoff

Fifteen-year-old Sarah, the daughter of Jewish immigrants, wants nothing more than to become an artist. But as she spreads her wings she must come to terms with the secrets that her family is only beginning to share with her. Replete with historical details that vividly evoke the Chicago of the 1890s, this moving coming-of-age story is set against the backdrop of a vibrant, turbulent city. Sarah moves between two very different worlds—the colorful immigrant neighborhood surrounding Hull House and the sophisticated, elegant World's Columbian Exposition. This novel eloquently captures the struggles of a young girl as she experiences the timeless emotions of friendship, family turmoil, loss…and first love.

A companion guide to *Her Mother's Secret*
is available at www.alliumpress.com. In the guide you will find photographs of places mentioned in the novel, along with discussion questions, a list of read-alikes, and resources for further exploration of Sarah's time and place.

CPSIA information can be obtained
at www.ICGtesting.com
Printed in the USA
FFOW03n1741220515
13544FF

9 780989 053556